Twenty-two-year-old Simon White begs for a place on Captain Dinesh Martin's pirate ship, the *Arrow*. When he proves hilariously inadequate at most tasks, he finds himself in the captain's quarters as cabin boy, housekeeper, and bed warmer.

Captain Martin used to be a British naval officer, until he became disenchanted with the hypocrisy, racism, and classism of the institution and embarked on a life of piracy. He runs an organized and efficient vessel and prides himself on the men with whom he surrounds himself. He is esteemed and admired, and he gives them as good a life as they've ever known.

But Simon has more than a few surprises up his sleeve, including some frightening powers, and Dinesh learns that sometimes a pretty appearance and amenable disposition can fool even an experienced man of the seas.

A FLASH OF GOLDEN FIRE

FIRE

The Arrow and the Flame, Book One

AE Lister

A NineStar Press Publication
www.ninestarpress.com

A Flash of Golden Fire

First Edition, June 2025

ISBN: 978-1-64890-876-7
Also available in eBook, ISBN: 978-1-64890-875-0

CONTENT WARNING:
This book contains sexually explicit content, which may only be suitable for mature readers. Depictions of graphic violence and death, and mention of the obliteration of a town.

*To everyone who has wanted to get away and live
by their own rules.*

This being the record and early life of Mr Simon Bartholomew White, as recorded by same, in his seventy-third year, on the Isle of Singapura, China, circa 1833. This story will be scandalous and disputable; however, it is true, according to my best recollection. My mind remains sharp in old age, despite—or perhaps, because of—a life of 'sinful' occupation and adventure.

My beloved Captain Martin—may he rest in much-deserved peace—would be proud and would corroborate every word of it.

"Where there is a sea there are pirates."
Greek Proverb

Chapter One

Salvation

Port Royal, 1781

The sea smelt of salt and death.

The bustling port city on the southern shores of Jamaica ran with booty and blood. The Brethren of the Coast or, more familiarly, men of dubious employ, otherwise known as pirates, came to the city to trade the goods they had amassed at sea in questionable circumstances. Of course, there was honour among thieves and all of that, but there were also short tempers and ravenous appetites for more than food and good ale.

Food and ale...

I licked my cracked lips and huddled deeper into the threadbare jacket I'd pulled off a washing line an hour earlier. It was the only clean thing on me, in fact. My other garments were stained and filthy, like my frigid skin.

So far, this coastal town hadn't fulfilled its imaginary promise of a fresh and welcome start. I'd left the town of my birth to embark on a new life, thinking that my luck might be better in Port Royal.

Born in Spanish Town to missionary parents, I had been orphaned at twelve, following a calamity that had left them dead, and I was lucky enough to have been taken in by a friend of my mother's, who saw to it to educate and care for me as best he could. My life was decent, though dull, until the age of twenty-one when he died of yellow fever, and I was forced to look to my own means for survival. I should have found my own way before that advanced age, but Carago had enjoyed looking out for me, since his wife had died in birthing his only son, who had lived for three days before following her.

Perhaps my childlike attitude and spoilt sense of entitlement were due to Carago's fatherly indulgences, although innocence had flown from me long before his passing.

So far, in Port Royal, I'd been attacked at knifepoint by a fearsome fellow the night after I'd arrived and also robbed of all my belongings but for a meagre allotment of coin that I'd hidden in my boot. He'd left me with a sore shoulder, a black eye, and a newfound respect for, and fear of, strange men.

In Spanish Town, my encounters with strange men had been more cordial, although nothing I would ever have described to Carago, who, to my bad luck, had held a similar attitude to those of my father and wider society. An unruly mop of red hair and a face full of freckles had ensured me a boyish countenance that I'd likely retain into middle age—God willing I got there to enjoy the benefit. Men liked the look of me, to be frank, and I hadn't lacked for companionship, although only in brief, physical bursts that had still proved rewarding.

I'd heard of the Brethren of the Coast—supposedly a breed of men who'd taken to a life of piracy with a different kind of philosophy, holding themselves to a higher standard than the average swashbuckling vagabond. If these visionaries did, in fact, exist, and if I could *find* one of them and beg for a place aboard his ship, perhaps I could prove my worth and gain passage off this pisspot of an island. A life at sea was a much better prospect than one on land at this point, and I was ready for an adventure.

I ducked into a tavern called The Penny Whistle to get out of the rain that now came in torrents, but not before I became soaked to the skin and chilled further. Quite a sorry thing to be so adrift at twenty-two, bedraggled and wet and without prospects.

The tavern was warm, at least, and nobody turned me out. A fire roared and crackled in a large hearth, in front of which a motley group of strangely attired men were seated at tables, their attention captured by an imposing figure who stood with his elbow on the mantle as he regaled them with animated voice and gestures.

I slunk to a stool by the bar and sat, my stomach cramping as the scent of cooking food filled my nostrils. I soon found myself as transfixed as the others.

The man was everything a pirate captain ought to be.

He was of indefinable race—likely a mixture of at least two. He was exceptionally handsome in a way far beyond his physical appearance, which was unique and appealing. And he was an excellent orator, regaling his audience with honeyed words and dramatic cadence.

He wore the jacket of a British officer, although the item had seen years of wear, and the badges had been removed, or torn from the cloth. The garment looked fine on him and gave him a ruffled distinction. His shirt and breeches were navy issue as well. He looked more put together than his crew, who sported the mismatched garb of unaligned men of the sea. He had the accent of a British officer and the elocution of a magistrate.

The serving wench made her presence known, approaching the captain, laughing in the way women do when they want a man to think of them fondly. But as far as I could tell, her charms weren't working upon him.

The crew was another matter.

"Oy, my darling, come here and perch on me knee awhile," a heavyset fellow suggested, leering at the young woman and waggling his eyebrows.

"Now, now, Mister Denbrooke. What would your wife think?" the captain said with an indulgent smile.

"My wife, Captain Martin," Mr Denbrooke said, "is probably spreading her ample thighs for the butcher *and* the baker at the moment. So she wouldn't care a damn."

Captain Martin. I'd been right in my supposition.

"Oh, go on," the girl said and flounced to the bar where she frowned and pretended to be unaffected by the captain's disinterest.

Everyone laughed and the captain grinned wider.

"Never was able to keep her satisfied," Mr Denbrooke continued. "I've only got one cock, and she likes to have three at once."

The men laughed and Captain Martin nodded.

"Hmm. Well, I can't fault your wife for that," he said.

The men laughed harder and some even hooted, and my foggy brain couldn't keep up.

I concentrated on dealing with the hunger pangs that assailed me and rehearsed ways I could approach this formidable man who took up space with such entitled ease.

"Hello, my name is Simon White. I'd like a position on your ship." Or, perhaps I should say, "Simon White here. You gotta place for me on board?" or "I'm strong and quick—when I'm fed, at least—Are you taking on crew?"

None of these were likely to get me what I needed, so I sat there, suffering, whilst they shoveled beef stew into their gobs and tore up whole loaves of bread to devour amongst themselves. My mouth became dry as I watched. What I wouldn't do for an ale or even a paltry glass of water.

There were things I'd thought about doing. Things that men paid dearly for in the back alleys and the whorehouses. But I couldn't bear the thought of trading an activity I enjoyed so much for food and drink or coin. I hadn't gotten to a point so desperate to fall into that. If I could only get onto Captain Martin's ship, I wouldn't have to contemplate a life of whoredom.

"I know you're watching me," Captain Martin said.

It took a moment to realize his words were directed my way.

"Why don't you grow a set of bollocks and come over, if you're so interested?"

I gaped at him through the pain of my empty stomach, surprised to be addressed at all.

"Hmm. Perhaps you are deaf...or dumb...or both."

His words were cruel but his attitude benign, as if he didn't really give a damn whether I responded.

Such a long spell since I'd said a word to anyone, I had to clear my throat before speaking. "I can hear you," I finally got out.

His eyes widened and a smile stretched his lips, like treacle spreading on a plate. "Well, well, well. The filthy cur speaks."

He was right about the filthy part.

"Stop hiding in the shadows. Show yourself, man," the captain said, beckoning with a finger.

I found myself obedient to his natural authority and worried about the reaction of his men if I didn't heed their captain's request. I pushed off the stool. My knees buckled, but I took a breath and fought the collapse, my heart beating a tattoo and my mouth dry.

I'd wanted the attention of the captain, but now that I had gained it, I wasn't at all sure what to do with his interest.

"Aw, leave him alone, Dinesh. He's as dirty as a stray kitten and likely as nasty."

I straightened and tried to smooth my filthy mop, as if to belie the statement, but my hands were just as grimy as my hair. Probably more so. Perhaps I should have stripped naked in the rain and taken a scrub brush to my skin. Captain Martin's men, who had gathered their garments from a variety of distant lands, were nonetheless cleaner than I'd expected a pirate crew to be. They regarded me with skepticism as I approached, and I couldn't blame them. I cleared my throat and summoned courage.

"My name is Simon Bartholomew White," I said, doing my best to level a steady gaze at the captain. "I'm looking for a place, if you please. I want to come aboard your ship."

He laughed. "What makes you think I have a ship?"

I blinked at him. Glanced at his men. I didn't know what to say. I scowled with frustration and tugged the leather purse from my boot. I held the pouch towards him with shaking fingers.

The captain regarded the offering with distaste, as if I were holding a dead rat.

"What do you have there, Simon Bartholomew White?" he said with some amusement.

His eyes—the colour of stormy seas—held untold depths.

"Enough coin to convince you to take a chance on me, Captain."

The purse held all I had, and I'd come close to spending it. But the benefits of one night's food and lodging were a waste when I needed a position in order to ensure my long-term survival. Then again, perhaps a bath and a full belly would have bettered my chances.

Some of the men laughed, and others cursed my boldness. The captain regarded me for a long moment.

"As it so happens, I do have a ship. Called the *Arrow*."

His men turned and chatted amongst themselves, losing interest in our conversation.

I tried not to sway on my feet. I was so tired and weak. I stared at the coin purse in my outstretched hand as it began to go in and out of focus. Was I about to faint?

The captain continued, "But why do you want a place on a ship you only heard about a moment ago? And only supposed before that?" he asked.

He looked me up and down with more skepticism than his crew had given me.

Perhaps this was a useless endeavour. How could I convince him that I'd be an asset?

He raised his eyebrows. "In search of a wild life, are you? Dreaming of glory and women?"

No.

"*No,*" I said as emphatically as I could. "I just need a place, sir."

My legs trembled and my heart quailed. I was a grown man, truly, but I'd never felt more like a child than I did at that moment.

"Any place," I whispered.

Some indiscernible emotion crossed his face. Disdain?

Sympathy? Interest?

He took two steps toward me and plucked the purse from my hand. He stroked it with his thumb and fondled the contents through the soft leather, narrowing his eyes in contemplation.

When he met my gaze, a spark passed between us.

Then he averted his gaze and tucked the purse into the pocket of his fine jacket.

"Off with you, Mr White. I'm not in need of men," he said.

He pulled out a chair and sat, straddling the seat as he prepared to address the others.

A desperate rage took hold of me. He'd taken my coin—all I had left to my name—and for a moment, it had looked like I might be in luck. The spark that had ignited at his look became a lightning rod of rage, giving me a burst of strength and a tendency to recklessness.

I gazed wildly about me, spotting a half-full tankard of brown ale that might or might not have been his. I grabbed the cup and threw it at him, uttering a string of curses and insults, demanding he return my coins, or I'd set his ship ablaze by morning.

None were more surprised at this turn of events than I, except perhaps for the captain himself. The tankard bounced off his middle, and ale splashed onto his fine clothes and up to his chin, the crash of the cup to the floor heralding the return of my sanity.

What have I done?

Captain Martin stared at me with apparent calm as the frothy liquid spread over his clothes. He reached under his jacket, pulled out a flintlock pistol, and aimed the barrel at my head.

"I suppose you're going to beg for mercy," he said in steely tones that suggested pleading might be my only option.

But I was all-in now, and there was no going back.

I kept my voice low. "Give me back my coin or bring me aboard."

I didn't have anything to lose now that he had my money. If he didn't do either of those things, then he might as well shoot me and be done with me.

I stared at Captain Martin, and he stared back. He was probably as surprised as I that I wasn't backing down. But strength had come from somewhere, and a sense of destiny held me straight and sturdy in front of him and all his crew. If I was meant to die now, then so be it. I'd not shed any tears for this place.

Captain Martin narrowed his eyes as the crew looked on with baited breath and, no doubt, a yearning for blood. I closed my eyes, ready for the end.

My own quick breaths hung in my ears as I waited.

"I'll not waste a bullet on you. Come aboard, then. If you don't prove your worth to me in a week, you'll walk the plank."

I let out my breath and opened my eyes. We stared at each other, neither willing to back down, but at least he hadn't shot me.

He tucked the gun away and folded his arms on the table.

"Pull up a seat, Mr White."

I blinked, my heart rate slowing, but hesitated because I didn't understand what was happening.

"Sit. Down." Captain Martin said, as one of the crew members grabbed a chair and scraped its feet over the floor so that the thing rammed into my leg.

I sat.

"I said you can come aboard," the captain repeated.

I nodded, licking my cracked lips. I realized at that moment that I'd almost hoped for the bullet.

The captain lifted his hand and whistled a sharp note.

"Bring Mr White some ale, and more for me. And a bowl of

stew for him too." He ordered in a gruff timbre. "He's crew now, and I'll not have him starve."

A fortunate thing I was sitting, because the thought of food and ale made me lightheaded. And now I felt bad about dousing him.

"I'm sorry…" I muttered, gesturing to his soiled clothing, and he laughed.

"Cooled me off." He waved a hand in the air. "I'm sorry I almost shot you." He glanced at his crew and turned back to me. "Have to keep up appearances, you see."

I nodded.

The crew went back to their discussion as if Captain Martin hadn't almost blown a man to bits in front of them. Perhaps indicative of the life I'd be leading that the possibility of bloodshed didn't cause a stir.

Captain Martin held my gaze. He pulled the coin purse from his pocket, hefting the little sack and stroking the leather.

My breaths quickened and my cheeks flushed.

"Simon Bartholomew White, you have a fair set of bollocks on you," he said, grinning.

He fondled the pouch, toying with the coins inside, as I felt a swelling in my groin. Then he tossed the bag toward me. Instinctively, I caught it and held the leather purse in my open palm with a feeling of disbelief.

"You can keep that."

"Thank you," I whispered, my fingers trembling. My brain was hazy with hunger, and I thought I might faint. I tucked the small AE bag of coins into my pocket as the barkeep, in his soiled apron, sauntered over.

"Here."

He slammed a bowl of stew and a spoon down in front of me

and then a tankard of rich brown ale. He handed the captain a soft cloth.

"Yours is coming in a minute, Din," he said to the pirate captain, who nodded, wiping at the front of his shirt.

"And another round for the crew, if you don't mind, Will. We're pulling anchor tomorrow morning, but we have the night yet."

The men around us lifted their tankards and shouted "Hoorah!" and "Cheers to Captain Martin!"

Captain Martin smiled at me then with a kindness that took me by surprise. "Drink up and eat your stew, Simon."

I stared at him, still stunned to be alive and at the mercy of this man who stirred my blood and had offered me hope. Then I wrapped my hand around the spoon and started to shovel the steaming stew into my mouth. The scalding food burned my lips and palate, but I was so fucking hungry the pain didn't matter. I gulped the stew down, making embarrassing sounds and hissing at the heat.

When next I looked at Captain Martin, he regarded me with a strange sort of pity in his expression. I didn't have the energy to protest, but I glared at him over my spoon, angry that he had to see me like this.

As if he realized my thoughts, he shifted his attention back to the crew and began to regale them with more bawdy and exciting tales. Mesmerized once again by their charismatic and well-spoken leader, they ignored me as I ate and drank.

Carago had told me that pirates were an uneducated bunch of immoral vagabonds, and most of the crew fit that description. But Captain Martin had a turn of phrase and a way of speaking that made me imagine him in a schoolroom as a child and then, as a young man, learning to read and write and figure, just like the most respected magistrate in the town. How did a man like that end up leading a swarthy crew of misfits that I was soon to join? I was eager to find out, and certain he'd had some kind of a career in the British Navy. He'd abandoned his post for some reason, or perhaps for many.

As the nourishment filled my belly and the ale revived my spirits, a different kind of ache assailed me. I needed to know more about Captain Martin.

*

The *Arrow* was anchored offshore. She was majestic and glorious, and contrasted many of the other vessels in the harbour. I'd expected her to be smaller. As I stood on the shore that morning, after a night sleeping under a bridge with a full belly and a destination, I couldn't help being impressed at the size of her.

Her hull and rails were painted a bright, rich red with a stripe of yellow between the gun decks. Her masts were black and sturdy. Even in mid-repair, she was beautiful.

As I gazed, transfixed, at the ship that was to be my home for the foreseeable future, a man bumped into me from behind, and I scrambled for balance.

"Pardon me."

The man was carrying a pile of rolled sailcloth and gazed at me with recognition. "Oy, you're Simon White, ain't you? The captain said to look out for you."

"Aye."

I was wary of the captain's men, unsure if they wanted me aboard or would rather see me starve in Port Royal. But this fellow, with curly brown hair and a substantial beard, smiled warmly.

"Name's Martinéz. She's grand, isn't she? The *Arrow*."

"Aye."

He lowered his voice. "Stolen from the British Navy."

"Ah." That made sense.

"Come on. I'll take you to Donatello, who'll have somethin' for you to do."

"Donatello?"

"Quartermaster. He runs things."

"Oh. I thought that Captain Martin—"

Martinéz laughed. "Oh, he's in charge, but Donatello does most of the hands-on work."

"I see," I said. "Does the captain have a connection to the British Navy?"

Martinéz gazed at me with respect. "Aye. He used to be an officer, but he got tired of the job. Wanted more of a free way of living, I suppose you could say." He waggled his eyebrows.

"So he turned pirate."

Martinez shook his head. "Oh, no, don't call him that. He won't like it, even if that's what he is." Martinez held up his hand. "Now, I don't mind the term, myself. But he calls himself a privateer, e'en though he ain't got a writ from any government. He's a proud man, Captain Martin."

We stared at each other for a moment whilst I tried to process what he'd said.

"Never mind. I'll let him explain his thinking. Though you won't see much of him, I expect. Donatello will probably have you working below decks until he finds out what you're made of."

Perhaps I was lucky that the *Arrow* was so large, as her substantial size meant they could always use an extra hand. I was determined to prove useful.

The crew had recently availed themselves of a trio of goats and five chickens, of which I was promptly put in charge by Donatello because, when asked, I admitted to some experience with animal husbandry. Unfortunately, that had largely involved cows and horses, but I'd figured I could extrapolate my knowledge to goats and chickens without too much of an issue.

I might have overestimated my skills and underestimated the challenge of keeping three goats entertained and in line in small quarters.

*

I'd hoped to be able to learn more about Captain Martin once I was aboard his ship. In fact, I didn't get near him for weeks.

The *Arrow* pulled anchor and sailed out of Port Royal the day I boarded, and low winds meant we didn't make huge gains for that first week. Even during the second and third week, the ship meandered among the islands in the southern Atlantic Ocean, minding her own business and steering clear of any encounters. She flew a Dutch flag as a decoy, so nobody dared approach us, and we minded our own business. I was relieved, although the rest of the crew grew bored with the situation. There was much work still to be done on board. The major repairs had been completed while at anchor, but there were countless minor tasks and maintenance work to be continued. The exciting and adventurous stories I'd heard of a pirate's life had not materialized.

"Excuse me. Pardon me," I stammered, pushing my way through the deckhands as they tried to swab the foredeck.

"Bloody hell, boy, get that feckin' goat outta here!" A burly, tattooed man yelled.

"Not again!" someone muttered. "Can't ye keep her tied up or somethin'?"

"Sorry, sorry. Excuse me. Lillith, get back here! Leave them be," I shouted, dodging bodies and trying not to slip on the soapy boards.

"Jesus, the bloke's gone and named the beasts," someone else said.

"He's touched in the head, I reckon," a fellow laughed.

I turned my head to give the man a piece of my mind and lost my footing, falling onto my arse and sliding until I was flat on my back. A massive shadow blocked the sun.

"Simon Bartholomew White, what the fuck are you doing?"

Captain Martin stared at me from above.

He wasn't wearing his jacket, and his faded cotton shirt gaped open, revealing a tawny chest feathered with dark hair. His long black locks were tied with a ribbon, but loose strands draped rakishly around his comely face. He looked like a disgruntled angel come to carry me to hell.

By now I was in fine condition, a regular diet of bread, cheese, and meat giving me a more manly shape. I'd regained my energy and ability to function. And also my contrary attitude.

"I'm trying to catch that fucking goat," I said, sitting up and checking to see if I'd hurt myself. Before I'd finished a mental inventory of the pains assailing me, Captain Martin grabbed a fistful of my shirt and pulled me up with the ease of a man used to physical labour.

"I thought you said you knew how to manage animals."

"Well, I do," I said, crossing my arms over my chest. "But, apparently, not goats. Turns out they're bleedin' arseholes with shit for brains."

Captain Martin's lips quivered with either fury or amusement, and I couldn't for the life of me tell which.

At that moment, Lilith gave a tremulous bleat from somewhere ahead. We turned toward the bow, to see the blasted white and brown creature tangled in ropes and chewing on the edge of a sail.

Captain Martin levelled a stern eye to me, and a part of me rose to greet that look. I wouldn't dare to say which part. Now that I was feeling better, my other appetites had returned in full force, which was dangerous on a ship full of men. However, I only had a yearning for one of them.

"Go get her. Put her somewhere secure. Then come to my cabin, Mr White."

Oh, fuck it. Was he going to make me walk the plank?

"This ain't my fault. I've tried my best to—"

"I'm not discussing this here," he said and walked away.

"Yes, Captain," I said, my face red from the running, the tumble I'd taken, and the rampant lustful thoughts that assailed me.

Why did I have to be like this? Another man would be quaking with fear at being caught failing at his duties. But all I could think about was that I'd finally have a private audience with the captain. Hopefully, I could convince him of my worth so he wouldn't toss me overboard.

I took the thin coil of rope out of my belt loop and attached the clasp to Lilith's halter.

"Come on, you lousy trollop. You're getting me in bad with the captain and everyone else."

I tugged on the rope, but the goat planted her feet and bleated, calling everyone's attention to my predicament.

"He can't even get a goat to move. How's he gonna survive when there's more at stake?"

"What was the captain thinking? Allowing that man on board. He's barely bigger than a lass. And less useful, if you get my meaning."

"Oh, aye. Although Captain Martin might not agree. And I can tell you what he was probably thinking."

Laughter.

I glared at the offending animal and channeled my rage and annoyance into my voice.

"Come the fuck on, you cunt!"

I gave the lead rope a huge tug, and the beast finally budged, dodging past me, bleating and pulling me along as she headed for the door to the stairs.

"For fuck's sake," I hollered, tripping over my feet and almost falling as I held onto the rope for dear life and ran back with her to the holding pen.

The two other goats, Monty and Gordon—neither of them near as much trouble—were happily munching on some branches. I took Lilith into the pen and tied her to a beam. She bleated happily and joined her friends in stripping leaves and chewing on the bark.

"Good. Stay the fuck here now. I'm trying to make a good impression."

She bleated what was probably an impertinent response.

"Right," I said, clapping my hands together.

Anticipation and excitement filled me at the thought of speaking to Captain Martin in his quarters. I wished I'd some cleaner clothes to wear.

I hadn't had a good wash since I'd first come on board, when I'd been provided a tub of cold water and some clothing: a pair of simply made trousers, a length of rope for a belt, and a linen shirt, along with a pair of leather shoes that fit all right, but which I never wore.

I'd got a wool jacket, too, for colder temperatures, and I couldn't fault the captain's generosity. I'd worn the clothes for three weeks, and since I worked with animals, they were probably a bit ripe. But there was nothing for it, and I had to show up to the captain's cabin in the only togs I had.

Chapter Two

The Captain

His cabin was at the stern of the ship, and guarded by a fellow known as Boone, an intimidating giant of a man whose job was to protect Captain Martin at all costs. Since he could shrivel my bollocks with a steely eyed look, he was well placed.

"What you want?" he grunted. He was sitting on an upturned barrel by the door of the captain's quarters, picking under his nails with the sharp edge of a massive knife.

"I was told to come to Captain Martin's quarters," I said in a voice that made me sound much less sure of myself than I'd planned.

He gave me a skeptical glance.

"Ya were, were ya?" he said. "Now what would the captain want with you?"

That was the fucking question, but how should I know?

I shrugged. "No idea. But I'm here, ain't I?"

Although Carago had taught me to read and write, and I knew how to conjugate and had a good grasp of proper English grammar, using a more common vernacular allowed me to blend in. All the better to surprise people with my level of learning and sophistication later on.

He gave me a salacious grin, his gaze running over me from top to tail, making me feel like a piece of meat. Normally, I'd respond in kind if I found a fellow attractive, but I wasn't sure Boone wasn't measuring me for a cook pot rather than implying a different kind of interest.

"That you are, my boy. That you are. Now give me the blade and any other weapon you've got on you."

"What makes you think I have a blade?" I asked, trying to act insulted.

He held out his hand. "Give it. Or I'll not let you in."

Probably a good practice not to let a crew member into the captain's quarters with a weapon. I hitched up the corner of my tattered shirt just enough to pull the sheathed dagger out of the waistband of my trousers, giving the handle an affectionate stroke before I passed the weapon to Boone.

"You got anythin' else on ya?"

I shrugged. "Only a cock the size of a summer squash. Would you consider that a concealed weapon?"

Boone blinked, then let out a belly laugh that shook the floorboards.

The door to the captain's rooms swung open, and we both started. Boone's expression turned serious.

"What's going on out here?" Captain Martin barked.

"Just shootin' the breeze, Cap'n," the swarthy man muttered.

"Here. Fella had this on 'im." He showed the captain my knife in its leather sheath.

Captain Martin didn't appear surprised. He held out his hand for the weapon, and Boone gave the knife over.

"Right." He glared at me. "You. Get in here."

I straightened up and glared back. "My name is Simon Bartholomew White, thank you very much."

The captain's bodyguard made a strangled sound, and Captain Martin narrowed his eyes.

"I know what your name is. Get in here this instant."

His tone brooked no argument, and I recalled that my life was entirely dependent upon his favour, so I stifled my indignation and followed him, offering a secret prayer to whomever might be listening to keep me safe and give me what I needed.

He held up the knife as he shut the door. "For protection?"

"Yes, sir. You can never be too careful."

"You can have your knife when you leave my quarters. You won't need a blade here." He sniffed the air and wrinkled his fine nose. "Jesus, you stink."

Not an auspicious beginning.

"Well, I ain't got a change of clothes, you see," I said, crossing my arms.

He examined me with a shrewd eye, taking in my ragged and lowly appearance, I was sure, and probably wondering why he'd saddled himself with me when he could have left me to rot in the Penny Whistle.

So I did what I always did when I wasn't sure of myself and acted like a twat.

"Why are you looking at me like that? Ain't you ever seen a pauper before?"

His eyes went wide and I thought I'd caught him off guard

with my cheek. I doubled down, taking in my surroundings.

"Hmm. Not bad, I suppose. I thought you'd have fancier digs than this though."

There was, in fact, a fairly impressive four-poster bed in the center of the room which made my mind swirl with all sorts of possibilities.

I walked to an ornately carved dresser and swiped a fingertip over the carved top, then squinted at the admittedly minute layer of dust the wood had gathered. "And a better housekeeper."

For a moment he looked like he was about to shout obscenities and throw me over the rail. A shock of terror hit me, and I wondered if my big fat gob had got me into trouble again.

Then his expression relaxed, and he laughed. I couldn't tell if he was amused at me or amused at what he was going to do to me, at first.

He shook his head in mild annoyance and brushed past me to plunk himself down in a luxurious wood and leather armchair by the bank of windows that looked over the sea.

"Now that you mention it," he said, "I *could* use someone to keep this cabin clean. Maybe you'd be better at that than you are at tending goats."

Ah shit.

I shrugged. "Well..."

I hadn't banked on being pegged as a scullery maid, but the situation was my own fault for complaining about the state of his cabin. Which actually wasn't bad, really. In fact, the rooms were substantial, and I wasn't sure how there could be so much space in the ship when the crew were all crammed in hammocks in the lower berths. Everything here was polished mahogany or lacquered pine, and there were fancy linens and cushions spread about. The captain enjoyed his comfort.

The windows let in plenty of sunlight and gave him a view of the open sea at the stern.

"Nice view," I commented.

"Thank you. Now take off those filthy clothes, Mr White."

My mouth went dry, and a zing of electricity zapped me from my sternum to my bollocks.

"Beg pardon?"

He crossed one booted foot over the other.

"I'm not convinced you don't have another blade hidden on your person."

"I can assure you, Captain, that I—"

"Strip. Now." He gave me an offhand smile. "Don't worry. You'll find that nudity on a vessel of this sort is a common thing. There isn't a lot of privacy."

I had figured that out already. However, stripping below decks for a quick wash was rather different than being told to take off your clothes in a man's private quarters. Then again, I only hesitated because I was having trouble controlling my physical response to Captain Martin's presence, and I didn't want to give anything away. But in this situation, obedience was required.

"Right," I said, taking a deep breath. "You asked for it."

I grabbed the hem of my shirt and tugged the cloth over my head, shaking out my dirty hair as I revealed my upper half.

He tried, but couldn't hide his astonishment. A burn scar like mine was a startling sight.

Perhaps the horrible disfigurement would distract him from other revelations. The ruined skin was a part of me and of what I'd been through. The fact I'd survived and not died of horrible infection was a bloody miracle.

The captain leaned forward and squinted as I untied the rope belt holding my trousers up, then shoved them down and off. I stood there naked in front of him, my cock behaving itself for the moment.

He didn't say anything, which was worse than if he had remarked on the obvious blemish. He stood and approached, then hovered his fingers over the rough skin on my hip.

"You can touch it," I said, my voice barely there. My gaze flashed up to meet his. "It doesn't hurt. Not anymore."

Although I was slight and of average height, Captain Martin didn't tower over me. I had to look up a bit; that was all. He gazed at me and I felt my cock swell and twitch. I closed my eyes, knowing that the truth of my feelings would be revealed before the end of this interview.

His fingertips traced the outline of my scar. The damaged skin was sensitive in places, but the phantom pain had mostly vanished. I tried to stay still as my body responded to his proximity, my nostrils picking up the scent of his clean sweat, and my prick stiffening even more.

Would he be offended by the thought that I was swollen for him? I had the sense that Captain Martin was a man who lived his life the way he pleased, and that he held no affection for, or interest in, women. But I could have been mistaken.

"Burn?"

"Yes, Captain," I said, breath hitching as he continued to trace the edge, where it rose past my right nipple and swooped under my arm.

"Turn," he said.

I obeyed, and he continued to where the scar descended down over my right buttock. I gasped. I'd not been touched that way in a long time.

"How did this happen?"

Perhaps he hadn't yet noticed my indecency.

"Fire," I said.

"When?"

"Ten years ago. I was twelve."

"How old are you now?"

"Twenty-two."

"You don't look that age."

I leveled a steady gaze at him. "Don't I?"

"Are you lying to me, Mr White?"

"No, Captain. I ain't got proof, but that's my age."

And then, his gaze shifted to my lower half. I held my breath as he stared at my standing prick.

"That's interesting."

I took a deep breath. "Is it?"

"Then again," he murmured, licking his bottom lip and continuing, "Some men your age will swell at anything."

"Aye, Captain. Some men will."

He brought his gaze back to mine, and there passed between us the confirmation of an unspoken secret. He smiled for a brief moment.

"Hmm," he hummed. His gaze returned to my scar. "It doesn't hurt?"

"No."

He frowned. "I should whip you for letting that goat chew my sails."

I gulped. "Yes, Captain."

I wasn't exactly agreeing with him, and I definitely didn't want that. I didn't think he was serious.

"But...you look rather a delicate fellow," he said, gaze sweeping over me as if he was only now allowing himself the pleasure of seeing me in my nakedness.

"Thank you for your mercy. I promise to do better."

He waved a hand in the air as if the whole goat thing was inconsequential after all.

"May I put my clothes back on, Captain?" I asked, feeling rather vulnerable and still not completely sure he was 'on my side', so to speak.

"No, I'm afraid not, Mr Simon Bartholomew White. You must continue to stand for inspection."

My eyes went wide. "Inspection!"

His lips twitched as if he were trying not to smile. "Oh yes. I inspect all the men who come aboard this ship, in one form or another."

"All the men?"

"Well, perhaps only the ones who interest me," he admitted. "In the way that you do."

My heart rate pounded in my ears, and my cock was at a full stand. He met my gaze again and more than a spark leapt between us.

"May I ask, Captain, in what way do I interest you?" I said, with breathless anticipation of his answer.

He let himself smile then. "Well, definitely not in your animal handling capacity."

"No," I agreed. "Not that." I swallowed thickly. "Then... how?"

Captain Martin and I gazed at each other with much silent messaging.

"Oh," I said. "That."

He raised his eyebrows. "You understand me?"

"Aye, I think I do. But perhaps you should say what you mean out loud, in case I am mistaken." My voice wavered, and I truly hoped I hadn't misunderstood him. But best to be clear.

"All right, Simon Bartholomew White. I agree that we should

speak plainly, in a situation such as this."

He stepped closer to me. So close that his hip nudged the tip of my stand, and I gasped. I tried to step back, but he took my wrist and kept me in place, his gaze drilling into mine.

"You interest me..." he murmured, "as a man who might appreciate certain intimacies that I enjoy sharing on occasion...with other men...who share those affinities...if you understand me now."

All of a sudden I found it hard to breathe. "Aye, Captain."

"And do you share those affinities, Mr White? Have you shared them...in the past...with other men?"

"As a matter of fact, Captain," I said, trying to steady my voice, "I do. And I have."

"I see," he said, with a detachment that belied the way he was looking at me now—with excitement and satisfaction and, well, need. I was quite familiar with that look, as a matter of fact. "Then stand for inspection, Mr White."

"I...am standing?" I didn't quite know what he wanted.

"Well, I'm asking you to stay still, as best you can. For I am going to inspect you *completely*."

"Oh, I see."

"In fact, come over by the window, if you please. The light's much better there."

He stepped back and guided me to the bank of windows, the pressure of his hold on my wrist gentle, but firm. The day was bright and the sun high. Beams of light flooded the floorboards and made them warm beneath my feet.

He released me but told me to stay where I was. I was completely under his spell and waited patiently as he brought over a full washbowl from his bedside table, and a cloth.

"This water is clean, in fact, as I haven't had time for a wash yet this morning," he said as if I cared a damn. Whatever water was in that bowl was cleaner than anything I'd touched over the last few weeks.

"Yes, Captain."

"Well, you're filthy, Mr White. And since I need to inspect you anyway, I might as well give you a quick once-over with a wet cloth while I'm at it."

"Yes, Captain."

"At some point, you'll need a proper bath with soap and hot water. But this will do for now."

"I didn't realize the crew were allowed baths," I admitted as the captain wetted the cloth, wrung it out, and held the damp rag in front of me.

"Well, they aren't. A wash in a tin tub is a luxury afforded to some. And any man who desires to share my affections had better be clean; that's all I'll say. Now close your eyes, Simon."

He gave the instructions with such gentleness I obeyed without question. He drew the cloth over my face, down my neck, and behind my ears, humming a low melody in his throat.

"Can't do anything about that mop of hair right now, I'm afraid. But at least I can clean the rest of you."

"Aye," I whispered, feeling looked after in a way I hadn't in a very long time. I did recall Carago treating some injuries of mine with such care when I was young and I used to roughhouse with the local children, many of whom had treated me badly. That is, until I'd found my voice and my courage and put up a good fight. Then they'd stayed away from me.

His touch was so gentle that it took me quite by surprise. His manner had been abrupt and at times cruel during the time I'd been aboard, albeit I'd only observed him on rare occasions and always from a distance. But I'd heard the screams of a man who had been punished for hoarding weapons and trying to plan a coup, and the crew had told me of his experience afterwards. They'd all voted for the fellow to be disciplined and tossed over the side because he'd brought distrust and danger on board. The captain, to my knowledge, hadn't done the act himself. Still, he had commanded that it be done and watched that the punishment was carried through.

For such a man to be so careful with me now, cleaning the grime from my body with a wet cloth while he took the opportunity to examine me in such an intimate way—was a revelation, really. I'd half expected him to bend me over the edge of his fancy bed, once he'd discovered we shared a certain predilection, then fuck me with little preamble. Apparently, he had a bit more class than that.

Perhaps he had plans to do more but wanted me clean and lulled into complacency first. Well, his plan had succeeded, but he needn't have bothered. I wasn't a maiden who needed to be seduced, and I decided he should know that about me.

"You know, you don't need to go to all this trouble," I muttered, watching him clean the dirt from the skin of my arm.

"Oh, I assure you, I do," he stated, gaze intent on his work.

"Well, I know I'm in quite the state. But what I mean is, you could have had someone dump a bucket of seawater over me instead, then summoned me here for a proper fucking." I shrugged. "I wouldn't have minded."

He huffed a laugh. "Really, Mr White? I'm not such a beast as all that."

"Aren't you?" I asked, and the tone of my voice must have given me away.

"Unless... Is that the kind of treatment you enjoy?" he asked, his question hanging in the air for a long moment.

"I...I don't need to be seduced, is what I mean. I like a good fuck, and I ain't got to be clean to enjoy a man's prick."

His face flushed now, and he stopped still, the cloth halfway down my thigh, his hand a length from my standing cock.

"Well, now," he said after a long moment. "That's good to know."

He continued, wetting the cloth every now and then, cleaning me everywhere but saving the indecent bits for the last.

"Turn around."

"I can do that myself, if you like," I offered.

"Oh no, I must insist," he said with the utmost seriousness.

I turned.

"Spread your legs and bend over at the waist. Put your hands on your knees."

I did so.

The sound of his breathing was loud in the quiet room. His hand landed softly on my arse, and he spread me open, using the wet cloth to clean me. "You're fresher than I expected, but one can never be too careful," he murmured as I tried not to moan at the pleasure his actions were giving me.

"Well…I always take some clean hay to the head with me. I'm not an animal."

I thought I heard him bite back a groan.

When he'd finished, he had me straighten and face him again. I stared down at my still dirty cock and balls, then glanced up. "Left the best for last, have you?"

He smiled and changed the dirty cloth for a clean one, dipping the soft rag into the cold water, which probably had a layer of grime on the top by now. No matter. I was cleaner than before.

"Well, that's up for debate," he said, eying my prick and grinning with embarrassment.

"Oh? You an arse man, then?"

"You could say that. I like nothing better than to sink my prick into a soft and willing arse, and I've been lucky to find a few aboard this vessel."

He followed his words by wrapping the cloth around my cock and giving it a hard stroke.

"Oh, fuck…" I groaned, my eyes rolling back in my head. The cloth was cold but the temperature didn't matter.

I expected him to let go, but he kept stroking me, up and down, gazing at me as he did. They weren't soft strokes either. He'd taken me at my word. The cloth soon warmed under the heat of his hand and my blood-filled prick.

I put a hand on his forearm to steady myself as I made embarrassingly vulnerable noises of pleasure. I'd been so aroused from the moment he'd commanded me on deck, and throughout the lengthy 'inspection', that his rough and direct treatment had an immediate effect.

"Oh! But I'm going to—" I was able to stutter, before my cock erupted over the cloth and his hand, and my body went rigid with the ecstasy of my release.

"Oh, what a good lad you are," he said, and those words sent further waves of pleasure through me, extending the moment as I hung there with my mouth and eyes wide open, shocked and stunned at the quickness of my culmination.

"Fuck," I gasped. "I'm so sorry."

He stroked me, still with the same rough movements, and I squirmed as my oversensitive flesh protested.

"Stop. Please, stop. It's too much…"

"Is it?" he said, giving me an amused look. "Oh dear."

My complaints didn't have any effect, and that made me like him even more. I had to withstand this torment for another few moments. Then he sighed and reluctantly took the cloth away, wiping my spend from his knuckles and throwing the soiled cloth into the bowl.

"Simon, don't ever apologize for your pleasure. Not in this room, at least."

I blinked, my breathing still ragged, my head scrambled. "Aye, Captain," I promised. "It's only…"

"What?"

"I thought… I thought you were going to tumble me."

"Is that what you want?" he asked, pulling his shirt over his head and undoing the belt of his trousers.

"Oh, aye. I hoped…that was what you wanted. Is it?"

"Oh, I do want to fuck you, Simon Bartholomew White," he said, pulling out a truncheon of a cock—hard and red at the tip and more than ready to give it a go. "But not today."

"Oh?" I said, my hearing gone as I stared at that perfectly sized specimen.

"I'm not going to take that liberty. Why, we've only just become acquainted," he said, as he gave himself a few rough strokes and reached for something on the table. He poured oil from a bottle into his palm and rubbed his hands together, gazing at me with a lazy kind of desire.

I was confused. "But…then why have you—"

"Kneel," he said. He pointed to the sun-soaked floorboards in front of him. The instruction sounded more like a suggestion, uttered without any threat behind the words, or any indication of urgency.

I knelt.

"Hands behind your head, Simon."

He stroked himself in earnest now, making little mewls and gasps of pleasure as he looked down on me. "You might want to close your eyes."

I didn't want to close them, entranced by the sight of him, except that I knew how it felt to get salty spunk in my eye. So I did and listened with increasing excitement to the sounds of flesh against flesh, the rustle of his clothing, the clank of his belt buckle as his movements became rougher.

"Oh God...oh, fuck...oh, Simon...oh yes..."

I felt the splash of his seed on my cheek and forehead, as Captain Martin uttered a long groan that became a whimper. By the time he was done, I was well and truly painted with globs of his semen.

"Oh, don't move. You look a picture. Keep your eyes closed. My goodness, but that was nice." He was breathless and full of self-satisfaction. I heard the sound of him tucking himself away and doing up his belt.

My cock was at a stand again, my previous completion forgotten as my insides screamed with need. But I obeyed, keeping my eyes closed while he washed his spend from my face.

"Stand up," he said, with a hand to my elbow. "Keep your eyes closed."

I stood with his aid, wondering why he wanted me blind, until my prick was enveloped in silky warmth.

"God! Oh God!" I cried out, eyes opening out of instinct as I gazed down at Captain Dinesh Martin of the *Arrow* giving me a hearty suck like a proper harlot. He had skill but I still couldn't believe he'd stoop to taking my prick in his mouth.

"Captain..." I gasped, putting a hand on his shoulder.

He pulled off, only to tell me to be quiet and not to spend, then went back to work.

Wait, what? Not to...not to *spend?* What on earth did he mean? And why did that command only want me to do so more urgently?

"But...why..." I grunted, as he got me closer and closer to the pinnacle and then pulled off.

"So that you'll remember this afternoon, and you'll remember me, once you've left this room. Now get dressed," he said and stood.

Chapter Three

Cabin Boy

I stared at him in shock. He was dismissing me *now*? But I was in a state of renewed tumescence and enjoying this visit very much. Turfing me wasn't fair.

"Leave? You mean, go back to the berths, back to caring for the livestock?" I didn't want to contemplate returning to my regular duties.

"For now. I have important business to attend to."

Where had I left my clothes? I looked around, locating them on a chair near the door, then met the captain's gaze with one of desperation.

"But...couldn't you...?"

He sighed and tilted his head, grabbing his shirt from the back of a chair and pulling the garment on.

"Well, I could. But I prefer to leave you in this state."

I gave my poor cock a few strokes and watched him as he buttoned up his shirt. "But, why?"

"Because frustrating you pleases me. Because I want to make sure you're thinking of me. Because the next time we're together, I'll make sure you're screaming my name into the pillow. If I even allow you a pillow."

Jesus fucking Christ.

"Now," he continued, gesturing to the chair. "Clothe yourself. I'll see to finding you some better vestments. I may have a position for you that's a step above looking after goats and chickens."

"Oh, aye?" I'd be happy for a different task, to be honest.

"Aye," he said, with a grin. "Do you think you could manage my rooms and help me with miscellaneous—" He looked me over again. "—tasks?"

I flushed, annoyed but entranced. "Of course."

"Hmm. Well, let me think on this enticing development."

"Yes, Captain," I said, resigned to being in a state of frustration for the foreseeable future. I started to walk to the chair where my clothes were piled.

"Oh, and Simon?"

"Hmm?" I said, turning back to him, hoping he'd changed his mind.

"Don't—" He gazed at my stand as if he wanted to pin my cock to the wall as a souvenir. "—take things into your own hands, if you understand my meaning."

I didn't quite understand.

"I beg pardon? What *do* you mean?"

He grinned with delight.

"That prick is mine. I own it now. And if I tell you to leave your cock alone, you leave it alone."

A thrill travelled up my spine as my cock swelled further. Well, this was a fine state of affairs.

"Wot? You mean, I'm not to toss myself off? At all? *Ever?*" *This is diabolical.*

He held up one finger, looking quite smug. "Not unless I give you leave."

My brain scrambled for purchase.

"But...when will I see you again? For that to happen..." I said, my voice trailing off in hopeless confusion and dismay.

"Never mind. Just be a good lad, and do as I've asked."

"I ain't a lad. I'm a full-grown man. Why should I keep my hands off?"

"Because I've told you to, Mr White. You may be a man—and I'm very glad you are—but I want you to bend to me. Do as I say, please."

"But..."

He sighed. "Do you like me, Simon Bartholomew White?"

"Yes, but—"

"Then show me you can be obedient. Because that would make me like you even more than I already do."

I stared at him, understanding now that this was some sort of test. He wanted me to prove I would obey him in sexual matters. In truth, I very much wanted to, in more ways than simply abstaining from self-pleasure. But the indefinite timeline worried me. I supposed I'd have to trust him not to make me wait too long for some relief.

"All right," I said. "But I should hope for some sort of a reward if I do as you ask."

He only smiled and gave a curt nod, appearing satisfied but not committing to anything on his end. Putting my filthy clothes back on and preparing to leave with a raging stand and muddled mind was a lesson in humility.

"Here," he said, and handed me my knife. "Wouldn't want you to come to any harm."

"Hmm. What if my bollocks go blue and fall the fuck off, in the state you've left me?"

He did me the courtesy of laughing at this exaggeration of my predicament.

"I suppose that's a risk I'll have to take. Goodbye, Mr White. Try to keep that bloody goat under control."

*

I went back to my hammock in the berth, with the stink of other men all around me, which solved the issue of the stand that wouldn't go down. But after a while, I became frustrated and felt more alone than ever.

Without the distraction of Captain Martin, things on the *Arrow* were as dull as dishwater.

I made sure the animals had food and drink each day and were soundly contained, but otherwise there was nothing to take my mind off wondering when Captain Martin would summon me and release me from this diabolical torture.

On the seventh day of my purgatory, I found myself seated at the stern of the ship, legs hanging through the rails, taking swigs from a jug of rum I'd nicked from Martinez when he wasn't looking. The weather was pleasant, and the rest of the crew were either napping in their hammocks or working on various repairs. The benefit of being invisible on a sailing ship was that you were never asked to do any work, of which there was plenty, and that nobody cared if you buggered off to drink yourself silly whilst moping about the state of your sorry existence.

I'd had the gall to hope for an upgrade to my lowly situation, and perhaps I would get one, but I had no idea how long the captain required to contemplate his decision. He had already taken more time than I'd expected. I lingered in a state of distraction. The rum soothed the edges of my discontent, and the view from my current perch was nothing less than spectacular.

Seagulls dipped and soared on the wind, shrieking their aggravation at each other. I leaned despondently against the railing and scanned the ocean's surface for anything of interest, almost hoping to see another vessel. Anything that might take my mind off of Captain Martin. Now and then I'd catch sight of a dolphin or a seal in the distance. At one point, I saw what I was convinced was the fin of a shark, but perhaps that was the drink. I lay on my back and looked up at the sky, snugging the mostly empty jug under my arm. The broad expanse above me turned all different shades of pink and orange and purple before the colours faded and I found myself gazing up at a blanket of stars.

The wind had died, and the ship rocked peacefully beneath me. I had no idea how long I'd been laying there. The nights were as warm as the days here in the southern seas, so I wasn't cold. And even if I'd been chilled, the drink was a simmering heat inside me.

I thought about my encounter with the captain, and wished I was still in his rooms. But no, he'd cast me out for his own amusement.

Part of me was annoyed and frustrated with the situation, of course. Another part of me felt inflamed by the thought that he wanted me to give over control to him. Control over my most private desires. Desires that he had an interest in possibly satisfying at some point.

I'd even taken the extreme action of giving my body a once-over with a cloth and cold water each morning, so that at least I'd be somewhat clean when I was summoned to his rooms. Some of the others made fun of me for being so fussy, but I told them to piss off and take their filthy selves elsewhere. I had to admit that keeping clean in this way did make me feel better. But my hair was still a disaster and looked nothing like its natural colour.

At the moment, I wanted nothing more than to slip my hand under the waistband of my trousers and stroke myself off. Most of the men were below decks by now, the ones up top were at the bow, keeping a lookout. But Captain Martin had forbidden me to do so. Was he truly making me suffer for his own enjoyment? Would he summon me back to his rooms to make sure of my obedience? Then again, perhaps he was deceiving me and keeping me in a state of self-imposed restriction for the amusement of pretending it had any other purpose than to frustrate me indefinitely? What if he'd forgotten about me and my prick entirely?

I sighed, running the tip of my finger along the skin at my hip, feeling my cock start to fill, and wondering how Captain Martin would possibly know if I tossed one off. Was the man a telepath? I didn't think so. He was awfully smart and capable, but I didn't think he had those kinds of powers. My visit to his rooms had been exciting, and our relationship held promise. But I was twenty-two years old. I was used to taking myself in hand at least a few times a day, if I could find a quiet corner. Even on a crowded pirate ship, there were places to hide and plenty of occasions to slip behind a box of stores and make quick work of a spill.

I slipped the very tips of my fingers under the waist of my linen pants, feeling my prick swell with the anticipation of a good going-over. At this rate, I was torturing myself because I didn't see myself disobeying him. Which was confusing because why should I be beholden to such a man?

He was the captain of the ship that had taken me on, but that didn't give him such intimate rights over me. Was there some secret pirate code—oh, excuse me—privateer code—of which I was unaware? I grinned at the thought.

We hereby decree that any man under the age of twenty-five when brought aboard must pledge to be abstinent, even from his own hand, unless the captain of the ship gives him explicit permission to— No, that was ridiculous. What fellow would agree to those terms?

Well, I hadn't exactly told him to go fuck himself, and perhaps I should have. Giving over that control was a tantalizing idea; to afford him so much power over my body. The thought of that kind of submission excited me, for certain.

However, I'd not anticipated being ignored for so long. For all I knew, he'd decided I wasn't worthwhile. For God's sake, holding back for this long couldn't be healthy. I was at my wits' end.

Hence the rum and my melancholy brooding.

And now my back ached from laying on the deck—my arse too. But I ignored the dull pain, as I was in a dizzy state of drunkenness, and the stars above were soothing and spectacular. I tried counting them, but that only made me tired, and I didn't want to fall asleep here. I must have closed my eyes.

And then a hard boot nudged me, and I woke with a grunt.

"What the fuck?" I blurted into the dark.

"Where did you get a jug of rum, young Simon?" Captain Martin drawled, reaching down and taking the item in question from me. He shook the bottle, the remaining liquor sloshing from side to side.

I held my breath, blinking up at him in the moonlight. Then I opened my mouth to tell him that the source of the drink was none of his bleeding business, when he grinned and popped the stopper. He lifted the jug to his lips and drank, side-eyeing me all the while.

I watched, remaining silent as his Adam's apple bobbed back and forth. He finished, replaced the stopper, and passed the jug back to me. I took it, cradling the bottle to my side like a trusted friend.

"What on earth are you doing out here?" he asked.

"I had planned to leap to my death, but the drink has soothed me."

He sat beside me, his back against the rail.

"Oh, my dear. Is it as bad as all that?"

I shrugged—as much as one can shrug while laying on their back. "You tell me."

"Me? What have I got to do with your somber mood?" he asked, taking some item out of his jacket pocket and putting the end between his lips. The flash of a match catching followed, and he lit his cheroot, puffing on the tip as the flame took hold.

"Bloody everything!" Honestly, how could he be so daft? "I've been patient. I've waited days for you to summon me!"

He gazed down at me.

"Have you?"

I blinked. "Have I? Have I? You told me to—"

"Yes, but I never imagined you'd obey me with such willing complicity."

"I—I—" I felt a fool. Except that he seemed inordinately pleased with me, and I couldn't discount that. "Well, I did obey you. And my compliance didn't come easy."

We both zeroed in on the tent in my breeches.

"Oh, my darling. I'm very impressed."

"I don't want you to be impressed! I want you to stop ignoring me and give me leave to—to—"

"Give you leave to what?"

I thought about what to say. I pushed myself up from the deck, leaving the jug of rum on the boards, and leaned toward him. I put a desperate hand on his chest, thrilling to the warmth and strength of him. "Please, since I've been so very obedient, can't I come to your rooms, Captain?"

He watched me silently, pulling on his cheroot and puffing smoke out in formed circles. Showing off. "Not tonight."

I couldn't believe he was still denying me. "You're such a prick!" I said, spitting with venom and pulling my hand back from his chest. I drew my legs up from between the rails and stood, albeit a bit wobbly. "I'm going to take myself in hand then. I ain't beholden to you no more, if you ain't keeping up your end of the deal."

"What, right this minute?"

"Aye," I said, meaning every word. I was already undoing my trousers.

"No," he said. "Wait."

I didn't want to. I was tired of waiting.

"Why should I?" I said, pushing down my breeches and taking my poor cock in hand. The relief was immediate, and I began to stroke myself back and forth. "Oh, thank fuck."

I recalled that I had an audience and looked over at him.

He was watching me, his eyes sparking with interest and some annoyance, but he didn't say anything as I pleasured myself. And I didn't give a fuck what he thought at this point. I needed completion so desperately.

I put my free hand on the rail and doubled my efforts, the pleasure like a delicious wine that I'd saved for just the right moment. I held Captain Martin's gaze as I worked myself, my breaths blending with the soft slap of the waves on the hull as the *Arrow* glided slowly forward.

"Stop."

One word, uttered in a commanding tone by the man who was in charge of this ship and my life, as little as my existence mattered.

I stopped. I let go of myself as if my cock was a heated coal from a recent fire. I stuttered a broken gasp and had to clamp down hard on myself, or I would have spent into the air at the look on his face at that moment.

"Oh...fuck..." I cursed, trying to hold onto my control.

He watched me for a moment. Then his arm shot out, and he grabbed my breeches, pulling me over to where he sat. I didn't know what was happening. I watched as he tossed his lit cheroot over the side of the ship, grabbed my hips and tugged me forward, his mouth covering my cock as I grasped the rail for purchase.

"Oh! Oh! Oooh..." were the only sounds I was able to make, besides gasps and choking noises as I went rigid and erupted down the captain's throat. Fireworks exploded behind my closed eyes as the captain milked my eager cock. The culmination lasted forever, perhaps because of the length of my abstinence, or due to the way Captain Martin was sucking and licking and swallowing it all.

I leaned on the rail, gasping for breath as the ecstasy faded and, once again, the captain kept up his attention past the point of comfort. I tried to pull away but he held me fast, making a noise in his throat that sounded like a laugh.

"Oh," I said again, breathless and spent. "Please. Please... stop...stop..."

He took pity on me and let my softening cock slide out of his mouth.

"Mmm" was all he said, licking his lips and swallowing my remaining spend.

"Bloody hell," I cursed, tucking myself away in case anyone happened to come by. "What the fuck was that?" I gasped, my legs trembling with the relief of days of built-up tension.

"I believe the term for the act is 'gamahuche'."

I held up my hand and took a step back. "Yes, but why here? Why now?"

After all this time!

"I didn't want your sweet essence to go to waste," he said, using the tip of his finger to wipe some of the seed from the corner of his mouth. "Or to splatter the side of my lovely ship."

I stared at him. He stared at me. Then I rolled my eyes.

"Oh for fuck's sake," I said and slid down to sit on the boards beside him. "You lost your cheroot."

He gave me a devilish grin. "Your prick is much better than a cheroot."

"Then why did you wait so long to come find me?"

"You know, I am a very busy man, Simon." He fished in his pocket and brought out another cheroot, flourishing the thing at me before putting the tip between his lips.

I watched as he struck a match against his boot and lit the end, pulling the smoke into his lungs as he closed his eyes.

"I'm sure. But I was going mad!"

"Better now though?" he asked, as he opened his eyes and gazed into mine.

"Yes. Much."

He blew smoke in my face. "I like you, Simon. But I need to decide if we should enjoy more time together."

"I...thought I was going to be your cabin boy."

"Perhaps you shall."

"But...when will you know?"

"Hmm. Well, perhaps tomorrow. Or the next day." He gazed

down at me with blithe curiosity. "You'll wait for me to decide, won't you?"

I wanted to say no, I wouldn't fucking wait for him. What kind of a mad fellow did he take me for? He could go fuck himself.

But what I said was "Yes."

*

I barely lasted two more days as I waited on tenterhooks with my needs rising again. He hadn't technically told me to keep my hands off myself, but I did—out of some misguided need to prove myself or prove I could obey. I tried to focus on the animals, and that did help, but they were hardly a distraction from my lustful thoughts of the captain.

Finally, I'd had enough.

The animals were my only solace. Perhaps they could be my salvation.

I glanced around to make sure nobody was nearby, then casually undid the knot in Lilith's tie down.

"Oh, Lilith, look. Your rope's come undone. You're free."

She didn't move.

"Lilith. Don't you want to run up on deck and cause mayhem?"

She grunted and chewed on the frayed end of the unbound rope.

"For fuck's sake."

I looked around again, then slapped her on her flank—not too hard, but enough to get her moving. She bleated with indignation and took off for the stairs to the deck.

I gave her a bit of a head start and then went after her.

"Oh, Lilith, you stupid bloody goat!" I grouched, so nobody would know I'd set her loose. "Not again!"

As I ran up the steps, curses and cries came from on deck from crew who'd been startled by Lilith's mad dash for freedom.

"Sorry, sorry. Pardon me. Excuse me," I said, dodging bodies as I chased her. As I ran, supposedly with steadfast intent, I tried to glean where the captain was. I hoped he would spot me.

"Mr White!"

The familiar voice and stern tone assaulted me with waves of delight and welcome alarm. I didn't care how mad he was, he'd seen and acknowledged me. Hopefully, he'd recall our conversation in the moonlight.

I stopped dead, leaving the goat to career past the yardarm, and turned toward him. The rays of the sun made a kind of a halo around him as I squinted and brought my hand up to shield my eyes.

"Yes, Captain?" I asked, hearing the first strains of "Amazing Grace" play in my head.

"Get that blasted goat, put her away, and come to my rooms. We need to discuss containment, and how to manage errant beasts."

As he spoke those words, he gazed at me in a way that left no question as to which errant beast he was referring. A thrill passed through me and my cock filled. Again.

"Yes, Captain," I said, with plenty of false humility. Inwardly, I was jubilant. My plan had worked.

"Duncan, grab that bloody goat! Take her downstairs and tie her up, for fuck's sake. I need to teach White how to do a proper knot."

"Aye, Captain."

I made my way downstairs. Boone was outside Captain Martin's rooms, as usual.

"You again," he said.

"I'm afraid so."

"He ain't here."

"He told me to meet him here. With some urgency, in fact."

"In trouble again?"

"No doubt." I said, grinning.

"Jesus, yer a prat. Well, you may as well go in, I suppose."

He held his hand out toward me with the palm up.

I rolled my eyes and pulled out my knife, passing the weapon over.

"Had to use it yet?" he asked.

"A few times," I said with mock gravity. "To get a second helping of potatoes."

Boone *almost* smiled.

I opened the door and went into the captain's rooms, for the second time. The quiet and peace of his quarters felt like a benediction. I wasn't sure where I should wait for him. Should I strip naked and surprise him that way? But what if he brought someone with him? Perhaps disrobing was a tad risky.

Suppose he had ordered me here to tell me he'd changed his mind, and I wasn't to be his cabin boy after all? I didn't particularly want to have that conversation buck naked. I'd best hedge my bets and keep my clothes on, as malodorous as they were. I could always strip later as a calculated move to influence him.

Waiting was not an activity I did well. I soon became restless and then distracted by a large map of the world spread out on Captain Martin's desk. There were pieces of wood in the shape of miniature boats, placed at various spots, as if he were preparing his fleet for an attack. They might have marked where they'd seen other ships, unless Captain Martin was still a navy officer who was pretending to be an ex-navy officer who was pretending to be a privateer-slash-pirate.

I was too clever to believe that. Although the story would make for a wonderful and thrilling adventure novel.

The tiny wooden boats were so fine. I picked up one to examine it, noting the detail and the workmanship, and that the map must have a magnet beneath it and each of the figures as well, as the wee sailboat needed more force to pick up than I'd expected. When I went to put it back, I couldn't remember the exact spot the miniature boat had been in. I frowned, my gaze traversing the map and wondering how much time I had until the captain—

Booted footsteps sounded outside. Then a familiar drawl.

"Is White here?"

"Aye, Captain. He's inside."

Well, blast. I frantically tried to remember where the little boat had been, hovering my hand over the map.

"I'll take the knife," Captain Martin said. "There's no need to confiscate his blade again. He'll do me no harm."

But how could he be so sure? He obviously wasn't afraid of me in the least. And he was right, I'd ne'er harm him. Not with a knife. He already knew to be wary of tankards of ale.

"Aye, Cap'n," Boone replied.

I closed my eyes and placed the miniature boat down in a random spot, hoping he wouldn't notice, and turned around as the door opened.

"Oh, hello," I said, putting my hands behind my back and smiling with the pretense of innocence.

Captain Martin frowned. "What have you done?"

"I—beg your pardon? What do you mean? I just got here," I said, unable to keep from glancing at the map. And I knew right away I'd made a mistake. Captain Martin was astute and not easily deceived.

"Simon Bartholomew White. Did you touch my charts?"

I stuttered a laugh. "Of course not. Why would I do that?"

"Move."

I closed my eyes in defeat and moved to the side, muttering a curse.

He went past me and examined the map. He immediately found the miniature that I'd put back in the wrong place and picked the tiny object up.

"You're lucky that I, at least, remember where this goes," he said, putting the small boat in a different spot and eying me with disapproval.

"Yes, Captain," I grunted, adjusting my stand in the fabric of my trousers, which proved the wrong move.

"You need to learn to keep your hands to yourself, Simon," he said. "And I know just how to teach you."

My eyes went wide.

Captain Martin smiled with the expression of a man who was about to lay into a holiday feast. "Now, where's the rope."

Rope? My cock jerked.

And he knew exactly where the rope was. He strode over to a chest of drawers, tugged open the bottom drawer, and pulled out a rolled up length of black rope and tossed it onto the bed. The coil landed with a soft thud.

"What are you going to do?" I asked, my brain short-circuiting as I imagined all the possibilities.

"I'm going to tie you up and fuck you, Simon," he said, in a manner he might use to say he was going to dip down to the galley and grab us a snack.

I swallowed, feeling a thrill all through my body.

"Do you consent?" he asked, with a hopeful expression.

"Consent? To what you just said, you mean?"

Captain Martin walked up to me and stood so close I could

see the pores of his unblemished skin and smell the manly scent of him. His eyes were pools of heat and desire.

"Do you consent to being tied up and fucked, Simon? Contrary to what you might think, I don't like to force myself on other men."

I wanted to say, 'Of course, let's get started.' But, instead, I crossed my arms over my chest and said, "Well...I suppose so." I didn't want to appear too eager. "If you must."

Captain Martin smiled and crossed *his* arms. "Not good enough. Perhaps you should go."

"Oh!" I exclaimed, uncrossing mine. "You see, what I meant to say was 'yes, Captain'."

He waited.

"I consent," I finished, making my willingness abundantly clear.

"All right. Now tell me what you consent *to*, Simon Bartholomew White."

I cleared my throat, heat rushing into my cheeks. "To being tied up and fucked, sir."

"Excellent. Now take those nasty rags off, so I can have them tossed over the side of this ship. Hopefully, that doesn't kill half the sea life nearby."

That was a low blow but, no doubt, a reasonable concern.

"Yes, Captain."

Once I was naked, Captain Martin took charge like we were going into battle. Perhaps that's how he thought of this sort of thing.

"Now lean over and hold your calves. Spread your legs."

Well, he was getting right to business. Since I'd had to wait so long for this much-anticipated private interview, I didn't exactly mind.

I blushed with humiliation, but a giddy sense of excitement filled me as I obeyed.

The captain was silent.

I craned my neck, my dirty hair falling over my eyes. "What's the matter?"

"Nothing," he said, placing a hand on one cheek and spreading me. "I didn't expect you to be so clean. Have you been washing?"

Pride and relief filled me. "Aye. With a cloth and water each morning."

He smoothed a thumb down my crack, making me shiver.

"That's very commendable and appreciated."

"I did it for you," I admitted.

"For me? Not for yourself?"

"Well...it did feel good to be clean, in general, or as clean as I could manage. But my endeavours were in case of exactly this circumstance, really," I admitted, gesturing to my nakedness.

He smiled. "I was going to clean you off again, but there's no need. I'll arrange a proper bath for you later, so you can do something about your hair."

"You are so kind," I said, with a sarcastic lilt to my voice. I felt rather insulted, even though I did look forward to bathing, particularly if the captain planned to watch.

"You can stand up now."

I did and turned to face him.

"That brings me to my next point. If it's kindness you're after in terms of intimacy, I'm afraid I'm not your man." His gaze pierced me with a brutal and frank level of honesty. "I like the men I fuck to be restrained, as you will see, and I'm not the most gentle of lovers."

A shudder wracked me.

I nodded. "Well, it just so happens, Captain Martin, that I'm rather fond of a man who knows what he wants...and isn't afraid to take the pleasure."

He smiled, as if he'd just been given an unexpected gift, and held my gaze. The sexual tension felt thick in the air between us.

"I should give you a word, in case you need me to stop whatever I'm doing. In case I'm being rougher than you like."

"Fair," I said, finding breathing to be difficult. I glanced at the rope on the bed.

"Good. I don't actually want to harm you. I do find, though, that a bit of...controlled pain...is inflaming to some..." He looked at me as the tip of his tongue traced his bottom lip, and his eyebrows lifted in a silent question.

"Aye," I said breathlessly.

"Do you like a bit of pain, Simon?"

"I like to be manhandled. Beyond that, I have yet to explore," I admitted.

He smiled slyly. "Well, I have some experience in this area. And I'd like to explore that with you, if you're willing."

"Aye. As long as I have a stop word."

"So you aren't completely new to this sort of play between men, are you? Would you like to choose one?"

"Cribbage," I said without preamble.

"Beg pardon? Did you say 'cribbage'?"

"Aye. Horrid game. Makes me want to pluck my eyes out."

He tried not to laugh and barely succeeded.

"Very well. If you utter the word, I stop whatever I'm doing and untie you."

"Oh. So I'm only to use my word if I want *everything* to stop?"

He chuckled. "You sound disappointed. Oh, Simon, I believe

we're going to get along very well."

"I'm just thinking that I might have to slow you down or stop you, but I might not want to stop *everything*. Is that an option?"

"Of course. Let's leave it open, shall we?"

"Aye."

"Now go lay on the bed, on your back, and spread your arms and legs like a starfish."

He tied my wrists to the carved posts of the bed frame, then folded my legs over my belly and fastened my ankles over my head.

"This is quite...undignified," I commented, feeling well-displayed and expertly captured.

"Mmm," he agreed, gazing at me with more than a twinkle in his eye.

I focused on breathing through my nose, my eyes on him, waiting for what he might do next. He had me at his mercy, and yet I'd never felt so free.

I watched as he walked to the drawer that he'd left open and took out what looked like a leather riding crop, returning to me with a look of mischief and excitement in his eyes.

I stiffened as if I might try to escape.

"Now, don't worry. I know how to use this."

"Are you an equestrian?" I asked rhetorically.

He had the grace to laugh. "Oh no. I meant that I know how to use this on *you*, Mr White."

"Now, remember, I've never ever—" I began but was startled when he ran the folded leather tip of the crop over the sole of my foot.

"Ah!" I cried out, trying ineffectively to pull away.

"Oh yes. We'll start this way."

"Oh, no, no, no...please, no," I begged, squirming and writhing as I tried without success to get away. Propitious that he'd given me a word, because despite my frantic struggles and the instinctive protests against the tickling strokes, I didn't truly want him to stop.

I didn't say the word, even though I didn't know how much more of this torment I could take. And he hadn't even gone near my prick yet. All the same, my cock stood hard and leaking from his blatant control and sadistic goals. Pain I could have dealt with but the tickling was too much.

But I had waited so long to get into the captain's rooms and his graces, so I did my best to persevere, even though I hiccupped with sobs by the time he took pity on me and stopped. A humiliating and sobering turn of events.

"And I haven't even struck you yet," he said with a level of glee that left me no doubt about where this was going.

I'd barely let out a squeak of indignation when I felt the first swipe of the crop against my bare arse.

"My goodness, but you are perfect, Simon," he said, laying into my lily-white arse with a smug determination. The sounds of the crop slicing the air and landing with a snap filled my ears, followed by a sting so sharp the pain made me gasp.

"Oh, fuck...am I? Oh...ow, ow, stop, fuck! Captain, Captain, Captain!"

He paused. "Yes, White?"

His address took me by surprise.

"For fuck's sake, ain't we on a first name basis by now?" I asked from my captivity, my limbs trembling from the intensity.

He only laughed and continued with his treatment until I moaned in anguish.

"Do you need me to stop?" he asked.

I was making pitiful sounds and my answer should have been yes. But even though my arse was singing with pain, a warm glow had lit me up inside, and I couldn't say my stop word.

"Never mind, I'm done." He tossed the crop to the side and started undoing his trousers as my eyes went wide. "With the crop, at least."

My gaze zeroed in on his scepter of a cock as he pushed his breeches down and took the monster in hand.

"Do you want this?"

"Yes, yes, yes."

"Do you like the ropes?"

"Yes!"

"All right, then."

With his trousers still carelessly around his thighs, Captain Martin, with whom I apparently wasn't on a first-name basis and didn't mind at all, kneeled on the bed, took some grease from a conveniently placed bowl, and slicked his prick up with a stolid determination. Then he leaned forward, positioned himself, and sank into me like a churn into soft butter.

"Good God," he breathed as he settled into me.

I whimpered at the incredible sensation of finally getting Captain Martin's cock into me.

"Aye" was all I could say as he started to move, causing my eyes to roll back in my head. It had been a while since I'd been fucked, to be honest, and I'd been hankering after this man for weeks. Ever since he'd held a gun to my head in the Penny Whistle, of all things. Well, perhaps before that, but the threat of violence upon my person had sealed the deal. Call me mad, for I was.

I wrapped my fingers around the ropes and held on as he began to thrust. He was practised, for certain, and varied his motions between long, slow thrusts and quick, hard ones. By the time he spilled with a low groan, I was a writhing mess of desperate need.

"Captain... Captain," I panted, for I'd not reached my completion as of yet.

"Mmm," he grunted, continuing to push into me with a lackadaisical enjoyment and a self-satisfied smile. But those motions weren't enough to push me over the edge.

"Please!" I begged, squirming beneath him so he could feel the hot brand of my prick against him. "Oh, please!"

The smile that spread over his face as he gazed upon me was everything. There was fondness and affection and pride.

"Watching you beg, Simon... Why, it's the best thing I've seen in a very long time."

"Now we're on a first name basis?" I asked, my voice shrill with desperation. I was strung on a tight wire of coiled tension.

"Perhaps. Although I like it when you call me captain, and I'm not particularly fond of my given name."

"Oh," I said. "Well, then, Captain. Will you...please, please, please...help me?"

He didn't answer me, only smiled. All I could do was whimper. I was past the point of coherent desire. I needed to finish so badly, and I was terrified that he didn't even care. Or that he would enjoy frustrating me more than pleasing me.

He pulled out with a sigh, then spent too long playing with my hole and his seed, pushing it in and dragging the spunk out with his fingers.

"I could do this all day, Simon White. Perhaps I will." He leaned over me to whisper in my ear, still fiddling with my slippery hole. "I'll plug you to keep all that sweet stuff inside, and you'll have to go the entire night full of my essence."

I moaned, heady with the idea.

The captain chuckled and backed off, gaze fixing on where his fingers danced and delved, the filthy bastard.

"Of course, I'd have to clean you out first, with a hose and water. And you wouldn't be able to eat anything." He clicked his tongue and sighed. "Oh, what a time we'll have."

I made the most pitiful sound and rolled my head from side to side. Couldn't he see the state of me? Wouldn't he let me have some satisfaction?

He laughed. "But that sort of thing takes planning. So instead, I'm going to make you spend all over yourself, my pretty lad. These ropes have you in the perfect position."

He slipped his fingers back in and petted that tender spot until I writhed even more pitifully. Then he wrapped his other hand around my cock and stroked until I convulsed and screamed, spraying my belly and chest. I cursed him as he fondled my oversensitive bits with the cruelty of a true sadist.

He unbound me, told me to stay put, then left me tangled and ruined in his bedsheets.

My mind spun with everything that had occurred, and my body ached in all the right places. I lolled in the soft sheets and may have drifted off.

The clang of metal woke me, and I looked up to see two crew members hauling a large tin tub through the doors. I clutched the sheet as I sat up, ready to make a run for cover.

"Are you that scared of a bath, White?" the captain asked, his lip curled with amusement. He turned to the men. "Put the tub by the window."

Captain Martin was seated in the chair at his desk, holding a pen in his broad hand and gazing at me with fondness. He was wearing his trousers and shirt with a patterned robe overtop, held closed with a loosely knotted sash.

I recognized the men but didn't truly know them. They didn't appear concerned to find me naked in the captain's bed. I wasn't sure what to make of that.

After they left, another two fellows came in with pails of steaming water. They emptied one after the other into the tub.

"Thank you, Peters," Captain Martin said.

"Aye. And Lin will bring the clothes," he said. "Will that be all?"

"Yes, thank you. Now leave us."

"Aye, Cap'n," Peters said, glancing at me without any obvious contempt before he left.

I gazed contemplatively at the closed door.

"Do they know, then?"

"Hmm?" Captain Martin said, watching me with a sedate contemplation. "Know what?"

I tossed the sheet aside and got out of bed, trying to look seductive. I yawned and scratched an itch on my thigh. Then grinned.

"That you like to leave your seed inside other men until it trickles out in tiny bits and makes their thighs wet."

He gazed at me with a blatant hunger.

"Are your lovely thighs wet with my seed, Simon White?"

"Well, it's dried now and gone tacky."

"Well, then," he said with a satisfied nod. "Into the tub with you."

I swallowed, desire rising in me again. "Yes, Captain.

He stood, removed his robe, and settled on the edge of his bed, and watched me step gingerly into the hot water. The metal tub was only about half full and appeared barely large enough to sit in with my knees bent.

"It's not going to bite you. Get in."

"The water's hot."

"For heaven's sake."

I stepped into the bath with some care, then lowered myself down, hissing as my skin came into contact with the scalding water. I tried to remember the last time I'd had a proper bath.

For all that the tub was small and not completely full, this was a luxury I'd never imagined to find aboard a ship like the *Arrow*.

"Blimey, you got a fire going on a wooden ship? Ain't that a tad risky?"

"There's a proper stove in the galley, with safety modifications. Did you wonder how your food was cooked?"

"Now that you mention it, no." I shrugged.

"Here," Captain Martin said, tossing me a bar of soap. My hands went up instinctively, and I did catch the object; however, the thing slipped through my fingers and into the water with a splash.

"Blast," I said.

"Simon White, is there anything you're good at?"

I searched for the errant bar of soap, found the slippery thing, and brought it above the water's surface with a triumphant smile.

"Answer my question."

"Well, Captain, my tongue is a weapon I'm very proud of. And I've a practiced skill at cocksucking."

"Mmm. I'll put you to the test when you're finished in there."

Well, then.

"Are you good at following orders, I wonder?"

"Depends who's giving them."

"Stand up."

I stared at him as he sat on the edge of his bed in his black breeches and boots and white shirt, like some kind of deposed king or prince. I didn't want to defy him, but now that I was enveloped in cozy warmth, I didn't want to leave that comfort.

"But, I only just—"

"So, no." He rolled his eyes. "Stand up, Mr White. I want to see you."

I stared at him for a moment, deliberating if I should do as he asked. Since I was in his rooms, and he'd been the one to treat me to the luxury of a soak, and since I did have a stake in seducing the man, I stood, clutching the bar of soap to my dripping chest. The water sluiced off me, as the cool air of the cabin brought bumps to the surface of my skin.

"You are absolutely filthy," the captain murmured as if he were speaking words of endearment to a treasured concubine. "The sludge is literally running off of you."

The intimate tone of his voice, and the reference to the state of both my body and my thoughts, frankly gave me a heady, lustful feeling.

I frowned. "But...I've been washing! Every day, even. I told you."

"And while I commend you for doing so, I'm afraid a proper bath is needed to deal with months of bad habits."

"Bad habits! I was clean when I came to Port Royal, I can tell you. Then I was robbed and almost killed at knifepoint. I was destitute for weeks. The last thing on my mind was a bloody bath."

"Well. It's a good thing you're here, then."

I couldn't argue with that.

"Aye."

"Now, my filthy fellow, I want you to rub that bar of soap all over yourself. And, I do mean *everywhere*."

A jolt of desire travelled throughout my entire body.

"Yes, Captain," I said, and proceeded to do as he wished, slipping the soap under my arms, between my legs, and wherever I could reach. I held his gaze as I bent over and reached behind me, sliding the slippery bar between my arse cheeks. "Only, I can't see if I'm getting my hole clean enough."

My voice was hoarse and my breaths quick, as I dangled that little lure before him.

The captain was on his feet and coming over.

"Give it to me," he said, his voice a deep raspy thing that thrilled me.

I passed him the soap, my heart pounding, and my scrubbed cock thickening at the look of purpose in his eyes.

"Bend over and hold the side. Spread your legs."

I did, the water sloshing over the metal edge. I should have been cold, but the heat of my passion kept me warm.

"Good man. I see you *can* be obedient in some circumstances. Now stay still."

I gasped as he used his free hand to spread me apart, and the other to swipe the soap along my cleft in a way that made me shudder and moan. Then he pressed the piece of soap to my fresh-cleaned hole and teased the rounded tip back and forth, whilst I tried not to give away how much I liked the sensation.

"Look at your greedy little hole. So hungry."

His words excited me. I spread my legs wider.

"This is the finest castile soap, I'll have you know. Very expensive."

"Yes, Captain." I said. "Are you certain you want to use such a fancy thing on my arse?"

"Oh yes. Nothing is too good for this beautiful, luscious flesh of yours, Simon. Don't undervalue yourself."

"Oh...well...thank you, Captain," I said, genuinely bewildered and flattered at his comments.

"I had a naughty thought. And you needn't worry, as this

soap is made from the most benign ingredients and won't harm you in the least."

Harm me?

The tip of the hard bar pressed against my hole, and the captain rubbed back and forth with a steady and concentrated pressure, teasing me open. When I realized what was about to happen, a hot spike of heat flooded me.

Captain Martin, the tricky bugger, pushed the slick piece of soap right up my greedy arse.

"Oh, fuck," I whispered.

I was astonished at the turn of his profane mind. To think of a plan like this and then calmly and deliberately take action, as if it were the most ordinary thing in the world to slide a bar of expensive Castile soap up another man's arse, was...diabolical and dirty in a way that went straight to my heart. Not many people surprised me anymore, so when someone did, it felt like the most welcome discovery—especially when the substance of the revelation fed into my own perversions with such exactness.

The slick bar filled my gut, the way the feeling of connection and acceptance filled my soul. Here was a man after my own strange predilections, who might prove to have the very same ones, truth be told. This scandalous pirate captain, or privateer, whatever he was, who'd brought me onto his ship and into his bed, had exceeded all my expectations.

"Mmm," Captain Martin hummed, nudging the object further with his fingers.

"But..." I groaned, even though I loved everything about this. "Won't it get stuck?"

"Oh, I'm not worried," the captain said, rubbing the outer edges of my arsehole with a determined efficiency.

Easy for him to say.

"Oooh," I moaned, feeling a wee bit scared but excited at the same time and so heated I thought I might light myself on fire. "Please..."

"Please what, Simon White?"

"Help...me?" I didn't know quite what I was asking for. The reassurance that the bar would come out, perhaps? But did I really want that, when the soap felt so good in its present location?

Captain Martin sighed. "All right then. Up."

"Stand up?"

"Yes."

I straightened, which made the object feel bigger than ever.

"Push the damn thing out, if you're so worried about the situation," he said, crossing his arms over his chest, his solid prick a distinct outline in his breeches.

"P-pardon?"

"If you can take a shit, you can expel a bar of soap. It should slide right out."

Those words and the very idea of taking a shit worked to cause me to bear down out of pure instinct.

And Captain Martin was right, it didn't take much effort at all. But the pleasure as the thing exited my body and sploshed into the bathwater made me blush with shame.

"See?" he said, a little bit breathlessly.

"Aye," I sighed. "Jesus."

I almost didn't want to meet his gaze, but when I did, the fire in his eyes made plain his feeling about what we were doing. I wrapped a hand around my cock, giving it a pull.

"Hands off. That pretty prick is mine. Leave it be."

"Yes, Captain," I said, shuddering with pleasure.

He fished the soap out of the water and made me bend over again.

I stared at my wavy reflection in the water, as Captain Martin played with that bar of soap and my arse, shoving it in and having me squirt it out, for his amusement—and mine, of course. I'd never felt more like an object at the hands of...well, anyone...and the feeling of being owned and enjoyed made me giddy, to be frank. I'd never claimed to be a regular fellow. There really was no explaining this strange feeling, but I didn't want to question the sentiment anymore.

Somehow, Captain Martin understood me, and fed me his own strangeness in actions that were quite welcome and exquisitely thrilling.

"I think I must be all cleaned out," I said, with a laugh.

"Hmm. Can't ever be too careful."

He continued to play with me, until the bar of soap was a tiny sliver of its former shape.

"There we go. That should do the job."

"I reckon," I agreed, dazed and impressed.

"Now sit down and lean your head back."

Even though I'd not known him long, the captain's voice already felt like a siren's lure, and I succumbed to his demands without thought. I expected him to take down his trousers, and slide his cock into my mouth. Instead, he helped me to wet my hair, then used another bar of his fine soap to lather up the greasy strands.

"Just how red is your hair under all this grime, Simon Bartholomew White?"

"Quite a bright hue, when not full of shit," I said.

"I certainly hope you don't mean actual shit."

His deep voice rumbled pleasantly as he massaged my scalp. I closed my eyes, enjoying the care he was giving me.

"Well, you never know," I admitted.

I was rewarded with the captain's soft laughter.

"Up now."

I stood but wobbled as if I were coming out of a trance. His gentle touch had lulled me into laziness. Then Captain Martin poured clean, cold water from another jug over me.

"Jesus! That's bloody cold," I gasped.

"Don't want you to get soft with all this pampering," Captain Martin said. "I plan to use you well, and I'm not always gentle." He tilted his head, considering. "In fact, I'm not often kind when I have a willing man beneath me."

I blinked silently in bewildered awe. Had I created Captain Martin from my own perverse dreams?

His gaze was running over me as if I looked completely different now.

"What?" I asked, starting to feel a bit cold.

He passed me a linen cloth.

"Your hair is quite red, as you say. And there's not a part of you that's not covered in brown freckles, except for…" he gestured at my scar. "Well, that and your pretty cock. You look like a randy little rooster."

I gazed down at myself. He was right. I'd been called rooster before, but never with so much affection. And nobody had ever called my cock pretty.

"Dry off, if you please. Then, if you're so inclined, you can give me a demonstration of your one and only skill."

I should have known.

I swiped the water from my skin whilst Captain Martin disrobed. I tried not to stare at his beautifully masculine form but lost that battle.

He cocked his head at me. "When did you last have a haircut?"

"Quite a while ago. And not a very good one, as you can see."

"Would you allow me? I have shears and…well, not to be cruel but it's rather a disaster."

Well, this was a surprise.

"I suppose so. But not too short. I like it long-ish around my ears."

Quite a strange idea to let a naked man throw a towel over my shoulders, sit me in a chair, and take a pair of sharp scissors to my damp locks. I was nervous that he would make a mess of the task, not that he really could make my hair any worse.

When he'd finished, he put the shears down, ruffled my hair with a hand and passed me a looking glass.

The man who stared back at me was unfamiliar, but I liked the look of him. He'd left the length of my hair mostly alone, but he'd trimmed sections in a layered fashion to lessen its shapeless bulk. Feathery bits of copper framed my face and fell around my ears.

"Well?"

"Thank you. I like what you've done."

I tilted my head and angled it so that I could see a bit of the hair at the side and back. He'd trimmed the edges that sat against my neck and they reminded me of the fronds of ferns. It looked… much improved.

"Thank you."

"You're quite welcome. I can see your face better now. Your eyes look even more blue."

He gathered the towel off my shoulders, keeping all the bits of hair inside, and used a clean cloth to wipe my neck where the towel hadn't kept the bits of hair off.

"How did you learn to do that?" I asked.

"Oh, I have a great many talents," he said with a sly wink.

He lit some oil lamps since the sun was going down on another day, and the cabin filled with soft light. And now I could see him better.

The captain truly was a fine example of a man. Just enough muscle to win in a fight, with a lithe, feline grace of movement, and a majestic aspect that made me want to kneel.

He sat on the edge of the mattress, took himself in hand, and beckoned me.

"Come now. Impress me."

He held my gaze as I dropped the towel to the floor.

"You really are quite lovely under all that dirt. Such a pretty little rooster," he said, his tone relaxed and contemplative.

I didn't know what to say. I didn't want to reveal how touched I was at those words. It had been a long time since anyone had been so gracious to me.

"Do you think so?"

"Simon, you wouldn't be here if I hadn't found you charming, even in your previously neglected state," he said with a refreshing directness. "But now you're quite pretty."

"Pretty! I ain't no lass."

He grinned. "Thank heavens. But you're as lovely as one."

"I'm not. Truly, Captain, I think your brain is addled."

He quirked the corner of his lips. "Quite likely. At any rate, your beauty is secondary to your skills at the moment," he said with a pragmatic inflection that made me desperate to please him. "Get to work."

"Yes, Captain."

I crawled over the bed to him, then met his gaze as I took his offered prick into my mouth and swallowed him down in one movement.

He gasped, stuttered, then cursed.

I drew off him and grinned.

"Again?" I asked.

He blinked. "Again."

This time, he let out a deep groan and closed his eyes.

"All right. That's good. That's very good."

"More?"

"More."

I fellated him, using my best techniques, for a short time, enjoying the noises and sounds he made—soft sighs, gasps, and moans.

He grabbed a fistful of my hair.

"Ow!" The word was muffled by his swollen appendage.

"Stop messing about and get me off," he ordered, his tone desperate and firm.

"Uh-huh," I grunted, knowing the vibrations of my words were making him crazy.

I splayed my hands on his powerful thighs and got to work, licking and slurping and swallowing that club of a cock like my life depended on the task.

Perhaps there was truth to that idea. If I could please Captain Martin and show him my intrinsic value, even if only as a cock slut and bed warmer, then perhaps I could gain a permanent place on the *Arrow* and not be tossed off at the next landing.

The captain groaned, one hand on my head, watching me with heavy-lidded eyes and a perverted fascination.

"Christ. Christ. Christ," he muttered.

But I was barely watching him. My focus was my mouth, my throat, and that solid baton of his. I made fucking love to his prick with my whole heart.

"Oh! God! Simon!" he grunted, his fingers tightening in my hair, tugging just enough to make my own cock throb. He erupted, his seed streaming down my willing throat, as he groaned with the ecstasy of a sudden and substantial release.

He held me still and only let me go when I started coughing and sputtering. He pulled himself out and gave me a little slap on the cheek.

"Well done," he sighed. "That was quite satisfactory."

I gasped for breath. "*Quite satisfactory?*"

The nerve of him!

His face was full of amusement, and my anger died in a moment.

"Get under the covers, Rooster. You're bunking with me."

"Yes, Captain," I said, charmed by the nickname he'd given me.

"And, Rooster?"

"Yes?"

"Based on your wonderful performance as a soap depository and the skills you've recently demonstrated so"—his eyes twinkled—"satisfactorily..."

I frowned.

He continued, "I've made the perhaps rash decision to claim you as my own."

"Your own? But what does that mean? Do I get a say in it?"

"Of course you do. Despite having a questionable means of employment, I'm not a scoundrel." He examined me with much thought. "What say you?"

"To what exactly? You haven't explained."

"To being my cabin boy and my housekeeper and my willing catchment when I've need of one."

"How fucking romantic."

He laughed.

"I'm not trying to seduce you, Rooster. I want to fuck you.

And I want to play with you. And I want to own you, in a manner of speaking," he stated. "In return, you get to live here, in my rooms, and enjoy all the luxuries you see around you, on a daily basis." He smirked as a tinge of pink crested his cheeks. "Well, at least on those occasions that you don't have a broom in your hand or my cock up your arse."

A testament to how much I wanted him that I disregarded the broom comment.

"Well, in that case—"

He held up his hand.

"*But*. If I catch wind of you offering your talents to any of the other men without my express permission or command, I will put you over the yardarm and whip you raw in front of them all."

My eyes went wide. "Truly?" I asked in an alarmed whisper.

"Perhaps not. But I will be sorely disappointed."

"Then, yes, I agree."

"You must speak the words to seal the deal."

I rolled my eyes. "I agree...to be your cabin boy and—" *I'm going to regret this part.* "—housekeeper," *But not this part.* "—and your willing catchment. Satisfied?"

"Oh, Rooster. I'm positive that I will be extremely satisfied with this arrangement."

Dear God, what had I just signed up for?

"And I hope that you will find some pleasure in being my devoted houseboy and fucktoy." He grinned, as if that really was beside the point.

I tried not to combust into an explosion of frustrated desire.

The captain gave me one of his shirts to wear and put on his embroidered robe. Then he had a few words with Boone—probably trying to convince him that anything he might have heard from this room had been a delusion of his own imagination. Then again,

I had the feeling Captain Martin didn't give a damn who knew what he got up to in his quarters.

The men came and removed the tub, then Mr Guthrie brought in some dinner for both of us—a tray with steaming plates of beef and chicken in a thick and savoury broth, which he put on the small table by the window and left.

I was halfway through mine when I realized…

"Hold on. This is chicken," I said, as the revelation hit me.

"Very good. I thought you only had one talent."

"Is this…one of *mine*?"

The captain looked at me strangely. "What do you mean?"

I put my fork down and stared at the meat on my plate. "Oh my God," I whispered in horror. "He killed one of my chickens!"

Captain Martin looked astonished for a moment. Then his expression turned to amusement. He laughed as if I'd told an amusing joke.

I scowled.

"Rooster," he said, smiling at the nickname that fit even more now. "That's what they're for."

"I thought you wanted fresh eggs!" I said, blinking back tears. "If I'd known they were to eat, I wouldn't have given them all fucking names!"

He sobered, but with some difficulty. "You don't mean to say that you named the chickens?"

I shrugged, a little embarrassed, but more horrified, at the situation. "I thought it a good way to make friends with them. I named the goats too, but that didn't work out as well." I gaped at him. "Will they kill the goats too?"

"Eventually," Captain Martin said.

"But…but…"

I thought about Lilith and Monty and Gordon.

"Finish your stew, Rooster. You've had a long day."

I crossed my arms. "No thank you. And, anyway, where did the beef come from? Is there a herd of fucking cattle somewhere?"

Captain Martin shook his head. "Just how large do you think this vessel is?"

"The beef. Where did it come from?"

"We looted it, like the goats and chickens. But the beef was already dead and butchered."

"Oh."

Captain Martin gazed at me with a tender expression. "Did you really name the chickens?" he asked.

I sniffed, overcome with emotion at the thought of the pretty hens. "Yes."

"What were their names?" he asked.

"Gladys. And Annie. Stefanie." My voice got rougher as I spoke because I didn't know who I'd eaten. "Elizabeth."

"Elizabeth!" he snorted.

I glared at him. "Frances. Mildred. And...Guinevere."

His eyes sparkled with amusement as he covered his mouth, presumably to hide a traitorous smile.

I wanted to kill him. Huge cock and commanding attitude aside, he'd colluded in murder.

"Simon," he said. "I'm so sorry. But we have to eat."

This was true, and meat was prized above all else. I couldn't blame the cook, in truth. But I wish I'd fucking known.

I nodded, too upset to speak and too tired to argue.

"Perhaps we should go to bed."

I felt as if the hot bath, the food, and the shocking revelation about my chooks had depleted me of everything I'd had left.

"Yes, Captain," I said. I walked to the bed and climbed under the covers, curling my body around a pillow and staring at the planked wall. I listened as the captain took the wooden tray with the dirty dishware and placed it in the hall, then closed and locked the door. He turned down the lamps and blessed darkness filled the space. I felt the mattress dip as he crawled under the sheets with me.

He sighed and pushed a stray hair off my forehead.

"Simon Bartholomew White. My charming little rooster. What am I going to do with you?"

"What haven't you done already?" I asked.

"I've barely started," he said and scooped me into his arms, pulling my naked body against his and kissing me below the ear. "Go to sleep now. We'll talk more in the morning."

The creaking of the hull and the softness of the mattress, as well as the deep breathing of the pirate captain, lulled me into the depths of slumber.

Chapter Four

Guinevere

I woke to sunlight and the sounds of muted conversation. The gentle roll of the ship and the captain's calming presence had soothed me into a deep and restful sleep—the first I'd had in a long, long while.

The winds had picked up, and we were moving at last.

It took me a moment to remember where I was, but the soft sheets and the lingering scents of sweat and our fucking reminded me. As did the fact that I wasn't sprawled half out of a hammock in the darkness of the lower berths.

I heard voices. One was the captain's, and the other I didn't recognize. I feigned sleep so I could hear what they were saying in subdued tones so as not to wake me.

"This is a safe spot?"

"Aye. It's quite sheltered, and I doubt there'll be any trouble. We can set here for a few days, clean and repair what needs done, enjoy the good weather, and then head out again, end of the week."

I opened my eyes and rolled over, squinting in the brightness and making out two forms standing by Captain's Martin's desk.

"Will we go to Tortuga?" the captain asked the fellow who was with him.

As my vision focused, I recognized the *Arrow's* quartermaster, Donatello. He wasn't a bad looking man either, and if I'd failed with the captain, I might have had a go for him.

"I think that would be wise. We can always raid a ship if we find a likely one, but we'll need proper supplies, which we can get there."

Donatello glanced over and saw me. His expression remained calm, as if discovering a young man naked in the captain's bed was nothing to remark upon.

He elbowed the captain's arm and gestured toward me. "The lad is awake, sir."

I went up on one elbow and scratched my scalp. "Hello."

Captain Martin smiled at me.

"Good morning, Simon White."

"Good morning, Captain Martin."

Donatello chuckled. "That's a very formal greeting for a cabin boy who's probably been fucked sideways three times by now."

The captain gave Donatello a look. "That's no reason to give up on decorum."

Donatello laughed. "If you say so."

I yawned and stretched. "He hasn't done it to me sideways yet, in actual fact. And he usually calls me Rooster."

At this, Donatello laughed louder and raised his eyes at

Captain Martin.

"Because of the—" I gestured at my hair.

"My goodness. That's gone quite red, hasn't it? And are those"—Donatello peered closer—"freckles?"

"Aye, they're freckles. It weren't all dirt, you know."

"You know, Rooster, you can call me Dinesh," Captain Martin said to me, coming over and sitting on the edge of the bed.

I shrugged and fiddled with the bedclothes. "I like to call you Captain Martin."

"That's fine. Whichever you like."

"Thank you."

He pointed to a pile of folded garments on the chair by the bed. "There are new clothes for you there. Do you have a pair of shoes that are relatively clean?"

"Aye."

"Do they fit?"

"Well enough."

"You'll be happy for them if you ever have to climb into the rigging. You need to wear shoes if you're going to be...uh...working...so close with me. Appearances must be kept up. Can't have you running around barefoot like a heathen."

I blinked at the captain. Appearances? "You had your bare cock up my arse, didn't you?"

He had the courtesy to blush as Donatello cleared his throat and tried not to laugh.

"Yes, but there was no risk of blistering or splinters."

He had a point. And I had a question.

"What you said about climbing the rigging... Do you think... Do you think I might have to do that? Is that a part of this"—I glanced at Donatello—"job?"

"Well, you never know what you might have to do on a vessel

such as this. We're a crew, and everyone does what they have to do, in times of need," the captain said. "But it's not a task I'll expect of you on the regular."

I nodded.

I had just the slightest issue with heights, so I was hoping I'd *never* be called upon to climb the rigging. I'd watched the others scrabble up the ropes, and that alone terrified me. I half expected someone to come crashing to the deck every fucking day. But the seasoned crew members scampered up and down like spiders, as if they'd been born to the task.

"Rooster, this is my quartermaster, Anthony Donatello. Anthony, this is Simon White."

Donatello gave me a little bow. I couldn't help but smile.

"Hello," I said.

"Mr White," Donatello said, the corners of his lips twitching. "How are you this lovely morning?"

"Well fucked, and I thank you very much."

Donatello's cheeks reddened, but he grinned. "I'd expect no less."

"Tony," he said as if to chastise Donatello for speaking the obvious.

"I'm sorry, captain. Only, I've known you for so long. And I do have ears, you know."

"So there's no confusion, Mr White is twenty-two, and here willingly. You know, I do have *some* morals."

"Of course, Captain. More than most, I suspect."

"That may well be. I do try."

I sat up but made sure the blankets were covering the important bits.

"What shall I do today, Captain?" I asked, my gaze drifting down his body.

He was dressed in a fine pair of black breeches that buttoned in the front, navy style, and a shirt made of some kind of rough-hewn fabric. A work shirt—not one of his fancy white ones with the full sleeves that made him look like an aristocrat. And he wore the boots, of course. I really liked the boots.

"Well, you'd better check on your chickens," he said.

Oh fuck.

I blinked back sudden emotion.

"We're under a light sail at the moment, which means we can relax for a spell. The winds are low and we aren't moving much. There are repairs and general maintenance that need doing. And my cabin requires a good dusting."

For fuck's sake!

"Yes, Captain," I said, gritting my teeth.

"And bring your belongings here."

I nodded. "Yes, I will. But...what if everyone finds out?"

The captain frowned. "Finds out what?"

I glanced at Donatello, then returned my gaze to Captain Martin. "You know...that I'm...serving you in those ways..."

"It's difficult to keep things from the men, Rooster. I'm sure they know already."

"What!"

"Perhaps not all of them, but rumours do circulate."

He and Donatello went back to looking at the maps and discussing our future route. I assumed he didn't want me to get out from under the sheets until they were finished and Donatello had left, so I spent some time enjoying the comfort of my predicament.

I sniffed under my arm to see if the bath I'd had the night before had done anything. I did, in fact, smell much better. The scent of Captain Martin's expensive soap lingered. I recalled what he'd done with it and marvelled again at the man's perverse ingenuity. I spread my arms out to each side and stared up at the ceiling of wooden boards, puffing air from my mouth to lift a piece of errant hair off my forehead. I hoped they wouldn't be much longer. I wanted to get dressed and go see about the chickens.

When they'd finally gone, I slipped out of bed and examined the togs on the chair. There was a striped white shirt, a dark blue short jacket, and tan breeches with brass buttons on the side and on the front flap. *Not bad, not bad.* There was some kind of soft undergarment, but I dismissed it out of hand. Who wanted to bother with another layer? Not me. And stockings. Maybe my boots would be more comfortable with stockings. I'd never had such fine things in my life.

I put everything on, feeling strange and as if I was living another's life. The breeches fit well and ended about two inches above my ankles, so I didn't have to roll them. The shirt was a bit large but I tucked the tails into the breeches and rolled up the sleeves, and the garment looked all right.

There was a looking glass in the corner of Captain Martin's room. I went over and examined my reflection.

In all honesty, I appeared as some deranged asylum escapee, dressing up in fancy clothes that didn't suit. Perhaps I was so used to seeing myself in rags, I couldn't fathom the result of a set of fine togs. I made a face and held my arms up, making fists, to complete the effect. Then I sobered and tried to arrange my hair into a less wild arrangement.

Having been properly fucked before my hair had fully dried made that almost impossible, but I smoothed the strands where I could. The situation would have been much worse without the trim Captain Martin had given me, which had been very thoughtful. Thank goodness my beard hairs were slow-growing and I'd been able to snag a razor from another crewmate, one I kept wrapped and hidden. I had been amused to see him searching for the implement and then simply succumbing to the rampant growth of his whiskers. They suited him, anyhow, and he'd thank me if he knew.

I supposed with my stockings and boots on I'd look more civilized. The fabric of the breeches and the shirt was finer than any I'd had against my skin, and the fact that Captain Martin had arranged these to be provided made me go a bit soft in the chest.

I ate a roll and a slice of mango off the captain's breakfast plate, then stepped out of the cabin and closed the door behind me.

"And where might you be going, Mr White?" Boone asked.

The captain's guard was again cleaning under his nails with the knife. I wondered how he kept getting his hands so dirty when all I'd ever seen him do was sit in that chair.

"The head, actually. I need to piss and see if Captain Martin left anything up my—oh, never mind."

Boone looked satisfyingly shocked, but then the corners of his lips twitched.

"Fine. Although you're probably allowed access to the privy now. As a perk of being the captain's—" He looked me up and down. "—favourite."

The privy? My eyes went wide.

"You serious?"

"By my mother's left tit, I am."

I grinned and started to walk away, then stopped. "Um. Where is it?"

He gestured down a short hallway to the left of where we were standing.

"In the lower gallery. Down those steps. With a door marked "Privy". Can you read, Simon White?"

"I can read." I could read well, as a matter of fact. My mother had had a small library of books, before my father had destroyed them in a fit of pique. I'd never forgiven him for that transgression.

"Off you go then, Simon White. Don't get lost."

I gave him a nod and headed in the direction he'd indicated. I located the gentlemen's privy down three short steps, around a turn, and down three more, nestled in a corner of the quarter gallery, near another door marked "Wardroom". I didn't know what the wardroom was for, but the privy was what I needed, at any rate.

I pulled the latch and opened the wooden door, then stood there for a moment, gazing upon Shangri-La. Compared to the heads at the bow, this was a significant upgrade, and I couldn't believe my luck in gaining such privileges. Perhaps even worth having to do a bit of upkeep in the captain's quarters.

The privy was much cleaner than the head, for one thing, and enclosed so nobody could watch me shitting out the spunk and soap from an entertaining evening with the captain. The experience proved quite relaxing, as a matter of fact. I'd never taken a lovelier shit in my fucking life. I completely forgot about the chickens and stayed there for longer than required.

Then someone knocked on the door, and I remembered there were other people on board.

"Just a moment," I said, glancing about for a rag or paper to use to clean up. Someone had piled some pages from an old book on a small shelf nearby, so I used some of those. There was a bowl of water even, to wash hands, along with—*gulp*—a lovely bar of soap like the one I'd become quite familiar with in the captain's chambers. I'd never gotten hard from looking at a bar of soap before, but that's what happened. I willed my cock to behave, pulled up my breeches, and got myself to rights.

I pulled open the door to see Mr Guthrie, the ship's cook, waiting there. His eyes went wide when he saw me.

"I beg your pardon, sir. It's all yours," I said.

Mr Guthrie looked me up and down with a puzzled expression on his face. "Who the hell are you?"

"Simon White. I used to look after the goats."

His eyes went wider. "What are you doing here? This privy is for the officers and the captain."

He sounded genuinely confused and not enraged about my presence.

"Well, I'm the captain's houseboy now. So I'm allowed to use the privy."

Understanding dawned as Mr Guthrie looked me over again.

"Ah. He's got you kitted out well, I see. Well, mind that you treat him with kindness, Simon White. We're all quite fond of the captain."

"Oh, don't worry, Mr Guthrie. So 'm I."

I went past him and heard him give a soft chuckle. I was feeling quite cheery until I remembered.

Five minutes later, I found myself sobbing by the chicken coops.

The animals were kept in a corner of the hold, in wooden pens that I was supposed to fill with fresh straw every few days. Although I imagined this duty would be passed on to another poor sod since I'd be busy seeing to the captain's needs.

"Oh for fuck's sake, stop yer blubberin'." Martinez looked about to see if anyone else was near. "Did you get right fucked and now you're sad about it?"

Jesus. Did everyone know my private business?

I tried to be coherent and stop my embarrassing display. "I'm not sad about *that.*"

"Why're you crying, then?"

"You killed Guinevere!" It had only taken me a moment to discern which of my beautiful chooks had been dispatched.

"I killed who?"

"My chicken! The one with the golden feathers by her tail!"

"Oh my God. The lad's gone and lost his mind," Martinéz muttered.

Mr Jones, a portly fellow with a mop of red hair, freckles, and a friendly smile said, "Aye, that's what the captain's rod can do to a man. Ask me how I know."

"Not you too!"

"Oh, aye. T'was lovely. He's very romantic, in a filthy way and all. I won't forget the experience."

"Well, you'd better. I'd wager he's claimed Mr White," Martinéz muttered. "And he won't be lookin' for satisfaction elsewhere now, I reckon."

"Just as well." Jones sniffed. "I couldn't walk right for three days."

My sobs had died down whilst I was listening to this conversation, and I laughed outright.

"See, he's all right. He's just a bit daft about the chickens," Jones said.

"I'm not daft," I said.

"Anyway, I didn't kill yer chicken," Martinéz said. "'Twas Hillier."

"That bastard," I muttered, seeing Hillier across the room speaking with a few of the men. Hillier was an officer, well-liked, and good friends with most.

"On the captain's orders," Martinez explained. "For your supper, mind. Captain wanted you to eat well. You should be thankful."

"Oh I am. But she was beautiful, my Guinevere. And sweet. And I've eaten her," I said, ready to cry again.

Hillier came over. "What's the matter with him?" he asked of Martinez.

"You killed his chicken."

"Her name was Guinevere," I explained. "And she was lovely."

"Beg pardon?" Hillier said.

"He's very upset about the chook. Then again, he's been in the captain's chambers all the night, and he's probably exhausted."

They chuckled together.

Hillier put a kind hand on my shoulder. "Never mind. She doesn't know you ate her. And now you carry a piece of her wherever you go."

"Until he takes a shit," Martinez said.

"Well, all right. I was only trying to comfort the man," Hillier muttered, clearly wanting to be somewhere else.

I thought about what Hillier had said, and in a way he was right. I'd loved that fat little chook, but now she was gone, and a part of her would be with me always, in an intimate, spiritual way.

"Thank you, Hillier. You've eased my mind."

"Glad I could help, White."

I looked at the other chickens. "Are they all going to be eaten?"

He shrugged. "Probably. They haven't been laying all that well."

I'd known that. I'd thought that if I named them and sang to them in the mornings and at bedtime, they'd do better. But they hadn't.

"All right, then. I've done all I can for you," I said to the chickens and the goats. "But I'm moving up in the world, and I can't worry about you lot anymore." A harsh truth, but I needed to tell it. They might as well know.

And truth be told, Guinevere had been fucking delicious before I'd been made aware of the situation.

I went to the section of the hold where my hammock swung near a porthole and grabbed my boots and the razor I had stolen, wrapped in a worn piece of leather. Apart from my knife, and the new clothes on my back, I carried all that I possessed in the world.

I gazed with nostalgia at the lowly corner in which I'd been living for the past few weeks. Then I inhaled the scent of a hundred men sweating and belching and farting, and bid the place a good riddance.

"Don't forget about us, White," Martinez muttered as I passed by.

"I'll put in a good word for you," I promised.

I felt like the crew were silently judging me for trading my body for a better place to sleep, but which of them wouldn't have done so if their proclivities had lain in that direction and the captain had offered? It sounded as if more than one had, albeit temporarily. I couldn't explain that I felt more than a physical pull toward the captain.

Perhaps I was deluding myself, and he *was* just using me as a bed warmer and a housekeeper, and when he got bored of me or no longer found me useful or desirable, I'd be tossed aside. But I could enjoy myself in the meantime, learn how to be a privateer, take advantage of the comfort and privileges my place would afford me, and attempt to prove myself indispensable to him so that he wouldn't dismiss me. I had charm, vigor, a relentless appetite for activities between the sheets—and elsewhere—and a way of ingratiating myself to the men I admired. I had a feeling that at least in some way the captain and I were evenly matched.

I returned to the deck, noticing some men glancing my way and speaking to each other in hushed whispers. I glared at them and made kissing noises, and they turned away. Then a looming shadow blocked my path.

I looked up.

Hanes, a giant of a man with bulging muscles and horrible teeth, stared at me with disdain.

"You Captain Martin's whore now?" he sneered.

"He ain't paying me, although he is fucking me, and quite well, I might add. He won't take kindly to anyone laying a finger to me, I'll tell you that. So, bugger off."

I wasn't afraid of Hanes, even though he could probably squash me with one finger. I was under the captain's protection now, and they all knew of the circumstance.

Hanes looked me up and down, as if he wanted a turn. Then he smiled.

"Does Captain Martin know he's invited a hellcat into his bed, I wonder?" Hanes said, gazing at me with some level of admiration.

I blinked. "Get out of my way, Hanes. I've an urgent appointment with a feather duster."

Hanes's eyes went wide. "A feather duster! Jesus. I've not heard that one before. He does get up to some strange things, our captain."

"Not for that, you idiot. For dusting. I need to clean the captain's cabin." I waved a hand in the air. "It's a part of my new job. The boring part."

"I thought he *wasn't* paying you."

"He's letting me stay with him if I clean and manage his rooms and...take care of other sundry...things."

"Mm-hmm," Hanes said, nodding. "I'm sure it's none of my business."

"You're right, what I do for Captain Martin *is* none of your business. Now get out of my way."

"Hanes!"

Hanes and I jumped at the sound of Captain Martin's stern address. My cock twitched, and it wouldn't have surprised me if Hanes's did as well.

The source of my annoyance gazed up at Captain Martin, who stood on the upper deck by the railing like the ex-navy captain he was, commanding respect with his very stance and composure. I struggled to maintain my own at the sight of the man who had spent the previous afternoon doing terrible, wonderful things to me.

"Yes, Captain?" Hanes asked.

"Aren't you supposed to be directing the crew on the fore-deck?"

"Yes, Captain. Beg pardon, Captain." Hanes said, giving Captain Martin a quick salute and moving on.

"Mr White," the captain said. "I thought I told you to gather your belongings."

He spoke in a detached, formal way, in front of the crew—as if we hadn't been intimate at all and were barely on speaking terms. I knew he didn't want to bandy about his fondness for me, and that kind of detachment in a man I had filthy thoughts about, one who had been demonstrative in private, was beguiling for some reason.

I smiled. "Ain't got none but these boots. And my knife."

His face softened before he nodded. "On your way, then."

I turned in order to proceed, but he spoke again.

"And put those bloody boots on. I didn't arrange for those

fancy clothes so you could continue to go barefooted. You'll get a nasty splinter and bleed all over my ship."

"Yes, Captain," I said and gave him a quick half smile before I made my way back to his cabin.

Boone saw me coming.

"You again," he said.

"Yes. You'll be seeing quite a bit of me, I'm afraid."

"I figured. After the things I heard in there yesterday," he said, gesturing at the captain's door.

I blushed, remembering the noises I'd made and the things the captain had done.

"Don't worry. I ain't gonna tell anyone. The captain would have my hide." He made a flourish with his arm towards the door. "In you go, then. Door's unlatched."

"Thank you. And, uh, don't pay attention to any other noises you might hear in there, right?"

"Of course, Mr White." He tapped his forehead. "Discretion."

I grinned, feeling much better about Boone and his presence here. I went into the captain's rooms, latching the door behind me. I trusted him to keep the rabble out. The knowledge didn't escape me that I had been part of that group up until yesterday. But the latch on the door to these rooms afforded me a welcome sense of privacy that I'd not had for a very long time. Turned out that when you worked as a lowly member of a ship's crew, you didn't get your own space. But as the captain's houseboy, I would cherish this privilege.

I put my boots by the captain's chest of drawers, then looked about at his cluttered cabin. To be honest, I hadn't really taken in most of my surroundings when I'd last been here, being much too overwhelmed with the captain himself and what he had been saying and doing to me. And in the morning, with the reminder of what had happened to my chicken, I'd been preoccupied. I still came over emotional when I thought of having eaten my feathered friend. But I gave myself a silent scolding, because you couldn't afford sentimental musings when you lived and worked on a vessel like the *Arrow*.

The captain and his officers might think of her as a privateering vessel, but she was a pirate ship, in all fairness, as he had no writ from any king to give him any kind of legitimacy. I didn't hold that against him, of course, and I appreciated that he put himself and his crew on a higher level than common vagabonds. But pirates were pirates, after all.

The four-poster bed was rather ostentatious, of course, but had practical ramifications and certainly looked impressive.

What a contrast to the accommodations for the crew, which were rope hammocks hung close together in the hold or narrow wooden slabs bolted to the side of the ship, which were barely more than shelves with an edge to keep a body from rolling off.

The stout legs of the bedframe were bolted to the floorboards, which made sense and also helped with vigorous, uh, athletic activity upon the mattress. I gazed fondly at the rumpled sheets, then sniffed the air. Since the windows were shut on a cool breeze, the salty sea air couldn't hide the tangy scent of our coupling. Did Captain Martin want me to strip the bed and wash the sheets? He hadn't mentioned it, and he'd listed off a collection of other tasks he wanted tending to. And anyway, we'd likely get up to the same nonsense later, so what was the point?

I gave the air another sniff and remembered the fancy chamber pot, with the hinged lid that fastened shut to reduce spillage in a rough sea. I tugged the porcelain bowl out from under the bed carefully—both of us had pissed before going to bed—and picked it up, holding the curved side to my chest in one arm as I opened the door.

Boone had a hand down his breeches, which he hastily withdrew when he saw me. He needn't have. Down in the crew quarters, the men fiddled with themselves all day and brought themselves off in the corners, muttering soft words of endearment to the memory of whomever they'd left at home. I didn't care a whit, honestly.

"Where can I dump this?" I asked.

He gestured to the bow. "By the head is the best place. Over the rail."

"Really? Not on the foredeck?" I asked, sarcastically.

He frowned. "You always this annoying?"

"So they say."

"Christ," Boone said, rolling his eyes. "The captain's got his hands full with you, then."

Oh, I'd say that the captain would have his hands *very* full with me. Every bloody day and night, if I had my way.

Chapter Five

Houseboy

It took me the larger part of three hours to tidy and dust the captain's quarters. Why so long, you ask? Well, Captain Martin had decided that his rooms needed a thorough going-over if I were to receive my own later in the day. He'd given me very specific instructions as to how he wanted the rooms attended to, including the implements that I was to use to achieve my ends. Boone knew where all the supplies were, and I wondered if he'd had this duty before I'd taken over. He gave me some clean linen rags for dusting broad surfaces, a painter's brush for dealing with cracks and crevices, and a push broom for sweeping, although I eyed the bristles with more lascivious thoughts for a moment.

The task of cleaning the captain's quarters turned out to be a less onerous job than I'd expected and a good way to acquaint myself with the contents of the room, which were varied and fascinating. The furniture—a mahogany desk and dresser, straight chair, and the carved bed frame, were high-quality pieces, especially for the sorts of men on the *Arrow*. Not that I was an expert on privateering vessels, but I had heard them to be sparse and utilitarian. However, if the *Arrow* had originally been a navy frigate, the captain's quarters would have been well fitted up, and it didn't look like they'd changed that.

There was a large spyglass on a stand by the window, and I took a moment to peer through the eyepiece. What wonderful luck if I'd spotted a ship or an island in the distance. But there was only a huge span of water, which should have given me comfort.

We'd yet to come into battle, and although an exciting prospect, I was terrified of having to expose myself to cannon fire and swordplay, not to mention small arms fire. I wasn't particularly practiced in the art of hand-to-hand combat, although I was good one-to-one with my fists and my dagger.

Truth be told, my best weapon was my tongue, and I didn't mean in the bedroom. I'd flattened many opponents with one or two barbed insults in my time. Confidence, mostly, and giving them a look down the nose so they felt inferior, even if only a ruse. I could indeed be a hellcat when I chose to be, but I didn't know if that would be helpful in a massive skirmish. Likely be too chaotic all around to get any good insults in, and the men we'd be fighting might not even speak English.

Basically, unless I came under protection of the captain or some of the crew, or hid away during the battle, I would almost certainly end up killed. Which was why my outlook on my life lately had more of a carpé diem theme. See? I did know a bit of Latin. I was better educated than most folks expected, thanks to my mother.

I tried not to worry about future skirmishes as I dusted the captain's desk, as best I could manage without moving the gigantic map and all of his things about. Next time, I'd tell him if he wanted me to do a good job of my cleaning, he should tidy up first. I wondered how that might go over. Probably a bit like this:

Me: "Oy, mate, you got to clean your stuff up if you want me to dust properly."

Captain Martin: "That's some cheek, you mongrel. Off the plank with you. But first, let me shove a bar of soap up your saucy arse."

Perhaps that was a better death than being skewered by a cutlass.

I finished the dusting, and I had to admit the place looked better. If I was going to be staying here, it was in my own interests to keep the place in good standing. I hadn't had such fine accommodations in my life so found the captain's quarters quite luxurious and exciting, above and beyond the thrill of Captain Martin's sexual interest in me and our exploits between the sheets.

I straightened the pillows and pulled the coverlet over the sheets that we'd stained with our lust, picturing everything that had happened between us as I looked forward to another evening of debauchery.

I headed to a door on the back wall of the cabin just past the bed, which I'd supposed led to a massive closet holding all of the captain's fine clothing. Instead, it opened on a large dining cabin with a table, around which a number of people could sit. Made sense for a navy vessel to have a room for secret conferences and battle plans and surely proved as useful for a privateer captain. Besides Donatello, there were several senior crew members involved in the daily running of the *Arrow*, and I imagined the captain held meetings here when needed. Perhaps on special occasions, such as after a fortuitous raid, the captain hosted fancy dinners here.

Mr Guthrie was proud to provide even the lowest crew members with tasty and nutritious meals. Presumably the officers dined on fare even more fine than I'd sampled so far. His breakfast had consisted of bread, jam, cheese, and a ripe mango, with a tankard of ale to wash the meal down.

The crew didn't get a proper breakfast, but most tended to save a bit of bread and cheese from supper. There was always one large meal in the middle of the day that was usually some kind of stew or fish to keep our blood strong. Mr Guthrie was a generous fellow, so if someone were truly suffering and went to the trouble to ask, they could usually get a tear of bread and a bit of cheese at any time of the day. Most of the crew were too busy to bother, and the amount that was regularly provided was enough.

The intrigue of discovering a whole other room was barely enough to console me on the realization that I now had more to clean. Likely used less often, there weren't as many knickknacks and objects to dust around so it didn't take quite so long. I finished quickly and was about to lay down on the captain's fancy bed and take myself in hand for a wee faf, when the front door opened, and Boone came in with a mopstick and bucket.

I was thrilled at first.

"Oy, wonderful! I've done the dusting and tidying but the floors could use a going-over," I said, thinking that he'd come to help.

He handed the mopstick to me and put the bucket down.

"Make sure to do a good job," he said and left.

I frowned. *Goddamn it.*

I'd been looking forward to remembering the captain's use of me the previous evening and enjoying a good wank.

I looked first at the bucket and then at the mopstick in my hand. I really needed to take the edge off, although why cleaning Captain Martin's rooms had so stirred my blood, I wasn't quite sure. I could be quick about the job, and the water in the bucket would still be warm.

I had a brief hesitation when I recalled the captain's prohibition on self-pleasure. But surely, what he didn't see, he couldn't know had happened. He had certainly proved quite clever but he wasn't all knowing and all seeing. And what he didn't know wouldn't hurt him...or me.

I didn't latch the door because that might make Boone suspicious. I rested the mopstick against the wall and crawled onto the captain's bed, reaching into my trousers. I closed my eyes and lost myself to the memories.

I became so entranced that I must have lost track of time, and was in the middle of a very vivid re-imaging of getting fucked in the ropes, when a sudden noise made me turn. I opened my eyes to see the captain standing just inside the door, as the mopstick handle lost its purchase and slammed to the floor.

"Blast!" I said, rolling onto my side to hide my leaking stand, and promptly fell off the mattress.

"Fucking hell," I cursed as the pain of a rough landing distracted me from my ardor.

The door shut with a loud thud, and the click of the latch echoed ominously. I squeezed my eyes shut as if doing so would make me invisible.

If only.

The scuff of the captain's boots on the wood floor and the sound of my frantic heartbeats were all I could hear for several moments. I cursed silently, not even trying to stuff myself away. Maybe the captain would be so distracted by my tumescence that he'd forget about the dirty floors and the unused mopstick.

The footsteps stopped near me.

I waited for Captain Martin to address me or to curse my name or to remark on the embarrassing situation he'd found me in. When he didn't, I took a deep breath and opened my eyes.

He was standing at the foot of the bed where he could see me, gazing upon my rumpled state with an indefinable expression. He folded his arms over his chest and simply took me in. Fuck it, he was a handsome asshole.

"Are you quite all right?"

I glanced down at my cock, which had barely started to wilt from its engorgement due to my vivid imaginings, even after the horrible fright of the captain's entrance and my tumble to the floor.

I cleared my throat. *Act as though nothing is amiss.* "Aye, and thank you for asking. Won't take a moment to finish," I said, glancing down at myself and giving the captain a suggestive leer.

He was unmoved. "Simon White. Were you having a wank in the middle of your duties?"

"Well, I was trying to. Until you came barging in."

He raised his eyebrows. "Barging in? To my own quarters?"

I wrapped a hand around myself and began to stroke, holding the captain's incredulous gaze. Probably a long shot, but I was an optimistic person.

"Rooster, get your fucking hand off yourself this minute."

Holy shit. I did as I was told, but my prick only stood taller at the sternness in his tone.

"Yes, Captain. Anything you say, Captain," I muttered.

"Get up and put your cock away. You have work to do."

"Truly, Captain? I'd much rather work on sucking your—"

"Stand *up*." His tone brooked no nonsense.

I scrambled to my feet and stuffed my now truly frightened organ back into my trousers, then fastened the brass buttons on the flap.

Captain Martin took me in.

"The clothes suit you. Disobedience does not."

"I'm still going to mop. I was just having a rest."

"Hmm. You didn't look very restful. And that's not what I'm mad about."

"Oh, I see."

"No, I don't think you do. That cock is mine, Rooster, and you're not to touch it without express permission, unless you're taking a piss and then only for a moment. No funny business. Because your pleasure is mine. We talked about this already. I thought you understood."

"I did."

"Clearly not, or you wouldn't have been about to spend when I turned up a moment ago."

"Speaking of which, my balls are aching a bit," I said, making a face and an adjustment to my trousers.

"Good," Captain Martin said. "Let's see how you feel after two weeks of not being permitted release."

My eyes about bugged out of my head and my chin dropped. "Two weeks? Are ye daft? I'll expire, surely, or go bleedin' mad from not being able to finish. That ain't healthy!"

Captain Martin's eye burned with fire and cruelty for a moment. Then he smiled. "Perhaps. Perhaps not. I'd like to find out."

"No, surely not. Not when we've just begun..."

His smile got wider. It could have been glee at the thought of keeping me from release or an indication that he might not have meant his threat.

"You are very lucky that we just began getting to know each other, Mr White. Because if this happens again, you will be put by for weeks without any chance at release."

The thought horrified me, but the idea also aroused me. That control over my most intimate parts and biological urges seemed a powerful cruelty. But I was confused.

"But how would you..." I whispered. "You can't be with me all the time."

"Trust me. I have ways of keeping you in line, Rooster," he murmured, as if he was telling me of secret pleasures he was privy to. Knowing him as I was beginning to, perhaps that was so. "And the first of those is punishing you when you do what I've explicitly prohibited. Especially whilst neglecting your other duties."

A bolt of fear sliced through me. Maybe being the captain's houseboy and seed-bucket *was* too risky. I fell to my knees in front of the captain, putting my hands together in prayer.

"Not the cat," I begged. "Please!"

Less than a week ago, I'd seen what Captain Martin had had Donatello do to a man who had stolen and hidden a brace of pistols. Perhaps he'd been planning some kind of mutiny, but the men gave him up at the drop of a hat because their loyalty lay with the captain. Donatello, on the captain's orders, had flayed the man with the cat-o'-nine-tails—a vicious implement designed to strip skin from a man's back and cause tremendous pain—until he'd lost consciousness, then tossed him over the side. I could still hear the screams.

Captain Martin sighed. "No, not the cat. That kind of punishment is saved for very serious offences. I don't like to do anything so cruel, but on occasion such brutality is necessary.

However, not in this instance."

"Oh fuck, thank heavens."

"Now take off your clothes, Rooster, and lay them neatly on the chair."

I blinked. "But I thought…"

He raised his eyebrows, and I determined it best to do as I was told, even though I didn't know what was happening.

"Yes, Captain."

He stood there and watched me as I stripped. I became more worried and chastened as each layer was removed and wondered what had possessed me to have a wank in the captain's bed, when he'd strictly forbidden me to touch myself. Eventually, I stood there, buck naked and terrified of whatever might be going to happen. My cock hadn't quite got the message though.

The captain eyed my prick with interest.

"Come," Captain Martin said, crooking a finger. I followed him around to the other side of the bed where the main space in the room was. He pulled the straight chair from his desk and placed it in the center of the floor, sat down, and patted his knee.

I stared at him, confused.

"Simon."

"Yes, Captain?" Desire, curiosity, and trepidation swirled in my gut.

"Bend yourself over my lap so I can give you the discipline you sorely require."

Wait a moment. Was he planning to tan my hide? Like I was a ten-year-old?

"Now hold on," I said. "I'm a grown man."

"Oh, I know that very well, Rooster. You wouldn't be in this cabin if you weren't. However, you have *acted* like a child, and you need to be taken in hand."

I was strangely affronted, even though an over-the-knee spanking would be a good deal less painful than the other punishments I'd imagined. Once again, my pride got in the way of common sense.

"You want me to go over your lap? For a *hiding?*"

"You can call it that if you like."

"What would *you* call it?"

He leveled a gaze at me, his palm sliding back and forth on his trousers like a restless dog on a leash. *"Deserved,"* he said. "And if you keep asking me questions, this is going to go much harder and longer than I'd planned." He leaned back and narrowed his eyes at me, then pointed at his knee and raised his eyebrows.

All right. Fine. If he wanted to play at this game, I could too. Perhaps if I acquiesced and squirmed and cried in a tempting way, he'd go easy on me. Perhaps he enjoyed having relatively young men over his lap with his handprint imprinted on their backside. Perhaps not the worst thing that could happen. Maybe if I could put on a good performance, he'd forget about the mopping and bend me over his bed afterward.

I stared at his lap, noticing the telling bulge in the fabric. Hmm. So this was making him aroused, was it? Now I wanted to bend myself over his knee, but I couldn't figure out how to get myself in the proper position without looking foolish. He took pity on me, I supposed, and took my wrist, pulling me so that I lost my balance and fell onto his lap with all the grace of a tethered donkey—and a similar sounding squeal.

Captain Martin adjusted my position and kept me from sliding off, whilst I stared at the wood planks beneath his feet, my cheeks flaring with the indignity of the position. However, the press of stiff heat beneath me certainly mollified my shame somewhat. If the captain was enjoying my indignity so much, well then, that made everything worthwhile. Captain Martin's thighs provided a strong support, but I wiggled nonetheless, satisfied to feel his cock throb and swell even more.

His fingertips on the edges of my scar made me jump. The damaged and reddened skin there was quite sensitive. He feathered his touch over the imperfection, as if afraid of hurting me, even though I was in this position expressly so he could do so.

I gasped and tried not to wiggle as he traced its jagged outline.

"Sensitive?"

"Quite," I admitted.

"I'll try to avoid the area. That leaves most of your spectacular arse available to my striking hand, at least."

"Spectacular, eh?" I asked, trying to keep from smiling.

"Oh yes. The prettiest I've seen."

"I find that hard to believe."

"I won't lie, Rooster, to you or anyone else. I'm generally honest to a fault, so if I tell you a thing, you can count on it."

"All right. I suppose that's reassuring."

I only hoped he didn't hold me to as high a standard because if a lie would get me out of a tight spot, I had no problem with fibbing.

My father had beaten me on occasion, but never over his lap like this. He'd taken me into the shed and strapped my backside with a leather belt, which had hurt like hell and had not been pleasant at all. I figured I could take a hand spanking, especially from someone like Captain Martin, who no doubt desired the fun more than the pain. At least, that was what I was hoping.

Captain Martin rested his broad hand on my buttock and squeezed, causing my cleft to part and flash him a glimpse of my tiny hole no doubt. He inhaled and his cock swelled more.

I wiggled because the anxiety and excitement made me restless. He sighed.

"Stay still."

"Yes, Captain. I'll try."

I didn't succeed. When his hand made contact with more force than I'd expected and a sound like the crack of a bullet leaving a musket, I yelped and scrambled to get away. But the captain held me with his iron grip and chuckled.

"When I give you a directive, my red rooster, my lovely little cockerel, I expect you to follow my orders, just like any member of the crew."

"Yes, Captain," I sighed, my eyes gone wide.

He started to spank me hard, again and again, mostly in the same spot. Jesus, he was strong. The sound of his palm on my skin alone caused the shame to rise in my cheeks—both sets.

"Do I need to gag you, Rooster, or can you keep quiet?"

Gag me!

"Um... I'll do my best, Captain," I said, my poor bottom stinging and aching.

"Right. Hold on."

I craned my neck to see that he was removing the white kerchief from around his neck.

"I'll be quiet. I'll be quiet!"

"Yes, you will. I'm going to make sure of your silence. Open your mouth."

I obeyed, my heart racing. Was this truly my fate? To be gagged and humiliated by the handsomest privateer I'd ever laid eyes on, purely because I couldn't keep my hands off my prick?

Captain Martin stuffed the kerchief between my teeth and tied the cloth tight behind my head.

"If nothing else, you're going to learn to take a hiding like the man you say you are. Now put your hands at the small of your back."

My eyes bulging and my lips stretched by the cloth, I did so. The captain took the wrist of my far hand and crooked my arm so I was held still over his lap, but he had access to my throbbing arse.

"Now count. I don't care if I can't make out what you're saying, but you might want to keep track. I'm giving you twelve."

"Twebb!" I exclaimed, the word muffled by the gag.

I'm pretty sure I felt him chuckle before he said, with more sternness that inflamed me, "Ready, Simon Bartholomew White?"

I started to protest, but too late. His hand came down, harder than the last time.

I grunted and counted into the cloth. It sounded like "Ubb."

"There you go."

He landed quick and brutal slaps against my not-so-innocent flesh as I tried not to squirm or shout. But that proved hopeless. Maybe that was why he'd told me to count, as at least I could yell out the number. By the time he landed the sixth, tears were escaping, and by the tenth, I was audibly crying and quite chastened.

Captain Martin could give a bloody good spanking, and I'd learned my fucking lesson.

Although my own stand had wilted somewhat with the effects of my punishment, the captain's was a ramrod beneath me. He untied the gag, hauled me up, and stood me before him.

"Are you going to do as you're told from now on, Rooster?" he asked.

"Aye, I will. Even though you appear to enjoy taking your hand to my spectacular arse."

He looked like he was either going to put me back over his lap or burst out laughing. Luckily, he did the latter.

"Well, I can't deny that. My you are a saucy fellow, backtalking me after a proper hiding."

"Only pointing out the obvious, Captain," I sniffed. "But I am sorry for disobeying you, and I will try to do better."

"See that you do. Your hand is much more useful to me wrapped around the handle of that mopstick than around your cock. And if you are going to be my—" He looked me up and down with the most sultry expression. "—assistant, I plan to make thorough use of you. Now grab that mopstick and get to work."

"Can't I get dressed?"

"Oh, Rooster. No. I'm going to enjoy watching you move around this room with a rosy-red bottom and a chastened attitude," he said with a smile, adjusting his erection and crossing one leg over the other.

The dirty fucking bastard.

I cursed under my breath.

"What was that?"

"I said, 'Yes, sir.'"

My arse throbbed with the remnants of my initiation to the whims of Captain Martin's discipline, but perhaps remaining unclothed would prove a mercy. I picked up the stick from where it had fallen and dunked the mop into the soapy water. I meant to throw an angry glare at Captain Martin—who had moved to recline on the bed—as I began, but when I saw him with his own cock in hand, watching me as he lazily stroked himself, the glare turned into a gape. Mother of God, the infuriating man was truly enjoying my debasement. The bastard was more perverse than I.

But two could play at this game. I went back to my lowly duties but made sure to sway my rosy arse in his direction.

"Oh, my goodness, what on earth is this?" I asked, planting my feet wide apart and bending at the waist to pretend to examine a dirty spot on the floor. "Looks like a bit of blood." I squatted down on the floor and reached around to scratch myself just above my arse crack, careful to avoid any tender areas.

I heard a soft moan from the bed. Aha. I had gleaned Captain Martin's weakness, and it just so happened to be my pretty arse, scar and all.

I straightened up slowly and shook my head. Then I swiped the mop back and forth over the imaginary stain, with a manufactured ferociousness that hopefully made my muscles bunch and shudder in an attractive way. I surreptitiously peeked behind me.

Sure enough, the captain's hand was moving quite quickly on his prick as he watched me with half-lidded eyes.

Chapter Six

Merrymaking

"Oh my, the air is so close in here," I muttered, wiping my brow and pretending to be suffering from the heat. I glanced into the bucket. "Huh. This water's gotten cold by now. I wonder if..."

I scooped a bit of soapy water in my hand as I turned to face the captain. He watched with an intense and captivated attention as I slapped my hand against my chest and let the soapy water drip down my body.

"Oh, that's much better," I sighed, following the trail of water with my hand and sliding my fingers down beside my now standing cock. Let him try to deny me now.

"You little fucker," Captain Martin said, giving me a look that expressed how much he wanted to either fuck me or murder me. I couldn't tell which.

"Oh, I'm so sorry, Captain. Did I interrupt your self-reflection?"

"Get over here," he said, stroking himself with some urgency. "No, wait. Leave the mop and come over here."

"Yes, Captain," I said, the glow of victory upon me. I did as he ordered and sauntered over to where he lay carelessly with his breeches down to his thighs, holding his gigantic cock as if he'd like nothing better than to beat me soundly with it.

"Get some of the oil and slick yourself up. Turn around so I can watch."

"Yes, Captain," I murmured, trying not to sound smug. I fought a smile as I poured some of the expensive oil into my hand. "Oops, it dripped onto my chest," I muttered, smoothing slick liquid over my nipples and pectorals, whilst I turned and spread my legs. I poured more oil into my hand and reached behind me.

"Oh yes. That's right, make yourself as slippery as a raw oyster for me," the captain groaned.

I rubbed the oil all along my crack and polished my arsehole like I might a prized gem. I was rather fond of the thing, to be sure.

The captain let out a grunt and a sigh. "Use your fingers to fuck yourself, now."

He sounded like he might erupt at any moment.

"Yes, Captain. Your wish is my command."

I bent over and played with my hole, spreading the oil around and sticking my fingers in to get myself ready.

"Oooh. Oooh," he moaned, the sound of his hand moving back and forth over his prick echoing off the walls. "Oh, fuck yes. That's perfect." He stroked himself a bit more, and then his hand froze as he grimaced and closed his eyes. "Stop. Stop. Don't move; don't move."

He was breathing heavily, and I wasn't sure if he was speaking to me or to himself. He attempted to slow his breathing and calm down, and I imagined he had come close to finishing and was trying to stave off.

When his eyes opened, they were dark and aflame.

"Now, get on my stand this instant. I want to fill you with my seed, you nasty, utterly delectable scoundrel."

Oh yes, he was getting to know me well.

I leapt onto the bed and crawled overtop the captain like a randy cheetah. He grabbed my chin and pinned me with a look.

"Stop fooling about and get on me, *now*. You've got three seconds, or I'll finish on your face, and you'll go to bed without anything else."

I loved the way he could barely speak without gasping for breath. The man was a slave to my powers of seduction.

"Aye, Captain," I said, getting into position.

I grabbed his cock, slicking the skin with what oil was left on my hand as he groaned and parted his lips, gazing at me like he wanted to slap me yet unable to do more than focus on staving off. It only took a moment to stuff his steel-hard member into my soft hole and sink down, the blissful look on his face my reward for any discomfort. There was so much fancy oil in play, however, that the burn was minimal and the feeling of being skewered was as good as I'd expected.

The captain's eyes rolled back in his head, and he let out a vulnerable whimper.

"Good God," he whispered as if he could barely function.

"Aye..." I stuttered in agreement, caught up in my own reaction to our joining, even though only the first few inches were in.

His hands gripped my hips all of a sudden, fingers pressing into my flesh with painful determination. He kept me still as he pushed the rest of the way in, impaling me with a ruthless efficiency.

I yelped, then groaned with exquisite pleasure.

"Dear God," I moaned, my eyes going wide and then hooded as the captain began to thrust and curse and pant like he was fucking possessed.

"Fuck, fuck, fuck," he muttered, taking lungfuls of air between words. "Oh fuck. Good God. Oh fuck, fuck, fuck!"

The captain became quite overtaken. And even though this meant he wouldn't last long, his urgency satisfied me in a completely different way. After only a few blissful seconds, he threw his head back—hitting the wall with a *thunk*—and let out an ecstatic cry that Boone and anyone else in the vicinity would have discerned with ease.

I watched him come apart beneath me, my mouth agape as I gasped and moaned. I went to take my cock in hand. Then I remembered his orders.

"Captain... Captain!" I panted. "Please, please, please," I asked, still held in his death grip on my hips as he plumbed me with slowing fervour.

I was close. I was so fucking close.

Captain Martin's cry of completion trailed off. He thrust into me again, then sank himself so deep I wondered if he could feel my tonsils, took my stand in hand, and got me off with three determined strokes.

I yelled with relief and ecstasy and watched my seed land on the captain's white shirt in satisfactory spurts.

"Oh, fuck, fuck, fuck," I sighed, riding my exquisite culmination in thankful bliss that quickly turned into the opposite as

Captain Martin, with an evil glint in his eye, kept his hand moving, deliberately handling the extra sensitive tip of my prick with purposeful delight.

"Oh, stop, stop, stop," I cried, trying to bat his hand away as I felt his cock slide out of me along with a puddle of his seed.

But he made me withstand this torment for a time before he relaxed his grip and let his hand fall away. He sank back against the pillows. "Oh my fuck, that was lovely."

I glared at him for a moment. Then I decided to forgive him his torturous games and melted against his chest and the damp fabric of his spoilt shirt.

I wasn't sure what his reaction would be, but I felt so boneless and fatigued that I couldn't really help myself. And he made quite the lovely pillow, to be honest. I snuggled against him, my nose pressed into his soft neck, and just about died when his arm came around me, and he kissed the top of my head.

"Simon White, you are a lazy, silly, aggravating fellow."

I grinned. He was getting to know me, and even though the words were cruel, the tone of his voice was fond.

"Yes, Captain. 'Tis true enough."

He chuckled, his body vibrating beneath me. He kissed me again.

"Have you always enjoyed having pricks inside you?" he asked with genuine curiosity.

I sighed. "Mostly. But it weren't always that."

"Pardon?"

"Well, I didn't have access to other men in such a way at first. So I used like, cucumbers and carrots and other likely things to see if I'd like the sensation."

"Carrots!" Captain Martin said, barking a laugh. "What on earth?"

"Well, they're the right size, some of them. And they're pretty fucking solid."

"I suppose they are. You're lucky you didn't lose one up there."

"A few times I came close. They're awful slippery when they're covered with lard," I murmured. "Speaking of which, that oil is lovely. Works very well to take your cock without any trouble."

"Why do you think I have it?"

I smiled, although he couldn't see. "Have you had that truncheon in every man aboard?"

Captain Martin sighed. "No, Rooster. Only a select handful," he admitted. "They aren't all sodomites, and I don't push myself in where I'm not wanted."

I nodded, more than a little relieved to hear that.

"And nobody cares that *you* are?"

"What...a sodomite?" he asked, blithely.

"A mag, a molly, a margery," I said, referring to the popular slang of the time. I rolled off him and grabbed my wilting cock, waving it in the air. "Mother Midnight, a creature."

"Good God. Do you know every term used in the alleyways?"

"Of course I do. Where do you think I've come from?"

He pushed himself onto his elbow and gazed down at me, stroking his fingers along my side to rest on my hip. He chuckled.

"You've got indents from my fingers here."

"Have I? Don't sound so surprised."

"Well, you're far too well spoken and literate to have grown up in the streets, Rooster. Don't play me for a fool," he said, sliding that hand over my bottom and slipping his fingers in the crack. He stretched me open and fingered my soaked hole, hissing with delight. "Mmm, so wet with my seed, you slattern."

I gasped as he played with me. "Aye, filled like a bloody custard tart," I stated with glee.

"Oh yes," he said, slipping a finger in, then another. "Goddamn it, Rooster. How on earth did I resist you for so *long*? Hmm? Even desperate and as filthy as you were, you lit a fire within me. And that flame only burns brighter now."

I glowed with happiness.

"But you ignored me. I was a nuisance, surely, more than anything else."

"I did think that. And you were. You are," he murmured as if they were endearments, while he probed my depths with his fingers, making me stutter and moan and my cock fill again. "Such a fucking nuisance."

He took my mouth with his and plundered me at both ends, sighing, then thrusting hard with his fingers.

I moaned and wiggled in his hold, letting him have me, letting him play. I loved being the captain's slut in his comfortable bed, filled with his seed, being frigged by his tireless fingers. I was in heaven.

A shout broke me out of my waking dream. It took a moment to realize the exclamation was a happy sound and not a cry of distress. The captain pulled back from my mouth and stilled his hand. He listened.

"Sounds like the crew is celebrating," he muttered, and sure enough, I heard the notes of Darcy's fiddle, and other sounds of merriment.

"Celebrating what?" I asked, then whimpered as the captain withdrew his fingers from my greedy arse.

"Who knows? Let's go find out, shall we?"

Part of me wanted to stay here in the coziness and comfort of the captain's quarters. But he seemed eager to join the fun.

He helped me clean up, sniggering about the amount of seed he'd dropped in me, the cheeky bastard. I imagined this would likely be a continuing theme with him, and I surely didn't mind it. There was nothing like being filled by a man you admired, especially when the courtesy made him so proud.

The captain stripped off his soiled shirt and dropped the garment into a basket in the corner. He found a fresh one in a drawer.

"Do you know how to do laundry, Rooster? We should wash these bedsheets once a week to keep the vermin and the smells away," he said as he drew on the clean shirt.

"I don't, but I suppose I can learn," I said since I was in a good mood and had decided to do what I could to stay in his good graces.

"That's the spirit," he said with a smile that was everything.

Once we'd dressed, I followed him out the door. Boone was sitting there as usual—did the man ever take a leak or a shit?—and now looked up.

"Boone, why don't you lock up and join the hullabaloo?" Captain Martin said. "We're going up, and I have the other key in my pocket."

"Thank you, Captain Martin. I was hoping to," Boone said and stood.

The deck was crowded with men in good spirits, holding bottles of whatever liquor they could get their hands on. I knew there was rum aboard, of course, but I'd also been offered drams of whiskey, and the cook served ale with every big meal.

There was singing and laughing and cursing. I didn't want to hang onto the captain like a dog, so I headed away when I saw Martinéz and Lahiri, but strong fingers circled my wrist and the captain pulled me back.

"Where do you think you're going, Rooster?"

I blinked at him. "I see my friends, Captain."

Captain Martin followed my gaze, then considered. His grip relaxed and let me loose.

"Only come back to me soon, please."

He gazed at me in a daft kind of way that made my heart flutter.

"Of course, I will. I just want to say halloo."

He nodded, and I left him.

"White!" Martinéz shouted as I neared. "You broke free of the captain's shackles, I see!"

"Ropes is more like," I said, grinning and rubbing my wrist as if there was a burn there. "He does like to keep me still when he's feeling amorous."

Lahiri chortled, his copper skin looking softer than a moonlit night. He was a delicate fellow—wiry, like me. I'd asked where he was originally from, and he'd said Kolkata in the East Indies, a very hot and crowded place. He liked the sea better and had hid away on a merchant vessel that had been overtaken by the *Arrow* a few years back. He'd skirted most of the fighting and had shown the crew to the booty on board their ship once the battle was won. Captain Martin had offered him a place, and he'd been crew ever since.

Martinéz was from Madrid and had been a member of a Spanish militia ship that Captain Martin and his crew had ransacked. There were several others on the *Arrow* who had deserted for Captain Martin, and for the opportunity to live in a different way, without the classism and structure of the Spanish military organization. Even though, to most Englishmen, the Spaniards were the enemy, if these men had abandoned their countrymen that was proof enough they were on our side.

All the folks on board, from what I'd gleaned, preferred a rebellious nomadic life on the seas to the restrictive lives they'd known. Myself included. So far, life aboard Captain Martin's ship had treated me better than anywhere else.

I sat my arse down on a sack of potatoes and stretched my legs. There was a lovely soft breeze, so the ship rocked peacefully on the current that carried her along. Half the sails had been rolled and tied, so that we drifted along at a sedate pace. It had been a day of hard work for most, and the fresh sea air did well to cover the smell of so many unbathed men.

The overnight crew were at their posts and seemed relatively alert, although most had cups or bottles in hand to partake of the festivities.

"The captain treating you well, then?" Martinéz asked.

"Oh aye. Keeps me in luxury, he does, except when we're fucking. Then he likes to treat me all lowly, like I'm his helpless slave." I grinned. "It's bloody perfect."

"Jesus. You're as filthy as he is."

"I think they're a good match," Lahiri said. "The captain likes to subdue his lovers, and Simon appears to like a good struggle."

"Didn't know how much, until him," I admitted, reaching for the bottle that Martinéz was holding. "He's got a wonderful way of making me wait."

"You behaving yourself?" Lahiri asked.

I pretended to be shocked. "I'll have you know, I'm a perfect angel with the captain."

Martinéz threw back his head and howled as Darcy started up with his fiddle again, playing a lively Irish jig that got a few men up to dance.

I glanced over to see the captain sitting on the boards, leaning against the rail beside Donatello with his legs stretched out. Donatello was speaking and Captain Martin nodded, then tipped the bottle to his lips. His Adam's apple bobbed as he drank, then he met my gaze and smiled as he lowered the drink.

I could not explain how that simple gesture affected me. I immediately wanted to go to him, so I made excuses to my friends and made my way back.

"Hullo again, Captain," I said, planting my feet apart on the deck in front of them.

"Hullo again, White," he said, offering me the bottle. "Sit a spell with us."

I took the offered jug and tipped it up, gulping a burning draft of whiskey into my gullet. I gave the container back and wiped my mouth with the back of my hand.

We stared at each other, and I swear to the Holy Mother that I wanted him to bend me over the side of the ship and fuck me in front of everyone. I hoped he had the same idea, but he kept quiet and simply delivered his lustful thoughts into my brain.

I took a deep breath. Everyone knew about us. They knew the captain was a sodomite and that I warmed his bed. I warred with myself for about two seconds before I stepped forward, a foot on either side of his outstretched legs. I sank so that I was astride them, my arse perched on his strong thighs.

"I missed you," he whispered.

I cupped his chin in my palm and leaned forward, touching his familiar lips with mine in the gentlest of kisses. When I pulled back, his eyes shone with happiness and surprise.

I started to get up, but Captain Martin's fingers wrapped around my wrist, and he tugged me forward so I fell against him. He wrapped an arm around me and took another swig of whiskey. I settled against him, content to be coddled by the man who'd cruelly tanned my hide and filled me with seed only an hour before. If this was pirate life, then sign me the fuck up.

There was audible laughter and muttering from some of the

others, but nobody made a fuss. If we'd done this in the middle of the Penny Whistle, the establishment where we'd first encountered each other, I'm almost certain that the law would have been called. At the very least, we would have been tossed out into the street. But here, in the middle of the ocean, on Captain Martin's ship, we were safe to indulge our feelings for each other.

The soft *da-dump, da-dump* of the captain's heart under my ear, and the jolly sounds of the fiddle and the stomping of boots soothed my restless mind. The captain shared his drink, feeding me like I was a babe in arms, and I thrilled to the gesture. I'd surely never felt so fucking safe and cared for in my life. I knew that Captain Martin was fearless and relentless in battle, and that he'd been responsible for the deaths of many a merchant seaman, and possibly several British Naval Officers as well. But he'd been nothing but kind to me, even whilst treating me like his personal whore. He'd never done anything cruel or vicious to me, and I truly had earned that spanking.

Going over the captain's fine lap and getting a hiding was nothing, compared to the actual cruelty I'd suffered at the hands of so many, in my short life. What we did together in that cabin was different, so different, and I'd fight anyone who denied it.

After a spell of blissful snuggling, I shifted to sit at the captain's side, and we drank and talked and joked with Donatello. Donatello and Captain Martin traded jibes and insults like very old mates often did, and I almost pissed my breeches a few times. Instead, I did like everyone else and pissed over the side, as the sun went down and darkness fell. Lamps were lit, and the merry-making continued into the wee hours. The sight of a deck full of drunken pirates singing songs and having fun, struck me as a delightful, wondrous spectacle to fall asleep to, leaning on Captain Martin's shoulder in the tranquil tropical night.

Chapter Seven

Catastrophe

I woke with the intense urge to piss. Too much rum and whiskey had filled my bladder and made my head ache and my stomach unsettled. And perhaps I was still drunk.

At some point, I must have fallen over because I was lying flat out on the deck. I pushed myself up and looked around. The captain and Donatello had fallen asleep together, with the quartermaster sprawled over the captain's legs, and the captain lolling against the rail, where he'd been most of the night. One of them was snoring—likely my captain.

The other men on deck were spread about, sleeping wherever they'd landed. Groups of them were piled up like a litter of puppies, and others had found space for themselves. It had been a joyful, happy evening, and I hadn't had many.

I sighed and stood, my head throbbing as the boat swayed beneath my feet. Or perhaps the deck was steady, and my addled brain made me think the ship was moving. The silence of the ocean at night stretched out from the bow and the moonlight made a pretty design on the surface. I turned and moved to the railing behind me, still entertaining visions of the festivities, so I waited until releasing a good stream of piss over the water to look up.

A great ship loomed on the horizon, heading in our direction. She was several leagues away by my estimate, but still too close. I almost choked on my tongue as I finished pissing and tucked myself into my breeches. I stumbled toward the captain.

"Captain Martin! Dinesh! Wake up, for fuck's sake. A ship, there's a ship, right here. Wake up! Wake up!"

"Hmm. Rooster..." he groaned. "For fuck's sake, let me sleep. I'll tup you later..."

"We'll all be dead by then. There's a ship! There's a ship, and it's gaining ground!" I raised my voice and let some of my terror come through.

His eyes went wide, and he scrambled up, peering over the railing.

"Fucking Christ," he cursed. "Where did she come from?"

He kicked Donatello, who groaned and joined us at the rail, holding his head. When he saw the ship, he let go of his head and gripped the wooden balustrade.

"They don't come in peace, Captain. Look," Donatello said, his tone foreboding.

Fluttering on the mast of the approaching vessel was a black flag, with white insignia of an indefinable design. But that was enough to know they were bandits, pirates, or vagabonds with no allegiance to anyone but themselves, just like us.

"Who's on watch?" Captain Martin asked, gazing around at

the sleeping men.

"Beatty," Donatello muttered. "He's there."

He pointed to a stout fellow sprawled fast asleep along the rail with an empty jug near him.

"Well, he'd better hope he's killed in the skirmish we're about to have, or the men will deal with him themselves," the captain muttered ominously. He reached into his pocket and turned to me. "White, run and get my spyglass," he said, pressing the key to his rooms in my hand.

"Yes, Captain," I said, my heart in my chest and the taste of bile in my throat.

I ran.

I ran so fast I almost tumbled down the stairs to the lower deck. The key stuck in the lock of the door, and I cursed, wiggling it frantically. I took a deep breath and applied the key with more deliberation and less panic, and the latch clicked. I pushed the door open, ran in, grabbed the glass, and ran back to the deck.

"Here, Captain," I said, passing the fine tool to Captain Martin, whilst Donatello roused the crew, wading in among them and kicking men with no ceremony.

"Get up! Get up, you buggers! Man the cannons! All crew to starboard!" he yelled.

Men staggered and scrambled, jumping up as they woke, no doubt with sore heads and limbs, but they rallied. They must have heard the urgency in the commands and realized this was a life or death situation.

The air filled with curses and cries as the men realized what was happening and saw the approaching ship themselves. I saw Beatty wake and leap up, his eyes wide and panic on his face. He met my gaze and I his, knowing the man's days were numbered. Doubtless he knew his fatal mistake too. He should have been on watch, even with a celebration going on.

In fact, the entire night crew had indulged in the drink and the merrymaking, and woke now to a terrible situation of their own making. They and the day crew ran to their posts to see what could be done.

Captain Martin lifted his spyglass. The moonlight lit the sky and the surface of the water with a brilliance we could thank our chances for.

Donatello returned to the captain's side.

"Can you make anything out?" he asked.

"No. It's all dark, as if they're asleep or adrift. But that's not likely."

"No. They're biding time, most likely. Hoping we haven't seen them."

"We almost didn't." The captain's gaze flashed to mine.

A great boom and a flash of bright light exploded over the waves.

"All hands to stations!" Donatello called. "We're under attack!"

"Hard to port!" Mr Dunn yelled. "No time to clear the decks. Just do what you can to get the cannons in place!"

Our navigator had been well in the cups but now took command of the ship with a justified urgency. The first cannon shot missed us, but another was launched that skimmed the bow and splintered a rail.

"To the guns! Fire when ready!" Captain Martin shouted, backed up by Donatello.

The *Arrow* slowly turned and presented her broadside to the other vessel, as their cannons were reloaded. We could see much activity on her deck now as the rays of the morning sun peeked over the horizon and the stars began to dim.

My heart leapt in my chest, as the smell of sulphur and smoke filled my nostrils. My belly reeled with the effects of the drink from the night before and with a sudden fear for my life. This was a wholly new experience for me and I already didn't like it. My instinct was to run below decks but I couldn't possibly display such overt cowardice. Besides, I needed to know the captain was all right. I want to say that I jumped into readiness to help defend the *Arrow*. However, I had no skills or training, and no idea what to do, so I decided it best to stay out of the way.

I crouched behind a barrel and tried to keep an eye on the captain and Donatello. I barely believed the *Arrow* hadn't disintegrated into a pile of splinters and flame because the fire kept coming. My ears rang with the sounds of shouting and cannon fire and gunshots, as our crew tried to defend us.

"Raise the white flag! Raise it now!" Captain Martin commanded, and I wondered at surrendering so quickly. Then again, I didn't want the ship to go down, and our position did appear hopeless.

"Surrender? Are you certain?" Donatello asked him in a loud voice that would carry over the sounds of destruction and men's shouts.

"We're outgunned, and they have the advantage. We can negotiate, perhaps. If they stop their fire, we can ask to board and discuss a fair solution. We have goods to trade."

Donatello nodded quickly and turned to the men. "Raise the white flag!" he shouted. "We'll negotiate a truce!"

The men hurried to obey, and soon our flag of surrender went up, flapping in the wind as the *Arrow* rocked beneath her assault. I prayed silently that the attacking ship would acknowledge the signal and give us mercy. I squeezed my eyes shut and tried to breathe, wondering if this would be my final sunrise.

And then the cannons stopped. The sound and smell of wood burning became noticeable and some of the men shouted to contain a fire. I opened my eyes to see the crew battling flames and to see that half of the aft rail had been blown away.

We waited with baited breath, but the attack was paused. The captain's gaze met mine, where I crouched near the barrel, and he nodded with a reassuring smile.

"Donatello," Captain Martin said, grabbing Donatello's arm. "You and I. We'll go in the skiff and bargain with them. Surely, we can come to an arrangement."

"Aye, Captain. Do you recognize the insignia?" Donatello asked.

"No. They're rebels like us. We must be prepared for anything."

"Aye," Donatello said gravely.

I scrambled out of my sheltered spot, wishing I had some skills in this area and not just a spectacular arse.

"I want to come with you," I said, breathlessly. Where this courage came from is anyone's guess, but for a tremendous need to be near to Captain Martin, no matter what.

He turned to me with regret in his gaze.

"No, lad. There ain't no point."

His words hurt me, but he smoothed my hair back from my forehead and kissed me there.

"Stay here, and wait for me. I'll be back."

"Are you certain?" I gasped.

He only smiled and gave me a salute. "Keep yourself safe, little rooster. Do that for me."

I nodded. My heart was breaking. Even though our union was only a few weeks old, I felt like a part of me was being ripped away. I was numb as I watched the skiff lowered over the side with Captain Martin and Donatello aboard.

I half expected the cannon fire to resume, and then we'd all be lost. But the slap of the waves on the hull and the murmur of anxious voices near me was the only sound, apart from my frantic heart beating in my ears. My belly roiled with heat and I felt like retching.

Donatello took the oars and rowed toward the other ship. The crew of the *Arrow*, including myself, gathered at the rail to watch. Several had their muskets cocked, ready for anything. Although I did wonder how effective muskets would be over that range.

The captain had handed me his spyglass, and now I raised the tool to my eye.

I locked onto the small skiff with the two important men aboard. It physically hurt to see Captain Martin so vulnerable, and I half expected the skiff to explode with cannon fire. The sun was peeking over the horizon, making a vivid and beautiful display over the sea, but I couldn't rid myself of foreboding.

A rope ladder came over the side of the other vessel and dropped to the water, and I breathed a sigh of relief. Our captain was an intelligent man and skilled in dialogue. I only hoped he could secure an agreement so that we might leave with our ship and our lives.

"Damn fools. They aren't going to negotiate," Martinez muttered, sending a chill up my spine.

I lowered the glass to look at him.

Hillier, who was next in command under Donatello, stood nearby with his musket raised, his expression grim.

"But they're welcoming them aboard," I murmured in a voice that aimed to be hopeful.

"Mmm, that may be. But I've my doubts as to their intentions," Martinez said.

I lifted the glass to my eye again, my belly swirling with renewed worry. If what Martinez said was true, the captain and Donatello were in a very vulnerable position.

The two men climbed aboard and soon vanished into a crowd of darkly dressed vagabonds. But surely they'd be all right. Surely they wouldn't be killed outright. There were rules of engagement, after all, even for pirates. Or so I'd assumed.

I jerked in fear as a dark and dangerous-looking fellow filled the glass. He was bearded and scarred and missing one eye. He looked toward the *Arrow* with a sneer, and I imagined he could see me watching. I gasped and lowered the glass, but then I couldn't make out anything.

I lifted the tool and peered through the eyepiece again.

The enemy pirate captain was speaking to his crew. He held up his arms and his men moved back, creating space around Captain Martin and Donatello. I prayed that one of them had a concealed weapon, although a small blade wouldn't make much of a difference. If that crew was out for blood, they'd get what they craved. For the first time, I cast doubt on Captain Martin's plan.

I watched through the spyglass, barely breathing, as Donatello and the captain spoke to the intimidating figure with some urgency. He nodded, then nodded again, and I could see that Captain Martin was encouraged. But then the villain shook his head and pointed back at our ship. His ragtag crew raised their fists in the air, and their cheer rang over the water.

"Fuck. Fuck," I breathed.

Two of the men grabbed Donatello and hauled him up onto a box, holding him steady as his wrists were roped together.

"No, no, no," I said.

"What's happening?" Hillier asked.

"They've got Donatello," I said.

"What do you mean?"

He grabbed the spyglass from me and lifted the instrument to his eye, just as a shot echoed between the two ships, and a man cried out in astonishment.

I watched from a distance as the pirate took out Donatello at close range.

"Donatello's gone. They shot him," Hillier muttered. He lowered the spyglass, his face ashen. "Fucking bastards." He turned to the others and handed the tool to me. "Prepare to fire! They aren't negotiating!"

"Wait! What about Captain Martin?" I yelled, lifting the spyglass to my eye.

I watched, my heart like a firebrand in my chest, as Captain Martin held up his hands and tried to reason with the other captain, the crumpled body of Donatello at his feet, blood oozing from the man's destroyed face.

"He's trying to reason with him! Hold on!" I said.

"Hold your fire!" Hillier said as the men prepared to do what they could. Captain Martin looked pale and desperate, but he was arguing and pointing at our ship. For a moment, his pale but familiar visage filled the spyglass, the face I'd touched and kissed so tenderly only half a day earlier.

Everything went dark.

My vision dimmed and my burning, furious heart put forth an incredible heat that took my breath and churned it like sparks of fire. The spyglass clattered to the deck as I grabbed the rail and glared at the distant ship.

I couldn't see a thing but the flames and fire that danced in my vision. A maelstrom appeared directly over the offending vessel—swirling and swooping dark clouds, vicious winds that tore their sails, lightning that crashed and struck their rigging. The sudden destruction satisfied some deep and dark part of me as an appropriate revenge for what they'd done to Donatello and were about to do to my beloved captain.

I wasn't cognizant of my actions, only possessed of a destructive force so strong that its violence and single-minded focus took me over. My hands and heart burned with the heat of my passion. A spark deep in my belly took hold and radiated outward to all of my limbs. Lightning crackled between my fingers.

Exclamations and curses came from the men around me. I stood there, hands two heated brands as they clutched the rail, the storm before us a reflection of my desire to smite them all, but for an image of Captain Martin's cherished face, and a memory of the way he'd held me in his bed the previous afternoon.

I was enraged past the point of reason that those bastards had probably killed him by now.

The storm was the only thing I could see with my eyes and the only thing I could hear. Then strange words came out of my mouth in a language I barely remembered. I understood them, even as I didn't know how or why I was saying them.

"Bring me the fire and the flame,
O'er the ocean, in my name.
Give me the lightning and the storm,
From the heavens, let it be borne.
Smite those who threaten what's mine.
They'll not have anyone this time.
Let the sea and the flame rejoice.
Let the ocean and sky make the choice."

I gripped the railing as the storm raged and howled, blackness and blue fire making a terrifying image. Then, as quickly as the gale had come up, it died down. The clouds became sparse and grey and through them could be seen the enemy ship. Aflame, and barely a vessel anymore, the smell of burning timber and steaming sulphur drifted on the breeze.

I blinked, coming back to myself with a horrible dread and shame that almost felled me. But I had to see. I had to see what I had wrought.

I lifted my hands from the rail and turned. Men backed away and crossed themselves or made other superstitious gestures. My palms ached and stung as I grabbed the fallen spyglass and lifted it to my eye.

I'd made the wrong choice, though my actions hadn't been a choice at all. Unfathomable power had overtaken me. A familiar phenomenon that hadn't occurred for a very long time, one that I'd thought had been laid to rest with my dear mother on that horrible day.

I couldn't see the other ship for the flames. Captain Martin was as lost as everyone else. No men were in the act of throwing themselves over the side because they were all dead.

It was a funeral pyre.

I tried to come to terms with the deathly vision, knowing I'd never see Captain Martin again and wondering how I'd survive.

"He's there!" Hillier yelled. "The captain! By all that's holy, look there!"

I gazed at Hillier, wondering why he was torturing me with impossibilities. Then I looked to where he pointed and saw a form bobbing in the water. But surely he was dead—a corpse tossed on the waves.

Then I heard a splash, and spotted three of the men swimming toward him.

"Lower the rope ladder! Do it now!"

A frail hope inside me broke.

They thought he was alive but that was an impossibility! I had put him in that maelstrom of death. I had murdered everyone aboard. I had torn that ship apart as if it were a child's plaything.

I had most likely killed him as well.

I looked at Hillier. He met my gaze with trepidation and alarm, which only made me feel worse. So I ran.

*

I hid in the hold, crouched against the slick wall, where my hammock still hung by the porthole, not ready to talk to anyone or offer any kind of explanation for what had occurred. I barely knew what had happened myself, and a similar thing had only occurred once before. This time, the release of my magic hadn't worked against me and left me with a vicious scar or killed me outright, although I wished it had.

But, perhaps I was wrong about that because my palms wouldn't stop stinging. I examined them in the light from a nearby oil lantern. They were indeed red and blistered. I hadn't been spared at all.

"Fuck," I said, as the pain worsened. As if seeing my injury made the destruction real. How had the railing not burst into flames? I didn't know if my recollection of events was accurate at all.

I gazed about myself, trying to focus and shake this inner turmoil. I didn't even know how much time had passed since the incident on deck.

I heard footsteps, and Martinéz came down into the hold as if he was looking for someone. But surely he wasn't trying to find me?

"Martinéz," I said, but my voice was gone. I cleared my

throat and tried again, with more volume. "*Martinéz.*"

His head swung toward me, and his eyes went wide when he saw me. He took a step back, and for a moment, I thought he might flee. He stood his ground.

"The captain," I stammered, my face crumpling into misery. "Did he...live?"

His eyes softened and his posture relaxed.

"Aye," Martinéz said, and I almost sobbed with relief. "Except for having watched his best mate killed before his eyes, and an entire ship burnt to timbers beneath him," he said, a statement of fact, and not an accusation. His voice was gentle.

I nodded and whispered, "Thank you."

He kept looking at me. He appeared to consider whether to say anything more.

"Are you all right, White?" he asked finally.

I didn't know quite what to tell him. Except that I wasn't all right at all. In so many ways.

"My hands," I whispered. I showed him.

"Christ Almighty," he said and crossed himself before taking a step closer. "You need tending. Let me get Faraday."

Faraday was a retired navy doctor who had come aboard the *Arrow* at one of her visits to Tortuga. Captain Martin had bribed him with a bag of coin to join his crew as he'd needed a surgeon.

"You don't have to," I said. "I know everyone's scared of me."

Martinéz gazed at me for a long moment. "We ain't scared, exactly," he said. "Only confused and a bit cautious. You can't blame us for that. You don't know what that looked like from where we were. I still don't understand what happened."

"If it makes you feel better, neither do I."

"That doesn't make me feel better at all."

I didn't know what to say to that.

"Are you a witch, Simon? Is that what you are?"

The word rang in my ears with all of its power and prejudice. I didn't want to believe that word applied to me. I averted my gaze and didn't answer.

Martinez sighed. "Anyway, I'm getting Faraday."

I didn't bother to reply. I went back to staring at the wall and wondering what I was going to do. Surely they'd send me off the *Arrow* at the next port. Nobody'd want me now.

Martinez left, and soon Faraday came, accompanied not by Martinez but with Hillier. The surgeon pulled a wood crate over and took a seat.

"Hello, White."

I glanced at him. Faraday was an average-sized man, with a snub nose that gave him a juvenile look, although he must have been in his mid-thirties. He had blue eyes and soft hands, and he'd treated me for lice, when I'd first come aboard, with more than average sympathy.

"Let me see those hands then."

I showed him.

"Well now. That looks painful."

The hurt was considerable, but I deserved to suffer for what I'd done.

"I've brought some linen cloths to wrap your hands. Best to keep the dirt out and leave the wound open to the air," he said. He reached for me. "May I?"

I nodded.

He took my wrists and examined them, turning them over to check the backs, peering through his thick glasses.

"Any other burns on you?"

"Don't think so."

Faraday wrapped my hands loosely with the clean linen. He

tied the strips in knots on the backs of my hands.

"There. That will keep them protected. You should have some willow bark tea for the pain," he said with a kind smile.

I was staring at my cloth-covered hands when I heard Captain Martin's voice. "He can have that in my cabin."

I looked up, slowly, as if preparing to see a ghost or a sworn enemy.

He stood there, watching me. He was all of a piece, and I let my gaze drag down his body to be sure.

"Of course, Captain," Faraday said, standing and giving me a nod. "Look after yourself, White."

"White will be under my care," Captain Martin said.

Faraday smiled, gave him a nod, and left us.

I don't deserve this. I almost caused your death.

I looked away and curled in on myself.

"Simon."

I didn't respond.

"Rooster," he said, in softer tones.

But that only made me more miserable.

He sighed. "Look at me."

"No."

Silence.

"You dare disobey a direct order from your captain, White?"

I couldn't ignore his commanding tone. I looked up at him.

His expression relaxed into pity. "What's wrong?"

What's wrong?

How could he ask that? Everything was wrong. Where had he been for the last few hours?

I blinked, trying to summon the words.

"I...I..."

I felt like an object was stuck in my throat.

I wanted to say that I'd almost caused his death; I'd produced the storm that had destroyed that vessel. Instead, my face collapsed, and I started to cry.

The captain spoke. "You saved me, Simon White. Somehow. I don't understand what happened any more than you do. But you spared my life and no one else's."

I shook my head. His survival had been a fortunate bit of luck. I didn't have that kind of control. Maybe I never would.

He bent down so we were at eye level. "Get up, Rooster, and come with me."

I shook my head again.

The captain sighed. "Rooster."

I kept crying, and now I'd started to shake.

"I'll carry you if I have to," he warned.

"No...just leave me here," I managed between gasps and sniffles.

"Nonsense," he said.

He scooped me into his arms, in spite of my pitiful protests. He carried me to his rooms, past curious and cautious stares from the crew. I hid my face against his shoulder and soaked the fabric with my tears.

Chapter Eight

Redemption

The captain stripped me, silently and efficiently, and put me into his bed. I fisted my hands to protect my palms and also to show my resistance to these circumstances. I didn't feel I deserved this kind of treatment.

Once I found myself underneath the soft blankets on the captain's bed, and the exhaustion of everything I'd been through caught up to me, I drifted into blessed unconsciousness as the *Arrow* swayed gently beneath me.

I woke to the sound of gulls shrieking outside the window and the dawn of a new day. When I raised a hand to my head, I felt the linen bandage and remembered what had transpired. Instantly, a cloud as thick and black as the one that had engulfed the attacking ship the day before enveloped me, and I rolled over, hoping to fall back into unconsciousness.

But Captain Martin had seen me open my eyes.

"Rooster, darling. I know you're awake."

His voice sounded close by, the puff of his breath tickling my ear.

I didn't respond.

He sighed and I blinked back tears. I couldn't get the fucking image of the maelstrom that had engulfed the ship the day before out of my head.

That storm, or spell, or summoning, had been *my* doing. And I'd killed so many people. I'd almost killed Captain Martin!

"Rooster, I want you to listen to me. And know that I am speaking as Dinesh Martin, captain of the *Arrow*, and also as Captain Martin, seducer and ravisher of Mr Simon Bartholomew White."

He waited and I could not stop myself from answering. He was the captain, after all.

"Yes, Captain," I whispered.

"I don't know exactly what happened yesterday. I'm not sure that you do either, although you appear convinced that the sudden and specific storm came from your hands."

Tears tracked down my cheeks. I nodded.

"Nobody on this ship is displeased with you. The crew is wary, yes, the way any inexplicable phenomena makes men uneasy. But they are also very thankful, Rooster."

"Donatello," I croaked.

"Yes. We lost Donatello, and I won't forget the pain of that. At least he went quickly," Captain Martin said. "I've put Hillier in charge of things, if that makes a difference to you."

I didn't respond, recalling the image of Donatello being shot. That shocking occurrence had ignited the flame in my chest, and I felt a remnant of that heat stirring now. But I took deep, calming breaths, as I'd learned to do years and years ago, to keep the dark magic as a glowing ember instead of a raging inferno.

I hadn't known Donatello in an intimate way, but I had known him to be a fair and diplomatic man. We had been friends, I think.

The captain kept talking. He stayed close but he didn't touch me.

Perhaps he was wary, too, and the thought distressed me. He needn't be. I'd as soon call a storm down on myself than hurt a hair on his head.

"Do you know, little rooster, that—traditionally—the fellow who is first to spy a ship on the horizon gets its finest booty?"

I didn't say anything, wondering where he was going with this line of conversation.

"Now, the only thing of value that survived our...encounter...is laying in this bed beside you. But I want to tell you that he's yours, if you'll have him."

The tears I'd managed to hold back returned, and I sobbed into the pillow.

"Oh, Rooster. Don't you see? We'd all be dead if you hadn't gotten up and looked over the rail. We're all alive because of you."

And now he did touch me. I felt the warmth of his palm on my shoulder, soothing me, and I didn't pull away. Soft kisses feathered along my shoulder blades, even as I sobbed and sniffled. I didn't deserve him, but I clutched onto those words and this kind treatment like a man adrift in a bottomless sea. I had been the one to alert the crew to the attacking ship. And the captain was right. We'd all have been lost if I hadn't.

That truth eased some of the pain in my heart.

"Come now. Turn and look at me," he said.

I forced myself to face him. I'm sure my eyes were swollen and red, my lips slack and ugly. But the captain's smile and the look of adoration in his eyes was better than any healing balm the doc could prescribe.

"There he is. There's my sweet rooster."

I didn't think anyone except my late mam, bless her heart, had ever called me 'sweet' because, normally, I wasn't. I was argumentative and a bit of an ass. But I'd take such coddling today. I'd take indulgence any day from Captain Martin.

He sobered and tucked a piece of wayward hair off my forehead.

"Listen to me and listen well," he said, speaking as a captain now. "Whatever happened out there at the rail is the reason I'm here right now. I don't know how, or why, but that storm never touched me. And if that—" He seemed to cast about for the appropriate word for the violence of the phenomenon. "—tempest...did somehow come from you, Rooster, you saved us all a *second* time."

The magic I'd summoned hadn't touched him? Those words gave me profound relief.

"Truly? You were safe the entire time I was—" I stammered, not wanting to say 'while I was killing them all'. "During the storm?"

"I was," he said.

Tears threatened again. "I thought... I thought I'd—"

"You thought you'd harmed me. But you didn't. You saved me, Simon White, and I shall forever be in your debt," he said, stroking my chin. "You saved the *Arrow* and her crew too. Those nasty vermin were out for blood, and whatever booty we had aboard."

The relief those words brought was a soothing balm to my rattled and fearful soul. For the first time since the incident had unfolded, I thought that perhaps I'd done the right thing, even if I wasn't sure exactly how.

The captain smiled, then appeared puzzled. He continued to speak in low tones.

"I felt wrapped in an invisible shield of some kind, seeing the lightning and the flames around me, watching the crew of that ship perish before my eyes. And then I was in the water." He narrowed his eyes. "And then I saw you, Rooster, standing at the rail, with a fierce and determined look on your dear face, surrounded by blue flames with orange ones shooting from under your hands." He frowned. "Your hands. Let me see."

I lifted them, palms up. The linen bandages looked clean and white, even against my pale skin.

"May I?" he asked, his fingers going to the knot on one of them.

I nodded.

As the captain carefully untied the knot, I realized there was no longer any pain from the wounds. And as he drew the cloth away, we both blinked in surprise.

The skin was reddened somewhat, but smooth. The blisters had disappeared. There was no sign they'd ever been there. The recently scalded skin looked better than the healed scar on my side and back that was ten years old.

I met his confused gaze with my own. Then he quickly untied the bandage on my other hand. He held them together in front of him, gaping at the healed skin.

"Faraday told me your hands looked like raw meat last night," he whispered, meeting my gaze again. "Is that true?"

"Yes," I said. "I don't know why they don't still."

"Is there any pain?"

"No."

He moved the pads of his thumbs over my palms, very lightly. "Now?"

"No. The skin is sensitive, that's all."

"Well. There is *some* kind of magic at work here." He was silent, still holding my hands. "Would you like to tell me what kind of supernatural forces I'm dealing with, Rooster? If you even know?"

His voice was kind, as if he were asking me about a regular occurrence, and not my questionable ability to call upon powers beyond nature.

So I told him what I did know.

"My mam told me that these powers were a gift from her. She didn't know why, and she didn't really understand her powers either. But she said she could feel them in me as soon as I was born, even though she was in denial for a long time. She didn't teach me anything, only subtly guided me when she saw glimpses of...these forces...rising in me. She wanted me to keep them hidden. From everyone, but especially from my papa."

I stared at the bed covers. I didn't like to think about these things. Most of the time, I pretended I was a regular man, albeit with questionable morals and even more questionable desires. But flesh and blood like anyone else. I didn't like to think of myself as different, and to be honest, these inexplicable powers frightened me. I didn't like to think I had so much influence on the world.

"Rooster, what happened when you were twelve?" Dinesh asked.

I'd known this question was coming. Why wouldn't he ask the most obvious question?

I took a deep breath and explained in the smallest number of words possible. "I tried to save my mother, but I wasn't able to."

The captain's face fell. "Oh, Rooster. I'm so sorry."

I nodded. "The power got away from me. The burn on my side was the least of what happened."

Captain Martin looked horrified. "But...you didn't—"

"My father was not a kind man. And he was afraid of her powers. He drugged her and killed her whilst she slept. When I woke to the horror, I couldn't hold onto my rage. The whole cottage, with her body and him in it, was destroyed, and I barely escaped."

"My God," Captain Martin said, his expression one of utmost sympathy.

"I've survived, somehow, on my wits ever since. I thought, maybe, the powers in me had died with her and my father. But it appears not."

"No," he agreed with solemnity. "It seems not."

I gently pulled my hands away and let them fall to my lap.

"Are you...are you going to tell the crew?"

"Tell them what?"

"That I'm a witch?" I asked, my voice barely audible. 'Witch' was the only word that made any sense.

"Is that what you are, Rooster?" the captain asked without fear or blame or anything but a casual curiosity.

I nodded with a sad smile.

"Among other things," I said, reaching out to touch the captain's whiskered chin.

"You mean, a sodomite and a very, very naughty young man?" he asked with real affection.

"Quite. But not so little," I said, glancing down at my swollen cock making a tent in the sheets that had come to take part in the conversation.

"No. Not little. And a very sexy fucking witch."

I loved him for that. For implying that my strange and

mysterious abilities only served to make me more interesting.

"Are you sure the crew doesn't hate me? They must have been terrified to see what happened."

Captain Martin considered. "I won't say they weren't. But these men have been through more than you'll ever know. It takes much to truly frighten them. And they are well aware that they wouldn't be here today but for you, Rooster."

I nodded. "Well, that's promising." I thought of the circumstances of our ambush. "Are you going to punish the men on the night watch?"

The captain gazed at me with kindness, perhaps that I'd think of others when I myself suffered.

"I made sure they understood the gravity of their mistake. But I think in all of the chaos and confusion, and because we only—" He cleared his throat and seemed overcome for a second. "—only lost one man, the crew is willing to forgive them. And so am I."

For some reason, that made me feel better, even though their actions had put us all in a vulnerable position.

"But how should I behave now that they know my secret?"

"Honestly? Just as normal would be best, I wager." He grinned and chucked me under the chin. "Go back to being the saucy little wise-cracking brat that you are, and they'll settle down and forget all the strangeness. These men are used to the changeable nature of the weather and the seas. Yes, they are superstitious, but they won't look lightly on the fact that you've saved us from certain death. And," he said, leaning in and kissing the tip of my nose. "Not to be incredibly vain, but they like *me* rather a lot. And you, somehow, protected me from...well—" He waved his hands around. "—from our bad luck. So I think you'll find yourself in high esteem among the crew if you can settle their minds that you're not about to bring a similar storm down on top of us."

His words were indeed a comfort. Except for one small thing.

"But, Captain, there will be a storm at some point, won't there?"

"Yes, I'm certain of it." He didn't look perturbed.

"Won't they think I summoned my magic again?"

He gazed at me with the gentlest affection. "Simon, the tempest that demolished our enemy was not a regular storm. Trust me. They know that. These men are familiar with terrifying acts of nature, but they've not seen anything like what you created in that moment. I think you're safe from being accused of anything else."

"Good," I said. "Only, I can't promise that what happened up there won't happen again. When someone I love is threatened, the force rises on its own and I have no control over my power."

I soon realized what I'd said and cleared my throat. *Step back, step back.*

"What I mean to say is, someone I *like a great deal.*"
Distract.

"And I like you very much, Dinesh," I finished.

"I like you very much too, Rooster. And I do owe you a great reward for saving our lives."

"It don't feel right to get a reward for what happened." I said in barely audible tones.

He leaned in, and the scent of his expensive Castile soap that held so many memories just about undid me.

"Pardon?"

"I don't know if I deserve a reward. I put all of your lives in danger."

"I'm done arguing this point, Rooster. Would you simply let me show you how I feel about you?"

I gazed at him, lost to those authoritative and luminous gray eyes. They were the colour of storm clouds, and they could see into my tumultuous soul. I had a connection to storms, you see.

I didn't know why my powers—or whatever they were—manifested that way, and I was rattled by what had happened. I could only hope that another ten years might pass before anything similar occurred, or that the magic would lie dormant in me forever.

But a privateer's life was a risky one, and I had a sense that if Captain Martin's life were endangered going forward, I would do whatever I had to do. I wasn't looking forward to any of it.

For now, he was safe, and so was I. How could I possibly stop him from kissing my face and my neck, my chest, the edge of the original burn, and then swallowing my cock whilst he held my gaze and blinked softly, like a cat drinking milk.

And milk indeed resulted, which I gave up in no time at all, since the vulnerability of the act, the generally excited state of my mind and body, and the skill with which he handled me, took away all of my defences. He kept me in his mouth until I became a boneless bag of skin, the tension that had held me in its deathly grip gone in a gentle overpowering that had needed no violence or restraint. I drifted on soft clouds until someone knocked at the door.

Captain Martin let my cock slide from his mouth. He gave me a pretty smile before lifting his head and gazing toward the door.

"Busy! Come back later."

He turned back with an impish smile that made him look like a troublemaking child.

"I've got a present for White!" said a voice that I recognized as Hillier's. "From the crew."

"Does he need the gift *this moment*?" Captain Martin asked, sounding annoyed.

"I've been tasked with delivering it, Captain, and I don't want to delay."

Captain Martin rolled his eyes and backed off, pulling the sheet and blankets to cover me. I was so relaxed, so content, and so relieved that I wasn't being tossed overboard that I remained on my back and watched him pull on a pair of breeches and walk to the door.

He opened it a crack.

"Well? What is this thoughtful token?" he asked. "Oh!"

The captain's laughter rang out, but Hillier shushed him.

I went up on my elbow, but I couldn't see past the captain's broad back. What on earth had Hillier brought me? The captain opened the door wider and stepped back. My eyes went wide as Hillier came in with a chicken tucked under each arm. And they were *not* dead.

"Your chooks were missin' you, young Simon," he said, coming in and putting them onto the bed with me. "The crew thought they might cheer you."

"Frances!" I exclaimed, jerking upright and spreading my arms, feeling such a weight lift from me that I could barely keep from laughing with joy. "Elizabeth!"

"I thought you might like to see a couple of them."

The chickens landed on the blankets, clucking and fussing as they wondered where they were. I saw the captain and Hillier exchange amused looks.

"Thank you, Hillier," Captain Martin said. "Please tell the crew they were well-received."

"You're welcome, Captain. How is he?"

I didn't listen to the captain's answer, because I was too busy hugging and petting my pretty chickens. What a comfort to see them! I didn't know when I'd become this attached to livestock, but I supposed once you'd named them, you were done for.

"Come here, my pretty things. Aren't you gorgeous, Elizabeth? And Frances, your tail feathers are turning a lovely shade of russet!"

"I'll leave you be," Hillier said. "Only, the crew were wondering where we're planning to sail to. They feel we need another conquest to replenish our stores."

"Yes, I agree. Put our destination to a vote. See what they want to do, where they want to go. And we'll abide by that."

"Of course, Captain."

"And please don't disturb me again unless the situation is urgent."

"Of course, sir," Hillier said and left us.

"Oh, you are such a pretty girl," I murmured to Frances, smoothing her ruffled feathers with my fingers. "What a good girl."

The captain stood there in his breeches, his arms crossed over his chest, watching me talk to my girls. I praised them and cooed to them, like a proud parent, and did feel much recovered. The crew had provided me a welcome solace.

"So, who shall we have for our dinner, then?" the captain muttered.

"You'll not touch a feather on them if you know what's good for you. And neither shall anyone else," I said, giving him a steely eyed glare. I was almost certain he was fooling, but just in case...

But he only smiled. "There's my feisty rooster. He's back, thank the Gods."

I clutched Elizabeth and Frances to me. "Yes, I am, and you keep your bloody murder hands off my chooks."

He held up his arms, trying not to laugh.

"I don't want any part of your chickens. I won't harm them. But they cannot stay here."

I shrugged, indicating that I wasn't in any rush to get rid of them.

"Well, I wager you've never had three such attractive guests in your bed at once, Captain Martin," I said with some smugness.

He actually blushed. "I've never entertained animals below the level of humans; that's a certain fact. However, there's a reason I keep such a large bed in my quarters."

I gasped. "Captain Martin! You fucking trollop."

He looked even more sheepish. "Guilty, as charged. But entertaining multiple partners on board gets a bit tricky when they are also your crew."

"I suppose so," I said.

"I'm happy to have one very lovely man on my bed, even if he comes with two rather scruffy-looking chooks."

I was pleased to hear the first part of that sentence, but moved to cover the ears of the chickens.

"How dare you. They aren't scruffy looking. Or if they are, it's because chickens weren't ever meant to live on the water."

"Granted. Perhaps we'd better put them out of their misery."

"No, stop that nonsense. Come over here and meet them properly," I demanded.

The captain indulged me, happy to see my mood improved, I suppose.

"Now, here, this is Elizabeth," I said, passing him the golden-brown chicken that chirped at the sudden movement. "Elizabeth, this is Captain Martin. He's responsible for the *Arrow*, and he's got an enormous cock. He likes to ram me with it, and I don't mind at all."

"Hello, Elizabeth," Captain Martin said, reaching out with a tentative hand to stroke her. "Will she bite?"

"Well, she's never bitten *me.*"

He didn't look reassured. But he made an attempt at friendship that was amusing to watch. "My, you are a pretty thing…Elizabeth," he said, acting like a reluctant uncle who'd had a baby passed to him.

"And this lovely russet beauty is Frances."

Captain Martin accepted delivery of the other chicken into his lap. Frances made hilarious clucking noises as if she was as excited as I would be to sit on Captain Martin's broad thighs.

"Lovely to make your noisy acquaintance, I'm sure," Captain Martin said, glancing up with a long-suffering look, as if he'd never had to deal with this sort of indignity in his life but would, in this moment, for me.

"Now, then, give her a kiss," I suggested, taking Elizabeth back and planting a soft peck on top of her tiny head.

"I'm not going to kiss her, Simon. She's lovely, but I don't fancy a feather in my mouth."

"Well, you aren't very adventurous, are you? I'll have you know there are a good many interesting things that can be done with feathers."

Chapter Nine

Witch

The *Arrow* became a flurry of activity while I spent a short time with my chooks in Captain Martin's bed. She was put into full sail and heading out on a more deliberate course. Orders were shouted, and feet stomped the deck as men hurried to follow them. The sails flapped as they were unfurled, and the hull rocked as we began to ride the waves with much greater velocity and purpose. The windows of Captain Martin's rooms had been opened to let in the fresh air, so all of this was a noisy hullabaloo that calmed me instead of making me anxious. We were moving forward, all had been forgiven, and I hadn't been cast as a menacing demon preparing to damn them all at the next opportunity.

Hillier was capable of manning the troops for this, as Captain Martin stayed at his desk, making notes in a leatherbound journal and glancing over at me occasionally. I judged him relieved that I was happy, and, frankly, the care he and the crew had given me in the wake of what had happened made me optimistic for my place here amongst them. I still felt unsettled and confused about what had happened. Then again, everyone else probably did as well. The important thing was that everyone but poor Anthony Donatello, God rest his soul, had got out of the chaos alive. I was trying very hard to focus on that.

After a little while, Captain Martin closed his book and said he must go up on deck and check in with Hillier. He suggested I get dressed and take the chickens back to their coop. I could tell their presence in the cabin made him uneasy, and I could see why, as one of them had already shat on the bedclothes. I recalled that I was the one in charge of the room's cleanliness and decided that the captain's suggestion had merit.

I pulled on my clothes, still getting used to their strangeness and feeling like someone else. Someone—probably Captain Martin—had placed my shoes beside the chair, so I gritted my teeth and put on socks and shoes. Seriously, what was I becoming? Perhaps appearing civilized and obedient would help the crew to accept me as a benign cabin boy and fucktoy, and not as a conduit of inexplicable supernatural power.

I took Elizabeth and Frances back to the coops and counted to make sure everyone but poor Guinevere, God rest her soul, was still alive and clucking, and hopefully laying eggs. A friendly man with ruddy skin and a limp, called Lancaster, had taken charge of them at Hillier's orders. I conveyed my appreciation of his care, told him all of their names, quizzed him to make sure he remembered, and made sure he was feeding them properly. His efforts to please me and the genuine concern he had for the animals reassured me.

The captain had implied he would take an hour or so and then meet me back in his cabin for some amusement if I was up for the pleasure. I definitely was, but I had time to spare so decided to go up on deck to get a glimpse of all the activity now that the *Arrow* was on the move. And also to prove to myself that the men didn't hate me.

As I emerged from below deck, I noticed a group of them huddled around the railing. One of them looked up and when he saw me, nudged the others, and they all moved away from the railing as if the wood had suddenly exploded. Which was when I realized I'd been standing exactly there when I'd been overcome with the magic.

Fuck.

I frowned and looked at the men. They averted their eyes and pretended to be engaged in conversation. I walked slowly over to the rail where they had been upon my appearance.

There, scorched into the polished wood, were my handprints. I checked my palms, which had lightened to a healthy and normal pink colour. They didn't hurt and looked to be fully healed.

I was obviously pleased, but the hastened repair also confused me. I still had the scar from ten years ago, and that looked a good deal worse than my palms, which were more recently injured. I stared at my handprints, recalling the horror of standing there with rage coursing through me, watching the vagabonds' ship burn and not knowing if Captain Martin was safe. The shame and fear were there at the edge of my emotions, threatening to drag me down.

But I remembered what the captain had said about being myself. So I made sure that the men were keeping me in their sights, and I deliberately placed my hands so they hovered over the prints on the rail. I gazed up at the sky.

"Oh, Grand Mistress of the Seas," I said in English, loud enough for the observers to hear. "Won't you smite the barmy blokes on this deck what think I'm the devil's minion? They're all a bunch of dirty devils themselves with nary a bright spot between them."

Then I turned and looked directly at them and cracked a huge smile, taking my hands away and rubbing my palms on my thighs.

"Not actually. I ain't gonna waste my energy on you lot."

Alarm turned to bashful realization that I'd had them on.

"Jesus, White, you almost made me shit my pants yestiddy. What a spectacle!"

"Well, I'm fucking sorry. I had to save the captain, didn't I? And all of *your* sorry arses."

They laughed with some relief as if the entire previous day had been a lark.

"Well, I won't get on the bad side of you after that," one of them said, crossing his arms over his chest.

I rolled my eyes.

Another bloke agreed. "Nor me either. I hope the captain knows what he's dealing with, that's all."

Be yourself. Be yourself.

"Oh, aye. He knows," I said, leering and tapping my forehead with one finger. "He's, um, very good at keeping me in line, I'd say. So, yes, you'd better be careful now to not upset either one of us."

"Oy, White. If you can do *that*, then we have the rule of the seas, don't we? No-one can threaten us."

I frowned. "It ain't like that, I'm afraid. I wish I could control the magic, but I can't. I don't rightly know how the force rises, and when it does, the power sort of takes me over. And I ain't myself whilst it's got me."

"You a bloody witch, then?"

The word echoed in my head, but I refused to run from its meaning.

I shrugged. "Maybe. Dunno. You wanna find out?"

The man shook his head and held up his hands. "No, mate. I don't want to know."

I wasn't happy that my powers were so mysterious, but I'd be glad to be left alone and not bothered. I prayed their superstitions wouldn't get the better of them. Sailors had all kinds of strange rules and beliefs, and I only hoped they liked me and liked the captain enough to disregard their fears as to any powers I may or may not have.

"Going back to the captain's quarters, now," I said, "So that I can ensure he is, in fact, unharmed and all of a piece."

Some of the men laughed.

"Sure, sure. You do that, Simon White," one said.

I wandered back downstairs and passed Boone who regarded me with slightly more respect. He nodded and gestured to the captain's rooms.

"In you go, then. He's been pacing the floors, waiting for you."

"Now, Boone, you are to ignore anything you hear in there for the next few hours. There may be pleading and begging and crying, but 'tis nothing more than the way we declare our feelings for each other," I said.

Boone rolled his eyes. "Don't worry, I ain't comin' in there for anything until you come out. I don't even want to think about what's going on between the two of you."

"Excellent. Ta-ta, then." I gave him a friendly wave, and then knocked on the captain's door before shoving it open.

"Right, I'm back," I said cheerily.

"Thank God," he said. "There's something here that needs tending."

I really, *really,* hoped he wasn't talking about the dirty bedding.

"I stripped the sheet off already, and we can put another one on. They only shat on the top sheet."

He stared at me with wide eyes.

"Pardon?"

"Oh, nothing, never mind."

"You mean the chickens? They *shat* on my *bed?*"

I laughed nervously and shrugged. "Well, they are difficult to house train. I'll wash all the bedding tomorrow. Promise." I crossed my heart to make the vow official.

He closed his eyes, shook his head, then opened them again. They blazed with desire.

"Take off your clothes, Rooster."

"Well, now," I said. "Yes, Captain."

The one disadvantage of my fine clothes—they made it harder to get naked when I wanted to. And, boy, did I want to. But now I wore a shirt that needed unbuttoning, and I wasn't all that used to fumbling around with tiny little ivory buttons whilst in a heightened state of need. They were very pretty buttons though, and I took a moment to admire them.

"Keep going."

"Yes, Captain," I said. I finished with the buttons, pulled the shirttails out of my breeches, and tossed the garment onto a chair. I had undone the flap of my breeches before I noticed the stunned look on Captain Martin's face.

"What?" I asked, thinking that he simply couldn't believe how utterly lovely I was.

"Simon," he said, his voice full of awe.

He lifted his arm very slowly and pointed at my midriff.

"The scar!"

I looked down at where the scar used to be and gasped.

The skin was smooth, and I could discern the outline of the old scar, but the raised edges that had made a relief map of my side were gone.

I held my breath.

What on earth?

I ran my fingertip over the surface. There was no pain, and the area wasn't as sensitive as before.

I lifted my hands and turned them. My palms looked completely normal now. Anxiety built in my gut, only because I was surprised and confused and didn't know what the bloody fuck was going on. I looked at the captain.

He stared at my midriff. And he looked as fucking confused as I was.

"What is happening?" he asked. "Why has the scar disappeared? How?"

I shook my head. "I don't know." I turned away from him and looked over my shoulder. "Is the skin the same on my back?"

The captain came forward hesitantly as if frightened of whatever powers had done this. I knew I was.

"Yes. The same. A little bit reddened, like your arse after a spanking. But smooth. And I can see freckles. It's the most remarkable thing," he said, reaching out a hand. "May I?"

"Aye."

He touched the skin on my hip with his fingers, then glanced at me. "How does that feel?"

"It doesn't hurt, but then, it didn't *really* hurt before."

Captain Martin slipped his fingers under the waistband of my breeches and pulled them down. He ran his fingers over my buttock where the scar stretched.

"It's not over-sensitive anymore. The burn has healed… somehow," I said.

"Hmm," he said. As if that was all there was to say. "Go and lie on the bed, Rooster."

I was more than happy to stop thinking about the scar. The imperfection had been a painful reminder of a terrifying incident, and I wasn't displeased that it looked to be fading. Even though neither of us could explain how this was possible.

"Aye, Captain."

I pushed down my breeches and then remembered that I had socks and shoes on. For fuck's sake. What a production this was going to be. I sighed, then bent at the waist with my arse in the air, trying to balance on one foot as I took off one shoe and sock, while the captain's soft laughter came from behind me.

He placed his hands on my hips, to steady me I supposed, then pressed his cloth-covered stand against my nakedness. I managed to get the rest of my clothes off, despite my lack of focus on anything but the Captain and his ready prick, and lay down on the bed, gazing up at the captain like a most willing sacrifice.

Captain Martin took his time removing his clothes, gazing at me with iridescent longing, then climbed on the bed and crawled over me. He kissed me sweetly on the mouth, and then he pressed his lips to every inch of that fading scar—soft butterfly kisses that made me sigh with longing. When he'd finished in front, he flipped me over and continued on my lower back and buttock.

He didn't stop there but had his way with me in a tender, lazy, sensual way that I would remember for a very long time.

*

"**A**nthony Donatello was an upstanding, competent, and compassionate man," Captain Martin began. "And I loved him dearly."

Sniggers and whispers could be heard from the gathered crew, despite the solemnity of the event.

Captain Martin stood by the rail, with an open Bible in hand. All of Donatello's personal items were balanced carefully on the rail, wrapped in sailcloth and gathered with one of the black ribbons that Donatello had used to tie back his hair. Three cannonballs were in the bottom for weight.

The captain looked up and eyed the men who'd been mumbling.

"Like a brother."

Silence, *cough, sniffle.*

"We commend his belongings to the deep in honour of the man we've lost," he said with great solemnity.

I blinked back tears and tried to bury the guilt that threatened to rise inside me. Which was silly, as Donatello had perished at the hands of the attacking vagabonds, and not as a result of my subsequent...spell...or whatever that storm had been.

Captain Martin looked down at the book in his broad hands.

"In God alone my soul finds rest. My salvation comes from him."

He closed the book, then placed his hand on the wrapped belongings, whispering words that nobody else could hear. Then he soberly pushed the package off the rail. The bag splashed into the waters below as Richard Darcy played a dirge on his fiddle.

The crew had voted for a return to Tortuga, and we were prepared to board and pillage any likely ships we encountered along the way. The recent battle had them spooked, and they needed to prove their might.

*

"Why, Captain Martin, you appear to have put me in a rather challenging predicament," I said about twenty minutes later as I tested the ropes that bound me.

"Mmm. I'm simply practicing my knots," he said as he finished and slapped me on the arse.

"What was that for?" I asked.

"Why, the fun of it, of course. We've had a trying few days."

We'd not encountered any other vessels as of yet, and the horizon looked clear as far as the eye could see, although rain splattered against the windows of the captain's quarters. The captain had decided that I needed a proper ravishing and he'd trussed me up good and proper. Only, now, he went and sat on the bed and picked up a large tome, opening the book as if he planned to enjoy the next few hours reading.

I was wrapped in strong, soft ropes and attached to a hook in the ceiling with one leg folded so that I could barely keep myself from spinning with my unbound leg. My arms were crossed at my back, and the captain had spent a good deal of time driving me into a state of desperate need.

"Oy, Captain. You can't just ignore me. Look what you've wrought!" I said, nodding and staring at my rampant prick, which jutted up good and pink and ready for more.

The captain did look for a moment, sighed wistfully, and went right back to his book.

Fucking bastard. He knew it drove me mad when he pretended to ignore me, and I was already on the edge of reason. I tried to think of other things because begging and pleading would only amuse him.

The place on my torso, where my old scar had been, looked just like the rest of me now. No one could tell there had been anything there at all. The moles and freckles had returned, too, which boggled my mind. I wasn't sure how I felt about the transformation, to be frank. That scar had been with me since my mother's death, and now I had nothing to remind me of her.

I didn't think anyone on board, except the captain, had seen the scar in full light, so no one was likely to note its absence. Faraday had sworn to the crew that my hands had been mangled and blistered, which was true. But I denied the truth, saying that Faraday had probably been uneasy about what he'd seen, and that had coloured his true perception. I told them that the captain had applied a healing balm to the skin, which had resolved the injury in no time.

I wasn't quite certain if they believed me, and perhaps it would have been wiser to simply admit I didn't know why the burn had gone away. But I was already drowning in uncertainties, and if that made *me* feel anxious, I could only imagine how the others might feel about the situation. I figured they'd be glad to latch on to a simple and ordinary explanation, as we all knew Faraday could be dramatic at times.

I struggled in the ropes and groaned with desire and frustration, glancing at the captain to make sure he noticed. I made a good show of my desperation and was rewarded when he closed his book and stood.

"Do you know what I plan to do with you, my little red cock?" he asked, playing on the slang for rooster and referencing my randy appendage.

"I wager the intention will be despicable and filthy."

"You do know me well," he said and smiled. "However, to begin with, I'd like to show you some items that I confiscated from a Chinese vessel that we looted several months ago."

My ears perked up. I had heard that the Chinese held

different attitudes about sexual practices than the uptight British.

The captain took a key from a hidden compartment in his secretaire and walked to the large wood chest in the corner of the room. He unlocked the chest and lifted the top on its silent hinges. He took out a polished wood box, about ten-by-ten inches square. He carried the item reverently in both hands over to where I was bound. He winked, held it up with the open edge facing me, and lifted back the lid.

Lined with red silk, snug sections contained a selection of objects in strange shapes, made with the same wood as the box itself and polished to a similar sheen.

"What on God's great earth?" I exclaimed. "They're lovely, but...what are they?"

Captain Martin gave me a knowing smile and raised his eyebrows. "I'm just about to show you. And, well, demonstrate at least a few."

He lifted the smallest of the items from the box and held it before me with a devilish look in his eyes. Shaped in an oval, like the others, and about the size of an egg, the thing, whatever it was, gave me a strange feeling in my belly.

"What do you mean, demonstrate?" I asked.

"Shush now."

I kept quiet, or tried to.

He removed a few of the strange objects and laid them out on the bed. I was beginning to have an idea as to their use. I'd spent a bit of time over the course of my life searching for things that might fit up my backside and be retrievable. Carrots had proved impractical after a most terrible incident, of which I won't go into detail. I'd learned that whatever went in there needed a handle of some sort, or my hungry arse would try to swallow the whole thing.

These objects were shaped like the dummies the nursemaids

used for babies to suck when their mother's teat wasn't available, except they were bigger and most likely made for a different orifice on adults.

Captain Martin came toward me with the smallest of the five objects.

"You're not going to stick that thing up my arse, are you?" I asked, sounding more excited than nervous about the idea.

"That's exactly what I'm going to do, Rooster. But if you don't stop asking me questions, I'm going to have to gag you."

I held my tongue, knowing that he was in earnest.

He held the egg-shaped item in front of me, turning it slowly, so I could see the object clearly from all angles.

"This is what I like to call a shit stopper, although it can hold other things inside a body, as well," the captain muttered, applying oil to the object whilst I watched and squirmed.

I was glad I'd had a healthy bowel movement earlier in the day. Now that I had access to a fancy water closet, my habits were more regular which proved easier to be clean and prepared for anything.

Such as the scandalous Captain Dinesh Martin of the *Arrow* pirate vessel—oh, excuse me—*privateering* vessel, determining to slide an egg-shaped piece of wood up my bottom for sheer entertainment value. I should have been prepared for this after the soap incident.

He used his fingers with some oil to prepare me to receive the strange thing. My cock bobbed helplessly as I wriggled with pleasure. The captain's fingers were long and agile, and he knew just where to touch.

"There we are. Now for the stopper."

I hung helpless in the ropes as he pushed the wet tip of the stopper against my eager hole.

"Mmm, that looks so perverse, Rooster. Relax now and let me push this in."

My hole stretched impossibly wide as the captain maintained a steady pressure. It felt like I was splitting in two, and then, with a woosh, my body swallowed the egg up. Thank God for the flange, which nestled comfortably between my cheeks. See? I was a greedy bugger. I groaned at the pleasurable feeling of being filled.

"Jesus, Mary, and Joseph," the captain hissed.

I moaned as the captain wiggled the thing to make sure the stopper was seated properly.

"How does that feel?" the captain asked.

"Bloody huge."

"Well, I know for a fact you like to have big things in your bowels," the captain said, as he spread my arse cheeks wide and tapped on the flat end of the egg. "Looks quite scandalous."

The vibrations echoed through me, sending sparks in every direction.

"Ooh," I moaned. "Help."

He laughed. "What on earth do you need help with? I'd suggest you relax, because I'm going to do a little reading whilst that lovely device stretches and prepares you for me. Then I'm going to fuck you, hard, whilst you're in those ropes, and leave a quart of spunk in you. Then I'm going to put the stopper back, and you're going to keep that spunk inside you until suppertime."

"Oh my God. So fucking filthy," I said with absolute reverence.

"Yes. And so are you, my dirty rooster. We're perfect together."

His words caused a glow of happiness to spread in my chest. "Aye."

Good thing I'd emptied my bladder before this game, as he

left me dangling and stoppered for a time whilst he went back to his journal. In truth, the ropes made a sort of a cradle for me, and my arse soon adjusted to the invasion. I must have drifted off.

A smart slap to the arse woke me.

"Aye, Captain. Sorry, Captain," I stuttered, not even sure what I was apologizing for.

"God, you've got a lovely arse, Rooster."

He cupped my buttock and jiggled the muscle roughly before slapping it again.

"Fuck," I said.

"Like that?"

"Yes. More."

"I'd be delighted."

He spent the next while alternately jiggling and spanking my arse, which made me discern the solidness of the wooden stopper in a way that sent ripples of pleasure throughout. He enjoyed eliciting gasps of pain and surprise, followed by moans and sighs of extraordinary pleasure from me. *Heaven.* He held on to the rope that secured me to keep me from spinning.

"Your arse is a lovely shade of pink now."

He tugged on the stopper. I groaned as he eased the thing out, my cock firm and dripping. But now I was bereft.

"Please, Captain."

"Please what, Rooster?"

"I want that big truncheon inside me."

"You do, do you? Well, isn't that convenient, because that's just what you're going to get."

The swish of oil on flesh preceded him nudging the tip of his battering ram at my rear entrance, hot and impossibly large. But the egg had prepared me, and he sank in with little trouble.

"Oh fuck, fuck, fuck," I muttered. "Oh God."

He was not any quieter.

"Jesus. Oh, Jesus, fuck. Fuck it. I want to ravish you."

"Yes, yes, yes."

"I'm going to fuck you now, Rooster. I shall flood you with my seed and perhaps even get you with child. You never know. There is some magic at work in you."

The very thought of the captain planting his seed in me proved intoxicating. Though I didn't think a babe would result, the idea of Captain Martin attempting such a thing aroused me to no end. He was a man of his word and did plow me to within an inch of my life, holding the ropes that held me captive and reaching places inside me that had never been touched before. Of that I was certain.

His sounds of pleasure and excitement were even more exquisite. I babbled, moaning and pleading for him to continue, harder, harder, more, more.

His breathing became more and more urgent, his grunts and exclamations more frequent. He had one hand on the rope and one hand painfully digging into my hip when he went deep and stilled, crying out as he emptied into me.

I felt euphoric and contented, in a spiritual way, as if I served as a vessel for an important ceremony. Except, now I was on the edge of completion. And I couldn't touch myself.

"Please, Captain. Please!" I begged.

He laughed softly, withdrew himself to my whimpered protest, and slipped the stopper back into me.

"Oh my God," I moaned. "Oh my God."

"There. A suitable vessel for my seed, you are."

He slapped my arse and walked around to stand in front of me.

"What the fuck, Captain?"

"What's the matter?"

"I need to spend. I'm so fucking close." I sobbed with frustration. "Please!"

"How can I say no to my beautiful Rooster?"

I laughed hysterically with relief as he poured more oil into his hand and wrapped his fingers around my cock, giving it several hard jerks.

"You'll have to be quick, mind. I've other things to do."

"Oh. Oh. Oh." I cried out. "Fuck. Fuck!"

His free hand slipped over my hip and found the base of the stopper, which he shoved and twisted.

I gasped as I spent in huge bursts that shot over his knuckles, my body spasming as the beam that held me creaked and protested.

"No, no, no!" I stuttered as the pleasure took me, protesting the way my culmination overcame me without my control. "Oooh!"

Finally, the intensity of the blissful spasms eased, and I became a boneless bag of jelly.

"There we go. Now you're happy, aren't you?" He sounded immensely pleased with himself.

"Aye, Captain," I said.

We stared at each other for a long moment.

"How long shall I be plugged then?"

"For as long as I desire. But I'll get you out of these ropes."

We looked at where the rope wrapped around the wood above.

"We were fortunate that beam held," the captain said.

"Aye," I agreed. "Good thing."

Chapter Ten

A-pirating

After we'd eaten our supper, he bent me over the bed and removed the stopper, describing to me in detail the sight of his creamy spunk dribbling out and onto a towel he'd placed there.

He promptly fucked me again and left more inside me, although this time he played with his seed before letting me tidy myself up. By the time he was done with me I was desperate again.

"Please," I groaned. "I can't stand this cruel torment."

"Oh, you poor dear. Come here, then. Sit on my lap."

I sat on Captain Martin's lap with my head on his shoulder as he jerked me off, with rough motions, whilst he whispered cruel and filthy things that he would do to me. When he was done, he cleaned me and tucked me into bed.

"Good night, Rooster. My sexy, little witch."

"Good night, Captain Martin. My lord and master."

He chuckled. "Oh, I like that. That'll get you whatever you want with me."

*

I woke to arguing.

Opening my bleary eyes, I saw the captain fastening his breeches and grabbing his shirt from the back of the chair. Hillier stood before the closed door.

"If it's so far away, perhaps we should try to avoid the vessel," Captain Martin said.

"I don't think we can, Captain. And the crew needs a battle." Hillier stated. He side-eyed me, acknowledged me with a nod, then returned his gaze to the captain. "They're all a bit spooked by what happened, and we need supplies."

"That's why we're heading for Tortuga," Captain Martin said, pulling on his jacket.

"Yes—" Hillier explained, while the captain gazed at me with a smile. "—but, the men don't want to buy supplies. They want to *steal* them."

Captain Martin closed his eyes, as if leading a ragtag group of bloodthirsty pirates was more than he could bear. He opened them and gave me a falsely cheery grin.

"Get up and get dressed, Rooster. We're going a-pirating."

"Coffee?" I squeaked. Surely we couldn't go into battle without breakfast. Not this time.

Hillier snorted a laugh. "Jesus. The freckled slut's been with you for a month and he's already turned into a pampered princess."

The captain folded his arms over his chest and sighed. He really did have the long-suffering attitude down.

I frowned. "Fuck you, Hillier. I was a princess before I ever boarded this ship. But you're right about the slut reference." I winked at him and wiggled my hips under the sheet.

"Christ," Hillier said, and his cheeks went red. "Get what you need and then come on deck. I'll tell the others."

"Thank you, Hillier," Captain Martin said.

Hillier left and I dragged myself out of bed. My cock was hard as was usual first thing in the morning, and before I could get very far, the captain had gone to his knees and dragged my shirttails up to my waist.

I gazed down at him in surprise.

"Someone mentioned breakfast," he said, wrapping his fingers around the base of my cock and taking me in his mouth.

"Fuck," I hissed. "I was talking about cheese or bread. Oh God."

The captain wasn't messing about. After a very short amount of time he got rather a good bit of nourishment to settle his stomach. He pulled off me and smacked his lips.

"That's better," he said, standing.

His cheeks were flushed and his hair mussed. He looked quite young in this moment.

"Yes," I agreed, my brain scrambled but my body singing with relief.

He pulled me against him and kissed me with sincere affection. I tasted myself on his tongue. "Go get some coffee and a bite of breakfast in the galley, then find me on deck."

"Yes, Captain."

I went to take care of business first in the fancy water closet that was honestly one of the best things about being the captain's boy. Lovely to be able to shit in peace. I spent altogether too much time there because of the comfort and coziness of the place.

Sure enough, someone knocked.

"Oy, there!"

Guthrie's voice.

"What's taking so long? Do you need help?"

"Why? Would you want to?"

"'Course not, you wanker. But hurry the fuck up."

I wiped my hands and fixed my breeches, then opened the door. Mr Guthrie stood there in a soiled apron, his hands on his hips. Perhaps a bit more wary than usual, but he'd called me a wanker, so he couldn't be all that frightened of me.

"Done?" he asked.

"Yes, Mr Guthrie."

I went to move past him, but he stopped me with a hand to my shoulder. "There's bacon and fried bread in the galley if you're looking for breakfast. The captain usually has a morning meal brought to his rooms, but he's rather busy at the moment."

I was a bit stunned by Mr Guthrie's generosity.

"Thank you. I *am* hungry. Is there coffee?"

"Of course. Help yourself."

"Thank you so much," I said, grinning like a fool. "Enjoy your..." I waved my hand vaguely at the water closet.

Mr Guthrie rolled his eyes and closed the door.

I went to the galley and had a couple of pieces of the fried bread and a mug of coffee. Only then did I feel like I could face chaos on deck, and the preparations for an actual pirate attack. At least, this time, we would be on the offence.

Shouts and directions from Hillier and the captain could be heard as I climbed the steps to the deck. Then the voices of other men giving directions to the men beneath them. The *Arrow* was a hive of activity.

When I emerged from the stairwell, I spied the captain

directing men near the bow and made my way over.

"Simon. Good. Stay close to me, will you?"

That I could definitely do. Or I'd try to.

"Yes, Captain."

He eyed me with concern. "Ever been in a battle at sea?"

I swallowed. "Only the...last one."

"Ah. Right. Of course. Well, this should go more smoothly. Although you have to be ready for anything in this line of...work."

"Work?"

"Yes, Simon. Work. Just because we go about things a bit differently than the Royal Navy doesn't mean there isn't some validity to what we do."

"Go about things a bit differently?" I said with incredulity. How dense did he think I was?

He narrowed his eyes. "Never mind. I'm not in the mood to discuss semantics."

"Aye, Captain."

Call it what he would, what he had planned was thieving, plain and simple. With a bit of murdering and maiming thrown in. I wasn't looking forward to it.

Captain Martin shouted out more orders, then turned back to me.

"She's a modest vessel, smaller than the *Arrow*, so victory shouldn't be too difficult for us. That said, there may be violence."

"*May be* violence? I thought that..."

"All right then." He sighed. Good thing he liked my arse so much because he looked vexed with me at the moment. "There probably will be violence, but I do try to keep that sort of thing to a minimum. If they will surrender, all the better. Then nobody needs to die."

"I—what? Aren't we...pirates?" The disappointment in my voice was ridiculous, considering my desire to avoid violence of any sort.

Captain Martin frowned. "Privateers, Simon. Not pirates. We've a little more class than that," he said, clearly not a fan of the term I'd used by mistake in his hearing. "And I'm a great believer in the power of intimidation."

Of course he was. If anyone could commandeer another ship without spilling blood, it would be Captain Martin. Even though the attempted negotiations with the last vessel hadn't gone as planned, I had utmost faith in Captain Martin's judgement. If he thought we could avoid spilling blood, I was in favor.

I knew by now that the captain's mouth had skills beyond what he liked to show me in the privacy of his cabin. He was an excellent orator and well versed at arguing a point with grace and precision.

Captain Martin filled me in on our quarry. She was still quite a ways off. Hillier estimated that we'd get close enough to announce our intentions in about an hour. She hadn't shown signs of alarm or avoidance, although they must know of our presence. The *Arrow* flew a Dutch flag when not on an aggressive approach, and we hadn't switched the decoy out for our own insignia yet. They likely thought we didn't mean any harm.

The captain gathered the crew below the forecastle, where he stood. He raised his voice so that everyone could hear and smiled as if he were preparing to host a grand party.

"Now, we will raise the black flag in one hour, once we are close enough that they can't escape when they realize our intentions are not entirely honorable."

Not entirely honorable. Again, I was amazed by the captain's flexibility of speech.

"I know you are men of great strength and fortitude, and with excellent capabilities in the area of hand-to-hand combat. And we will engage in combat with the men aboard that ship if we *have to*."

There were cheers. The captain raised his hand.

"However," he said, waiting for quiet before he continued, "If we can convince them to surrender without the use of brute force, I will award the crew of this ship a five per cent allotment of my share—*the captain's share*—of whatever we take. To be distributed evenly, on top of your individual shares."

There were whispers and amazed mutters.

"Five per cent?" one fellow said. "That ain't much, split amongst us all."

The captain kept smiling until other members of the crew began to complain.

"It'll take more than that for me to keep my killing arm still."

"I'll not be polite for five. Make it ten."

"Ten per cent! Ten per cent!"

I gazed about me at the men who adored Captain Martin, now complaining about staying their hands for a five per cent extra take. I couldn't fathom their reasoning.

Except that Captain Martin didn't look surprised or alarmed. He frowned as if giving the situation much thought. And in that moment, I knew that he'd started with five per cent because he'd anticipated the men wanting more.

He was a clever fucking man, my captain.

"Well. You drive a very hard bargain, you lot. Ten per cent of my share?"

"Ten!"

"Ten per cent! We won't stop for naught but that."

"Wouldn't be worth it for five."

The captain nodded and said very soberly, "All right. Ten per cent of my share, distributed evenly amongst you if you can keep the bloodshed to a minimum. And try not to kill anyone."

"Aye, but can I injure a man? There ain't no issue with maiming, is there?"

"If necessary, I suppose I'll allow it. But please, not a leg. An arm gone, that can challenge a man. A leg gone, and that's a much more serious matter, especially at sea."

There were concessions of agreement.

I stood there, mouth agape, as the reality of the situation became clear. I was on a ship full of bloodthirsty men, whatever they might be called, who were going to attempt to be moderate in their mode of attack. I should have felt grateful, and I did. But all the talk about maiming and the idea of anyone losing an arm or a leg by sword made me queasy.

Captain Martin came down off the platform. He went to the rail, his spyglass in hand. He'd requested that I stay close, which was no hardship, so I walked over to stand next to him.

"That was very clever," I said, crossing my arms and looking out to sea, where our quarry sailed steadily in the distance.

"I'm not just a pretty face."

"It's not your face I'm thinking about most nights," I said with full-on sincerity.

He looked at me with his eyes raised as if he couldn't believe my cheek.

I cracked a grin, and he matched it.

"Ah, Rooster. For once, I wish I wasn't a privateer captain."

I couldn't hide my astonishment.

"How now? Not a privateer captain? Don't be daft. What other line of work could you get into?"

He laughed. "Well, now, I've a mind to try my hand at

blacksmithing when all of this is said and done."

"Blacksmithing!" I pictured him in a leather apron, covered in grease, standing before an anvil, with a pair of tongs holding a red-hot piece of iron. Hmm, perhaps that wouldn't be so bad. "But you love the sea!"

"Do I?" he asked with amusement.

"I thought so," I admitted. "Don't you?"

"Aye. I do. But a part of me yearns for stability, Rooster. Not now. Perhaps not for years yet. But someday."

"In England?"

He shrugged. "Perhaps. Or Asia. Or some tropical country. I haven't decided." He eyed me carefully. "What are your plans for the future?"

I blinked. "I don't make plans that far ahead. I don't even have plans for tomorrow. I'm a live by the moment sort of fellow, I suppose. I ain't convinced I have a future, to be honest. Not the kind you're talking about."

"Don't be silly. You can do whatever you want, Simon. Don't let anyone tell you different," he said. "I used to think my life was the way it was because of God's plan. But I was dead inside, not really alive. Only going through the motions."

"Why did you stop being a navy captain?" I asked.

"The hypocrisy. The cruelty. Things I was required to do without a thought that I didn't believe in."

I didn't ask what those things had been. I'd heard stories of the way the navy kept their men in line. Didn't surprise me, really, that Dinesh had decided to have no more of that way of living.

"Here, on the *Arrow*, I run things my way. Our small community might be unconventional, but I've seen more acts of sheer bravery and honor on this ship than on any navy vessel I've been assigned to."

Hillier was still shouting orders to the crew, and men ran about, preparing our approach.

Captain Martin lifted his spyglass to the distant vessel as the *Arrow* closed the distance.

"Looks to be a Chinese vessel, but I think they've already been through a skirmish of some sort," he muttered. "Here, have a look."

He passed the glass to me, as if I had the same kind of credentials he did. My heart lifted, and I felt more like a man than I ever had before.

I took the spyglass from him and brought it to my eye.

As I scanned the ornately designed rail of the other vessel, my gaze landed on a person who was holding a spyglass in my direction. After a moment, their glass lowered to reveal the strangest visage I'd ever seen. The person looked neither male nor female. They looked too young to be the captain, with long waves of tangled hair kept out of their gaunt face with bunches of string. Their stature was small and sleight, and their handsome face was covered with geometric black tattoos. They stared at me, as if they could see me with their bare eye, when I needed a glass to see them. They turned to a stocky man beside them and spoke.

The stocky man held his hand out for the spy glass, and the person with the tattooed face gave it to him, then looked in our direction with a resigned expression. The stocky man, likely the captain or the quartermaster, peered at the *Arrow* through his spyglass, then shrugged and limped away whilst the tattooed man stared after him with a face full of worry.

"Looks like an easy mark," I commented.

They didn't appear to give a damn about us. I'd only seen a handful of men on deck, and there were chunks missing from part of the ship. A couple of their sails were torn.

"But I don't know if we're going to find much loot."

I lowered the glass and saw Captain Martin looking at me with amusement.

"What?"

"How the fuck do you know?" he asked.

"I beg your pardon. I don't. I thought you wanted my opinion."

"Well, I wanted you to be prepared."

"For what? A bloody tea party? They don't look all that frightening."

Captain Martin stared at me. Perhaps he was wondering what had ever possessed him to invite me aboard. "Give me that," he said, reaching for the glass.

I passed the shiny instrument to him.

"A bloody tea party," he muttered, lifting it to his eye and pretending to be annoyed as his lip twitched and I grinned, scratching my chin and gazing out at the fine weather. Quite a good day to attack a crippled ship, I figured.

Captain Martin observed the other ship for several moments. Then he lowered the glass and met my gaze. "How are you with a sword, Rooster?"

I blinked. "If that's a clever way of asking me about my skills in the bedroom, then quite good really."

The captain sighed. "No, I mean an actual sword. Can you defend yourself, if necessary?"

"I can wield a dagger. But I've never used a sword." I thought that was why he wanted me near him. Because we both knew I'd be pretty fucking helpless in a sea battle. Either that, or I'd call on my mysterious powers and kill everyone.

"Remind me to have you train with one of the men."

"Yes, Captain."

"For now, you have your knife. Just…stay alert. And be prepared for anything."

I grinned, trying to pretend I wasn't terrified. "Is that a clever way of—"

"Simon. Stop messing about. I don't want to lose you."

I stared at him, seeing genuine care for me in his kind expression.

"I don't want you to lose me either," I whispered.

He smiled and gave a nod.

I glared at him. "And you be fucking careful yourself. How would you spank me if you only had one arm?"

Captain Martin barked a laugh. "I'd figure it out."

"You would, at that."

Captain Martin checked the other vessel's location again, then turned to look at Hillier, who stood nearby with his arms crossed whilst men ran about doing his bidding.

"Now," Captain Martin said, and a chill went through me.

Hillier nodded and turned to face the main deck.

"*Hoist the flag!*" Hillier shouted. "*Hoist the colors*! Let's show them we mean business!"

"Aye, aye," men shouted in response.

More scurrying, and the pulling of the rope to lower the Dutch flag and hoist our own. I'd had yet to see the official privateer colors of the *Arrow,* so I watched intently as the flag went up. The broad banner snapped in the wind and became, for a moment, a confusion of shapes.

Once the flag reached the top of the mast, the tarred sailcloth straightened out in the brisk wind that was causing us to gain on our prey.

A white, crudely stitched skull, on a black background, with a thick red arrow going through the outline and a bleeding red heart at the bottom. The sudden reality of being part of a privateer crew, and not simply a member of a ragtag group of jovial sailors, punched me in the gut.

"Captain Martin," I said, my throat going dry. "Is it quite necessary to attack this other ship?"

He regarded me with a level of expiring patience. "We've been through this. The crew needs a distraction. And we need supplies."

"Yes, but, maybe we could simply *ask* if they have any to spare?" I suggested.

He stared at me, opened his mouth as if to speak, closed it, and lifted the spyglass to observe our quarry.

After a few silent moments, he lowered the spyglass and turned to Hillier, effectively ignoring me and my silly suggestions.

"They've seen our colours. Things are lively now. Send a warning shot over the bow."

"Aye, Captain," Hillier said.

"Give her a warning, now! Fire the cannon!"

I put my hands to my ears, as the men fired a cannon over the other ship's bow as ordered. The *Arrow* vibrated with the force of the launch. I only hoped they'd heed the message and not try to fight us.

They didn't fire back, and by the time we came abreast of her, it appeared they weren't going to put up a defence. But the captain didn't order Hillier to stand down.

"Wait a few moments to see if they hoist the white flag. If not, give them another warning."

"Aye, Captain," Hillier agreed, biding his time.

Captain Martin turned to me.

"Hillier's got a boarding party of the most intimidating crew members ready. They'll go first, and once they've secured the ship, we'll go. Or you can stay here. It's up to you."

I didn't want to be left here on my own.

"I'll go with you."

"Good. You'll need a title, I suppose, so they'll think you're someone important."

That hit me harder than I'd expected. He must have seen the look on my face, as he cupped my cheek and continued, "Of course, you're vastly important to *me*, Rooster, but I doubt that introducing you as my bedwarmer and cumslut would give you the status you deserve."

I stifled a laugh. "Yes, Captain. Understood."

"I'll call you my right-hand man and introduce you as Officer White. How does that sound?"

"Well, rather accurate, since it's usually your right hand wrapping around my sabre."

"Good Lord. Are you going to be able to keep your mouth shut?"

"Yes, Captain. That title sounds right swank."

"Yes, it does," he regarded me critically. "Get your jacket."

"Yes, Captain."

I ran back to his rooms and grabbed my fancy jacket off the back of the chair. Since the weather had been warm, I'd sort of forgotten about it. But I should wear the garment for this meeting. I glanced in the standing mirror and made some adjustments. The fine workmanship of the cloth and button closures made me look quite respectable.

A gigantic sound rang out and the *Arrow* shook right down to the timbers.

"Ready...and FIRE!" Hillier shouted.

Another loud bang and shudder.

A spike of fear shot through me as I hastened up the stairs.

The deck was a hive of activity. Men darted here and there in a kind of organized chaos. Captain Martin stood by the rail, looking through his spyglass at the ship that was now smoking, with half of its deck blown apart. Even though a part of me was terrified, I did notice that he cut quite a striking figure.

"HOLD!" Hillier shouted. "Rifles!"

The crew who were lined up at the rail shouldered their rifles and took aim. I was surprised by how close we now were to the other ship.

"Ready! Aim!" Hillier shouted.

Then Captain Martin lowered his glass and raised his hand. "Wait!"

"Stand down!" Hillier commanded, and I watched as thirty men lowered their muskets, obedient to the last.

A wooden oar waved over the deck of the other ship, with a white flag at the end of it.

By this time, I had reached Captain Martin.

"They've surrendered," he stated. "Hillier will send the armed party aboard, and then we'll go. He'll leave ten men here in case things go wrong, but I don't foresee any trouble."

We waited while Hillier took twenty men in a skiff that was lowered over the side. His boarding party rowed quickly to the drifting vessel. With skills forged from years of practice, the men climbed the ropes and netting at the stern like spiders, gaining the decks in no time and dispersing amongst the surrendering crew.

I expected to hear some alarming noise—musket fire, a scream of pain, perhaps a voice pleading for mercy. But all was relatively quiet.

Captain Martin kept apprised of what was happening with his spyglass, but he barely needed to use the tool. We were that close. Hillier must have given a signal because he lowered the glass with a smile and a nod.

"To the skiff, Rooster. But keep your guard about you," the captain said.

"Who's coming?" I asked. "Not just us two..."

"Guthrie will join us."

I nodded, but then frowned. "The ship's *cook*?"

"Yes."

"Are we having a picnic? On the other ship?"

Captain Martin turned, his eyebrows lifted in amusement.

"No, Mr White. Mr Guthrie presents a calm and wise demeanor when in a situation like this. He may be the *Arrow's* cook—a fact we shall not disclose to the other party—but he used to be a general in the King's Navy. He has...diplomatic skills." Captain Martin shrugged.

I blinked in surprise at this unexpected piece of news.

"Blimey. You're not having me on?" I asked with some incredulity.

"No. Not at all."

In fact, here came Mr Guthrie now, dressed as fine as the captain and carrying himself with a sense of import I normally didn't associate him with. As he approached, he gave me a smile and a wink, and I recalled our daily meetings at the water closet. His stately appearance showed how one's perception of a person could change in an instant.

"Hello, Mr Guthrie," I said.

"Officer White." He gave me a nod, then turned to Captain Martin. "Captain."

"Guthrie," Captain Martin said. "Ready?"

"Aye. I've got the beef marinating for later. Let's go."

The three of us descended the rope ladder to the waiting

skiff. Guthrie first, then the captain, and then me. I misjudged the distance from the last rung and tumbled into the boat, almost going over the side. But the captain grabbed the sleeve of my jacket and pulled me in.

"Watch yourself, White," he said, in a gruff voice that betrayed his affection for me in the way he struggled to keep the sentiment hidden.

"Yes, Captain," I said, reassured by his presence and his quick actions.

My gut was a coil of nerves as we rowed toward the other ship. But then Hillier's face appeared at the rail.

"Nice lot here, Captain. They're being wonderfully agreeable," he said, dropping a rope ladder that unrolled against the hull until the bottom touched the water near our skiff.

"I'm glad to hear it, Hillier," Captain Marin said. "Up you go, White. After Guthrie and before me, if you please."

I struggled to climb the ladder—which proved more difficult than I'd imagined.

"Everything all right?" Captain Martin asked from his agile purchase below.

"I'm fine. I'll manage."

"Wonderful. I'd like to be aboard by sundown, if you please."

I didn't risk taking my gaze off of what I was doing to send him a disdainful glare. Instead, I gritted my teeth and tried to move a bit faster. He'd be lucky if I didn't slip and fall, taking him into the drink with me.

Finally, we gained the deck, and Hillier helped me aboard.

"Officer White," he said.

Apparently, while I was retrieving my jacket, Captain Martin had informed them of my temporary promotion.

"Hillier. Thank you."

The captain came next.

"Welcome aboard the *Lantern*," Hillier said. "Her crew has given over with barely a skirmish."

"Excellent. You've done well."

Hillier beamed, glowing from the captain's good favour. I understood how that felt. Hillier then made introductions to the captain of the *Lantern*, a stout, short fellow with scraggly black hair and a fancy mustache.

"Captain Dinesh Martin, this is Captain Hu Zhang. Captain Zhang, Captain Martin of the *Arrow*." Despite Captain Zhang's haggard appearance, he pulled himself up and greeted us with a polite and careful grace. He had a heavy Eastern accent, but his English was strong and clear.

Hillier continued. "This is Officer White, Captain Martin's right-hand man, and Officer Guthrie, our navigator."

I smiled and gave Captain Zhang a wave, which may not have been the right sort of greeting as Captain Martin frowned and gave a subtle shake of his head.

I raised my eyebrows and shrugged, tucking my hands under my arms.

"Welcome aboard," Captain Zhang said. "We want no further battle. We have already been picked clean, but you are welcome to anything you can find."

"Thank you," Captain Martin said. "I'm sorry that your fortunes have been in decline. But your ship is now my property, and my men will search the vessel for anything we can use."

"I understand. We will leave you to the task," he said and wandered over to the tattooed person I'd seen through the spyglass.

Chapter Eleven

Squid

Istuck close to Captain Martin, as I'd been instructed. He put Guthrie in charge of the intensive looting, and he and I wandered the deck as he pointed out differences between the *Lantern* and the *Arrow*, both in size and the amount of battle readiness. There were fresh gouges in the wood of the deck and scorch marks in various places. One of the deck rails had been broken in half in a previous encounter. The *Lantern* and its crew had seen better days.

A tap on my shoulder caused me to turn.

Standing before me was the long-haired person with the face tattoos that I'd seen in the spyglass.

"Hello," I said, my gaze assessing them from a closer angle. They looked even more intriguing from this distance.

"Hello. Officer White?"

"Yes."

"And this is Captain Martin? Of the *Arrow*?"

"Aye, that's him."

"Can I help you?" Captain Martin asked.

The young fellow—for he looked no older than I—glanced back and forth between us before answering.

"I'm hoping you can, sir. My name is Squid."

"Squid?" Captain Martin repeated as I became even more fascinated.

He gestured vaguely at his face. "Because of the ink. And—" He gestured to the rest of himself. "—my shape."

"Ah, well I'm pleased to meet you, Squid," Captain Martin said.

Squid nodded, his fine eyebrows knitting together. He pushed a stray piece of hair off of his face. Squid looked as mysterious as his name. I couldn't pin down his nationality or his sex, in all honesty, although he was dressed like any fellow might be.

"And I, you," he said. "I was wondering if I might...have a place aboard your ship."

Captain Martin assessed him calmly. "And why should I bring you aboard the *Arrow*, Squid?"

"I'm strong. And skilled. And I want off this stinking pile of timber," Squid spat, eyeing the crew of the *Lantern* who'd gathered at the stern with expressions of displeasure.

"I need more of a reason."

"The *Arrow* is a much finer vessel than the *Lantern*," Squid murmured, glancing at our ship and then gazing at Captain Martin with a look of assessment. "And you are more of a man than any of us."

The captain preened under Squid's appraisal, and I rolled my eyes. Even though Squid struck me as an interesting fellow, I wasn't sure I wanted him on our ship.

I watched Captain Martin, half expecting him to laugh at this obvious manipulation.

"Convince me," he said.

Squid's fine eyebrows slanted. "I know how to do most anything, Captain. And I'm prepared to work where you want me."

"Why should I add to my already large crew just because you want to leave yours? How do I know you won't abandon us at the earliest opportunity?"

Squid appeared confused. "I'm prepared to give back what I'm given."

"Meaning..."

"If I'm given respect, I'll give respect. If I'm afforded courtesies, I'll return them. That's all."

Captain Martin nodded as if this was enough.

"If you're near the ladder when we debark, you can join us. But I'm not going to look for you."

"Yes, Captain. Thank you," Squid said, content.

I gaped at him. "But, Captain..."

"Yes, White?"

My gaze followed Squid as he strode off, presumably to go wait by the ladder.

"We don't know anything about this man. He could be a murderer!"

The captain stared at me, then tipped back his head and laughed and laughed.

"My God. No." He straightened and gave me the most endearing look, as if he couldn't believe how cute I was. "Technically, *I'm* a murderer, Simon. And Guthrie. And...most of them," He gestured to the crew members who were lugging things out of the

Lantern's hold. "As I recall, you, yourself, are responsible for the deaths of an entire ship."

I'd forgotten about that. I could hardly believe he'd throw that in my face.

"Yes, but...I was protecting *you*."

"I realize that. Men have many reasons for the killing they do," he explained.

"What I mean is what if Squid isn't like the rest of us?"

He looked at me strangely.

"In what way?"

"What if he's not a good person? Sure, the crew have shadowed pasts, but at heart most of them are decent. We don't know anything about this Squid person. And what kind of a name is Squid anyway?"

"What kind of a name is Simon?" he countered.

I gasped. "Simon is a bloody respectable and historical name, thank you very much. Squid is a...slimy and mysterious creature from the depths!"

The captain's amusement grew.

"What are you scared of? He looks all right to me. I have an affinity for unusual people. I do like to collect them." He eyed me up and down as if I were a piece of pottery on his shelf. I didn't hate his manner, but he was very distracting.

"Fine. Do what you want. But I don't like him."

"Noted."

"Humph."

"Oh, you are lovely when you're disgruntled. Like a prickly little pear."

How he could deliver an insult, combined with a complement, like he was telling me to pull down my drawers... *Goddamn it.*

I wanted to be angry. I was extremely offended by the prickly pear comparison. But he had also called me lovely, and right now he was looking at me like he wanted to rip off my breeches and bend me over the gunwale.

"I'm not... I'm not angry," I said. "I just don't know about Squid."

Captain Martin shrugged. "Maybe he'll change his mind."

We gazed along the rail to where the crew were hoisting belongings acquired from the *Lantern* down to waiting boats.

Squid had positioned himself at the top of the ladder, waiting for us.

*

Back on the *Arrow* with a number of items recovered from the *Lantern*, including one strange and contrary fellow named, ostensibly, Squid, we tried to satisfy the crew who were a little disappointed in the lack of blood spillage.

"Didn't even get to chop off a bloody arm! I thought we were pirates, not a band of sorry labourers." One fellow grouched.

"Privateers, you mean."

"Oh, fuck off."

Another man sighed. "Didn't have to take out my sword once. Not once!"

So much for allaying the crew's need for battle and blood. The *Lantern* had put up so little resistance, the matter had been like taking purchases from a store, without having to give over any gold. Satisfying on some level, but missing the visceral release of a hand-to-hand fight.

"Now, now," Captain Martin tried to assuage them. "I'm very pleased with how you all managed that. To think, your capabilities as negotiators and facilitators are growing by leaps and bounds. I'm quite impressed."

The crew blinked up at Captain Martin, half of them not even sure what those words meant. But they saw the admiration in Captain Martin's eyes, and the respect in his tone of voice, and responded to those honest words.

"Well, of course, yes, we could have chopped off a few arms. But in the end, we didn't need to, I suppose."

"Exactly," Captain Martin affirmed. "But they knew you were ready to do so and wouldn't hesitate. That, my friends, is called the power of intimidation. And it's a much more efficient way of doing business."

"Humph. Business. Are we businessmen, now? Not even privateers?" someone asked.

"We were always businessmen," Captain Martin said. "In the business of thievery and mischief."

There were chuckles. Someone added, "And other sordid activities," with a glance at me.

I stuck my tongue out at him.

"I didn't know we were collecting strays," Martinéz muttered, motioning toward Squid, who lurked by the rail, watching everything and looking unsure about where they should be or go, or whether they'd made the right decision to come over to the *Arrow*. And in that vulnerability, I saw myself from a few weeks ago, and my heart softened toward him.

"That's Squid," I said, loudly, so the person in question could hear me. "He'll be an asset to the *Arrow*."

I met Captain Martin's surprised but pleased gaze across the deck, and he smiled and nodded.

"Yes, indeed. Squid is a member of this crew now and is to be treated as such," he said.

Squid scowled and shook his head as if embarrassed to be

talked of. But he raised his chin. "I'll prove myself. Don't worry."

Martinéz snorted. "It's you should worry, if you don't."

Lahiri put a hand on Martinéz's arm. "Leave him alone. We were all strays at one point."

This was probably true and a good reminder to the crew.

Lahiri stepped forward and offered his hand to Squid.

"Welcome aboard. We're glad to have you."

Squid looked surprised, but he took Lahiri's hand.

"Thank you."

"I'm Lahiri. And this miserable bugger is Martinéz."

Lahiri beckoned to Martinez. Martinéz rolled his eyes and came forward and welcomed Squid, as well.

I exchanged a look with the captain, as the rest of the crew all came forward to welcome the new crew member.

"Hillier, how much did we get? Anything of real value?" Captain Martin asked.

"Aye, Captain. Quite a bit, actually. The rascal wasn't being entirely honest about his hold being empty, it turns out."

"Mmm. I suspected as much." The captain gazed over the rail at the *Lantern*, which was limping away on the wind, its tattered sails barely affording the vessel enough push to proceed.

I wondered what would become of it.

"Put Squid in charge of the livestock, Hillier. We'll see how he does with that."

I looked at Squid, who appeared even more perplexed as the last of the crew shook his hand and went back to their tasks.

"Actually, Rooster, why don't you take Squid down to where they're kept. You can introduce him to the chooks by name, in fact." Captain Martin frowned. "Hold on. Did you name the goats too?"

I rolled my eyes. "Of course, I did. How would *they* feel if I only named the chooks?"

Honestly, sometimes I despaired of Captain Martin's basic levels of decency.

He smiled at me as if I were his personal source of amusement. Which I suppose I was when it came down to the matter. I winked at the captain, making a lewd gesture with my tongue, before striding over to the strange-looking, tattooed man.

"Oy, then. Come on. I'll take you to the menagerie."

I wondered if minding the livestock was the default job for any new crew member.

"Rooster?" Squid asked with raised eyebrows.

I realized the captain had used his nickname for me. I gestured at my mop of red hair.

"You know. The hair?"

"Ah." If Squid had any questions as to why Captain Martin would use such a casual and affectionate name for me, he didn't voice them.

"Follow me," I said with a level of cheer that reflected my relief that there hadn't been any violent altercations, I'd been treated as an officer for at least a little while, and the men appeared satisfied with our easy take.

The crew carted the goods through to the captain's hold, where the entire take would be divided by share, with the extra ten per cent the captain had promised given to the crew. Hillier was in charge of this—the duty used to fall to Donatello.

I still felt a level of guilt about Donatello. Maybe if he'd been as dear to me as Captain Martin, I'd have been able to keep him safe. But then I recalled that Donatello's murder had caused the flame to rise in me, so perhaps I should think of his death as Donatello's final act—to be the sacrifice that helped me to save our captain and the rest of our crew.

I led Squid down to where the menagerie was kept.

"Mr White, are you actually the captain's 'right-hand man'?" Squid asked as we descended the narrow steps into the hull.

"Well," I said, "if you consider what most men do with their right hands, that's as good a title as any."

Squid uttered a laugh as we descended.

"I suspected," he said.

"That the captain likes to tumble me?" I grinned and winked, figuring I might as well find out now if Squid had any issues with oversharing, or the act of sodomy.

"It's rather obvious, ain't it?" he said, unaffected.

"Why? Do I walk strangely? Seeing as the captain's got a rapier the size of a torpedo, it's entirely possible."

"No, it's not the way you walk."

I stopped and turned. "What gives it away, then?"

"The way he looks at you."

"Like he wants to bend me over the rail and have his way?"

"Well, no. At least, that's not the impression I got when you came aboard the *Lantern*."

"Oh?"

Squid shrugged. "I figure he was keeping an eye on you to keep you safe. Because he holds you in high esteem."

I snorted. "I don't know about that."

Inwardly, I was beaming. Perhaps the captain really did care more for me than I'd imagined? I wasn't sure that was quite possible, seeing as I was nothing but a good fuck and a man of questionable and uncontrollable powers. I was a freak of nature with a talent for cocksucking and that was about all. I hoped Squid would have more luck managing the goats than I had.

"Here they are then," I said, when we had located the spot where the animals were kept. I'd seen the fellow who had been in charge of them on deck helping with the loot, and I imagined he'd already been told of his switch in duties. "You want me to tell you their names?"

Squid looked at the chickens, at the goats, and then at me. "Names?"

"Why is everyone so surprised they have names?" I said, reaching into the pen and pulling Elizabeth into my arms. "This is Elizabeth."

"Elizabeth. Really." He didn't sound impressed.

"Oh, fuck off. You're in charge now. I suppose you can name them what you like."

"No, I'm sorry. I don't mean to be rude. Do go on. I'd like to hear their names."

I eyed Squid carefully to see if he was putting me on for his own amusement, but he appeared sincere.

"This one is Henrietta. And this is Gertrude," I told him, pointing to the chickens, who evinced health and happiness, at least. And all present and accounted for as well.

He had put his hand over his mouth but looked to be paying attention.

"Unfortunately, we lost one to..." I cleared my throat, "A delicious dinner. Her name was Guinevere, may she rest in peace."

I crossed myself and blinked back a tear.

There was a strange noise that sounded like a sneeze but that I realized was Squid giving a stifled laugh that had mostly come through his nose. He dropped his hand and broke out chortling in earnest now, and I thought that a bit too much, actually. A chortle, sure. A laugh, I'd accept. But he was enjoying the story far too much. He put a hand on the corner of the wooden pen to support himself as the chickens clucked in a disapproval that mirrored my own.

"Hmm," I said, regarding him with distaste. "For a fellow named Squid, you've got a lot of cheek laughing at the names of my chickens."

I put Elizabeth down and picked up Henrietta. "I shan't tell you their names. Not if you're going to laugh at them."

Squid shook his head and tried to rein in his hilarity. "I'm not... I'm not laughing at the...chickens," he sputtered. "I'm laughing at *you*, Officer White."

He proceeded to clutch at his chest as he gasped for breath and laughed harder.

"Or should I say, Rooster?"

I glared at the man.

"Perhaps you should say goodbye," I said. "If the captain heard you making fun of me in this way, he'd turf you over the side."

I wasn't entirely sure that was true. He might just join in.

Squid sobered at that and reached out to me. "I'm so sorry. I really am. I promise to address you as Officer White henceforth. Please don't send me back to the *Lantern*..."

"I shall try to be the better man."

"It's only," Squid said, with a hint of emotion, "that's the first time I've laughed in—" He looked down at his hand and counted his fingers. "—one, two, three years."

I gaped at him. "You haven't laughed in three years? That's terrible."

"Yes. It has been."

My attitude immediately softened.

"I would... I would love to hold...Elizabeth...if I may?" he said.

"Of course."

I introduced Squid to every one of those chickens and then

to the goats, explaining how troublesome the goats were compared to the chickens. As if to prove my point, when I opened the gate to the goat pen, one of the mad creatures pushed past between me and Squid, bawling and scrambling across the hold as if escaping certain death.

"Oh fuck!" I said, shutting the gate and taking off after the errant creature, followed by the sound of Squid's scuffing boots as he joined me in the chase. "Fuck, he's going up on deck," I exclaimed. "Fuck, fuck, fuck."

Squid's laughter behind me indicated that he was not upset about this development in the least.

The goat—Lilith, of course—ran up the narrow steps past two crew members who cursed and threw me annoyed glares.

"Jesus Christ, White, get your fucking animal!"

"She ain't mine," I protested, running up the steps, closely followed by Squid who said, "Excuse me, excuse me," so many times I began to see the amusement in this ridiculous escapade.

As we followed the goat up on deck, I caught Captain Martin's annoyed look when he saw her. But before I could apologize or tell him to get off my fucking back, Squid shoved me aside and launched himself like a torpedo after Lilith.

I struggled to keep my balance and braced my hands on my thighs, breathing hard from all the running, and watched Squid go. Unbelievably, as Lilith was quite fast when she was on the run, Squid managed to get past her and cut her off just as she was heading for the steps up to the forecastle.

"Ho!" Squid yelled, then dove for the animal, who skidded on the slick boards as she tried to avoid him. They crashed to the deck in a cacophony of noises—Squid's grunts of exertion and, no doubt, pain, and the goat's squeals of astonishment.

Lilith brayed and moaned as if she were being murdered.

Squid yelled for some rope. One of the crew threw him a length, and he soon had her captured. How he kept himself from strangling the damned thing, I'll never know.

A round of applause greeted Squid's prowess as he stood there regarding me in triumph, holding the end of the rope while Lilith pulled to get away again. She bleated helplessly and then quieted.

The captain and I exchanged a glance. He appeared as surprised as I at Squid's talents.

"Take the goat back down, Squid," Captain Martin said. "And thank you for taking charge of her."

"Aye, Captain," Squid said. "You're welcome. I'll make sure she doesn't get loose again."

He tugged on the rope, and Lilith followed him obediently.

"White. Come with me," the captain ordered.

Four words I had never been more thrilled to hear.

Chapter Twelve

Important Ship's Business

Captain Martin led me to his rooms, where Boone was sitting once again, keeping an eye on things.

"Boone."

"Captain."

"Why don't you go find Guthrie and see if he needs any help in the kitchens?"

"Aye, Captain," Boone said, giving me a glance and then rolling his eyes. "I'll make myself scarce so's you can have your fun."

"That's not what—" Captain Martin started to say, but Boone only smiled and waved.

"Huh," I said, gazing after him. "What do you suppose he thinks we're going to do?" I asked innocently as if I didn't have a very good idea.

"Whatever he thinks, I can promise you it's nothing compared to what I've got planned for you, little witch."

My heart fluttered at the endearment. I liked the way he used the frightening word as a soft little name for me, when my powers were so mysterious and perplexing and terrifying.

I followed him into his rooms. As soon as I had shut the door behind me, he told me to take off all my clothes.

"My goodness. That's not very romantic, Captain," I said, shaking my head with disappointment.

His eyebrows stretched up so high I thought they might climb over his head. "We're on a pirate ship, Rooster, not a gondola on the Rio dei Greci."

I didn't know what that was, but I made sure to look affronted. "Excuse me. A *privateer vessel*, surely."

Captain Martin smiled. "Surely."

I took off my jacket and placed it on the chair at Captain Martin's desk.

"Would be nice to get a sweet kiss or a flower first," I muttered.

Captain Martin barked a laugh. "Honestly, you are the maddest fellow. Where the fuck am I supposed to get a flower out in the middle of the ocean?"

I quirked my lip at him. "And I thought you were a man of vision."

Dinesh leered at me as I disrobed. "Oh, I'm envisioning quite a lot right now. And what I'm imagining doesn't involve flowers or pretty words at all."

"Well, fuck me," I said, feeling my body ignite at those words.

"Don't worry. That *is* a part of the vision."

There was a rapid knock at the door.

"For fuck's sake!" Captain Martin said.

He marched over as I draped my jacket over my bare shoulders.

He leaned toward the door. "Yes?" he asked.

"It's me, Captain. Hillier."

"What do you want?"

"May I come in?"

Captain Martin glanced at me. I shrugged.

"If you promise not to be upset at what you see."

"Oh. I...yes, I promise," Hillier said, but he didn't sound all that sure of himself.

Perhaps the captain was only trying to get rid of him because I still had most of my clothes on.

Captain Martin opened the door and ushered Hillier inside. Hillier looked at me, saw that I had my jacket over my bare torso like a shawl, noticed my bare feet, looked at Captain Martin, and smiled with relief.

"You had me going there for a moment."

Captain Martin smirked. "What did you think you were going to see?"

"I...don't think I can say that out loud."

"Oh for fuck's sake," I cursed, throwing my jacket on the chair and starting to undo my pants.

"White. You can wait until I'm done with Hillier to finish your disrobing."

"But why should I? He seems to have expected to see me trussed naked from the roof. Surely standing here with no clothes on won't bother him."

"Rooster, keep your fucking breeches on."

I stilled my fingers and straightened, crossing my arms over my chest. I did feel a little self-conscious in front of Hillier, to be honest.

"What's the matter?" the captain asked.

"I'm terribly sorry to disturb you, Dinesh. You see...the men want their ten per cent now," Hillier muttered.

Captain Martin stared at Hillier as if he couldn't fathom the rush. "Right now? I'm a little busy..."

"Yes, well, I told them you were," Hillier said, clearing his throat. "And Torrington said, 'If the captain's too busy—" Hillier glanced at me with an apology. "—dipping his dick in that pretty witch—" I preened as the captain scowled. "—then we'll distribute the loot ourselves'." Hillier shrugged.

Captain Martin blinked. "We haven't even assessed the size of the haul."

"Yes, Captain."

Captain Martin thought about what Hillier had said. "Do you think they'd wait if I spoke to them?"

"Mayhap." Hillier let his gaze shift to me for a moment.

"Hmm," Captain Martin hummed. "What if you select some items of moderate value to give to each of the crew with promises of more to come once we take a cataloguing of what we found?"

Hillier stood a bit straighter. "Of course, Captain. If you'd trust me to do so."

Captain Martin put a hand on Hillier's shoulder. "Of course I do. I wouldn't have put you in Donatello's place if I didn't."

"Thank you, Captain," Hillier replied.

"And, Hillier,"

"Yes, Captain?"

"If anyone is looking for Mr White, let them know that I'm briefing him on some very important ship's business. We'll try to be quick."

Hillier grinned. "Of course, Captain." He nodded at Captain

Martin, grinned at me, and left us, closing the door quietly behind him.

"Hmm. I wasn't aware this was to be an important business meeting," I said as Captain Martin walked over to stand before me. "I don't think I'm dressed for it."

"Doesn't worry me," he said in tones that held a menacing note that thrilled me to my bits and back.

The energy in the room shifted, and my breathing quickened, my body on alert for what his closeness promised.

"What's wrong?" I asked, my words barely audible over my heavy breaths.

He quirked his lip as he reached out and took hold of my wrist, leading my hand to the front of his breeches and pressing my palm against the solid, hot mass of his covered stand.

"Oh," I said. "I see."

"Hmm. Would you like to?"

"Oh yes, please," I said.

Captain Martin's fingers flew over his breeches, and in a moment, he'd pulled out his cock, astonishing in its fiery rage.

"Hmm," I said, tilting my head to eye his prick from a different angle. "Does boarding vessels inflame your blood, Captain?"

He grunted. "Aye. Though not as much as boarding young upstarts like yourself."

I smiled, amused by his meaning. I closed the space between us and leaned against him, the hot brand of his excitement pressing into my belly. "Well...if you want to board me, you'll have to subdue me first."

His breathing quickened, and his hand wrapped around my throat, tilting my chin up and squeezing just enough to make me pay attention. I can tell you that one particular part of me became quite alert.

"My pleasure," he said, walking me backwards to the bed.

I stumbled and fell onto the mattress as he shoved me down and covered me with his much bigger body, a situation that I welcomed.

My fingers wrapped around his sabre, causing him to groan and push into my grip. He closed his eyes and grimaced.

"Careful, careful. It'll all be over before we start."

Oh, hell, no.

I released him immediately and stretched my arms over my head, blinking in mock confusion.

"What will be over, Captain? I thought we were discussing business."

"Business," he said, with some astonishment. "Simon White, are you being deliberately obtuse? Obviously, that was simply an excuse to make our meeting more legitimate to the crew."

"Oh no, Captain. I would never. Just, when you asked me to come to your rooms I imagined you wanted...well..." I raised my eyebrows, silently begging Captain Martin to understand that I desperately wanted to be the innocent virgin about to be despoiled.

It took him a moment. Finally, his confused expression softened with understanding.

"Ah, yes," he murmured, his gaze running over me, eyes blazing with sudden fire. "Well, you see, Rooster, I wasn't exactly clear about my intentions."

I batted my eyelashes at him, pretending to have not a clue what he was about.

"No? Well, I want you to know that I'm here for you...whatever you need."

Captain Martin let a sly smile form on his face as he settled himself against me, his cock a hard brand against my hip. I still had my breeches on—an unfortunate oversight. But that made playing the game a little easier.

"Well, I'd like to try something. You strike me a friendly fellow." He smiled, and the devilish glint in his eye was everything.

"Very friendly," I said. "To a fault."

"Mm-hmm. Well, so am I." He blinked slowly like a happy cat. "Do you know what two men who are...*very friendly*...can do with each other?"

"Hmm," I said, scratching my chin and doing my best to be adorably daft. "Play checkers?"

"No."

"Chess?"

"Oh dear, no. Much too dull. The game I'm thinking of is so much more exciting."

"Okay," I said. "How do you play it?"

He looked like he was going to start to laugh. "If I describe it, the game is going to sound very strange."

"Hmm. But how will I know what to do if you don't?"

He winked. "Oh, it's very easy. I'll do all the *hard* work."

"Hard work?" I scoffed, squirming underneath him. "That doesn't sound like very much fun."

"Oh, it is though. Very enjoyable."

"Hmm. I don't know." I pretended reluctance, though he could probably feel my rampant stand poking him.

"Let me show you," he said.

"Hmm. I suppose that would be all right."

"Excellent. But you must do as I say. Even if my instructions sound strange. If you trust me, I will introduce you to an enjoyable activity."

"How can I possibly resist?" I asked.

"I don't think you can," he said, pushing onto his knees and tugging at my breeches.

"Oy, what are you doing, Captain?" I asked with mock astonishment as he undid the flap. I went up on my elbows and gazed at him as if I really were a lily-white virgin who didn't know any fucking thing. The idea was ludicrous, but the entire fabrication did make for a fun romp.

"Shh," he said, undoing my breeches and pulling my cock out.

"Captain Martin!" I gasped.

"Oh, don't worry, my lovely boy. This won't hurt."

"Are you quite sure?" I asked, batting my lashes and uttering little gasps as he stroked me.

"Quite sure. I know what I'm doing. Don't worry. Am I hurting you?"

I looked down at his fingers sliding up and down my very willing stand and shook my head. "No. Not at all."

"Excellent. How does this feel?" He gave me a particularly long stroke that finished over the head.

"Oh! Do that again."

He grinned and repeated the motion. I half sat up again. "Oh, Captain. Now what?"

"Turn over," he said, releasing my cock and moving aside.

"Turn over?" I asked. "But why?"

"All will become clear. For now, it's because I want to have a look at your pretty arse."

"Well, then," I said, rolling myself over.

"Let's just get rid of these," Captain Martin said, pulling my breeches all the way off and tossing them aside. "Hmm. Look at you."

I wiggled my bottom and craned my neck so I could see the admiring look on his face. "Is my arse very nice?"

"Oh, my darling. You have the prettiest bottom I've ever had the pleasure of getting to know. I can't wait to show you what being very friendly with another man can be like."

"Yes, please."

"But first, a spanking."

"A spanking! Whatever for?" I asked, putting my right hand over my arse, palm up, to guard against him.

"Because I want to. Trust me, it'll warm your blood nicely."

"No. I don't want you to."

"Rooster."

"You can't make me," I said in such a way to make it plain that I wanted him to force me.

"Oh, think you'll find that I can," he said, lunging forward and grabbing my wrist, as he settled on his knees beside me. With one tug, he had me sprawled over his broad lap, then held my wrist with my arm bent at the elbow, so I couldn't possibly move. With his other hand, he began to stroke and slap and pinch the skin of my buttocks until I was writhing mass of sobbing emotion.

"Oh, please. Oh, please. This isn't as much fun as I expected!" I protested.

But Captain Martin laughed and kept going. When he finally stopped and simply laid into me with the palm of his hand, the change was a relief and a pleasure.

"Oh fuck. Oh fuck. Oh my God," I blurted as he held me still and spanked my arse like he had nothing better to do. "Oh, Captain. What a wonderful game."

The spanking stopped and if what I was hearing was an indication, Captain Martin scrabbled with the ties of his trousers.

"Oh no, what are you doing now?" I asked in a hilarious approximation of alarm.

"I am going to put my cock into your saucy arse and fuck you ten ways till Sunday. Now be quiet and spread your legs."

"Oh yes, Captain. This game has been lovely so far. I can't wait to find out what—" I stopped talking and groaned as his slick finger pushed inside me. "Oh God. Oh *God*."

Captain Martin gasped and went deeper. "Oh yes. Look at you squirm."

"Oh my God."

He prodded me with one, then added another.

I groaned and gasped and writhed, my cock leaking onto the sheet beneath me. I thought I might finish from only that and all the play-acting. I truly did feel like a virgin who'd never had anything in his arse before.

"Oh, oh, oh," I moaned, spreading my legs wider as he played with me. By the time he pushed three fingers up me, I was almost a goner. "Captain! I'm going to spend if you keep going."

"Don't you dare. No, no. You mustn't," he said, sliding his fingers out. "Get a hold of yourself."

"I'll try. I'll try," I said, lying as still as I could whilst my body throbbed with desperate need.

"Wait for me..."

In a moment, he had covered me, and his randy rapier was going in, in, *in*. So fucking deep, deliciously skewering me as I tried to keep breathing.

"Oh, Rooster, Rooster, Jesus..." he muttered, stuttering, gasping and groaning as he moved with much urgency. I didn't think it would take long for either of us.

It didn't.

Our cries of completion mingled in the pungent heat of the room as we gave ourselves up to the pleasure we made together. Trembling and gasping, we came down from the height of our mutual culmination and relaxed into each other.

I stretched my arms over my head, surrendering to the sense of boneless ease. Captain Martin—Dinesh—dropped down on top of me, the weight of him causing a woosh of air to escape my lungs.

"Heavy…" I squeaked. "Too heavy. Help."

He sighed and cursed, then rolled off me.

When I looked at the captain, he was blinking and staring at the ceiling, his chest going up and down, cock still hard and shiny with oil, with leftovers of his seed at the tip. The slick moisture of his release oozed out of me, and I shuddered with aftershocks of illicit pleasure.

"Oh, Captain Martin," I said, watching his lips twitch into a brief smile. "Dinesh." I spoke his given name again, savoring the syllables in my mouth. He looked over and met my gaze. "What have you done to me?" I whispered. "This isn't like any other game I've ever played." I was still playing the innocent and coquettish young man.

He gazed upon me with adoration and amusement.

"No, and you shan't play this particular game with anyone else."

"Of course not," I said, scooting over to lie on his chest. "The thing wouldn't be the same."

I reached down and found his victorious sword. He grimaced as I teased the overly sensitive skin.

"Is this what was inside me?"

"Yes. And it will be again. Possibly in about ten minutes."

I watched him squirm and protest under my touch, turning the tables until he stilled me with a hand on my wrist.

"Enough. Too much."

I afforded him mercy and withdrew my hand.

"Do you need to attend to your crew? Make sure there ain't gonna be a mutiny?"

He sighed, still gazing upon me with dreamy eyes.

"Let them fucking mutiny," he said. "Let them take over the ship and put me in a boat with only you, Rooster. I'd be more than happy."

"What?" My astonishment was genuine. I hoped he was joking. "And lose all of this luxury?" I waved my hand at the room around us. "Speak for yourself, man."

He sighed again and kissed me—so softly and sweetly that my heart melted. He pulled back and offered me a weary smile.

"Fine, then. I'll go deal with them. But you are to stay right here, my little red rooster, filled with my seed. I don't want you to get up. I want you exactly here when I return because I need to claim you again."

I smiled. I'd be wherever he wanted me. "But what shall I do whilst you're gone?"

"Think of all the ways I'm going to fuck you when I get back."

"Oooh."

He pushed himself up and backed off me.

"Spread your legs."

I blinked in confusion and then obeyed.

"Oh, fuck me. Look at that hole. Wet with my spunk." He inhaled a shuddering breath as he reached down and played with the juices there. I gasped and squirmed with pleasure and the thrill of debauchery. "Well filled, but there's room for more. Don't fucking move."

He got off the bed as I lay there, spread wide for him and anyone else who might walk in.

*

Luckily, nobody disturbed me but the captain when he arrived back and made good on his word.

As the *Arrow* made our way toward the island of Tortuga over the following week, the captain took his pleasure—and I got mine—several times.

Hillier had also begun to teach me the art of wielding a cutlass. However, after a few close calls we determined that we couldn't risk the loss of another quartermaster, and my lessons were ended, much to his relief. I was good with my knife and, of course, I had my magic.

The winds and the weather held, and by the time the moon had shifted into another phase, we drew near to our destination.

"Rooster," Captain Martin said with excitement after pushing open the door to his rooms, where I was renewing my battle with the persistent dust—where was the stuff coming from? "Rooster, you must come and see."

"See what?" I asked, jutting out my lip to puff a blast of air at my damp forelock. "Is there an orgy?"

He barked a laugh, but came in and grabbed my hand, pulling me out of his rooms—our rooms, I supposed they were by now—and up the steps to the deck.

"There had better be an orgy. I was right in the midst of—"

And then I caught sight of the turquoise water and the green and verdant island jutting up from the ocean like the shell of a monstrous turtle.

"Is that Tortuga?" I asked, in tones that expressed my awe of the island's beauty.

"Turtle Island. Yes, that's her. Isn't she beautiful?"

Men were gathered along the *Arrow's* rail, looking at the white sand and grey rocks and the miles and miles of green trees.

"Well," I said, folding my arms along the rail and giving the island a quizzical stare. "Doesn't look very civilized. We'll get lost in all that jungle!"

He laughed. "Oh, don't worry. We're not straying from the port town of Cayonne, which is just around the bend there. The village is somewhat more civilized than that jungle, at least in some respects."

"Oooh, that sounds lovely. Do we have time for a quick romp though?"

"Gods, Rooster, you're utterly insatiable."

"Well? Do we?"

We did have time, in fact. We left Hillier to manage and disappeared into the half-dusted depths of the captain's rooms, not coming up for air until Dinesh had fucked me twice and spent all over my face.

He sucked me until I spent all over my belly and chest, then passed me a handkerchief to wipe off. Ever the gentleman.

"I see you've succeeded in marking me as your own as we are about to head amongst vagabonds of all nations."

"Yes," he agreed, eyeing me with satisfaction. "You'll likely hold my scent for a while."

I rolled my eyes. "Is it too late to call for a bath?" I asked, using the handkerchief to give myself a cursory clean.

"Entirely. Do your best with the cloth and the washbasin if you must. But hurry."

"Why? Am I really coming with you?"

"Of course. You're my right-hand man, aren't you?"

I blinked, stunned. "I thought that was pretend."

He turned and winked at me. "The ruse worked so well, I've decided to promote you and make the designation permanent. I still expect you to warm my bed, of course. But only if you're willing."

I threw back the sheet and jumped off the bed, then strode over to stand directly in front of him, naked as anything, holding the soiled hanky.

"Of course, I'm yours. But I'm thrilled to be my own agent now too. Does this mean I'm an official member of the crew?"

He straightened and gave me an incredulous look. "You're a legitimate member of the captain's officers now, Simon. That's one step above." He smiled at me. "Don't let your new position go to your head."

"Since you insist on putting me in quite undignified positions on an almost daily basis, I'm sure that's not a worry at all." I smirked and eyed him up and down.

"What a naughty, naughty officer," he said in a sultry tone.

"Oh, now we have to play at that game too!"

Chapter Thirteen

Tortuga

Tortuga was a cacophony of chaos.

Never mind being on dry land after weeks at sea, on a ship where I was surrounded by men who had become familiar—a family, of sorts, I supposed—now I found myself uneasy around so many strangers. I stayed close to Dinesh, glad to have his staunch and stolid presence nearby.

Hillier had already arranged for part of the crew to go ahead and gather the supplies we'd need for the rest of our journey. Men were already bringing things back to the ship as the captain and I, Hillier, Mr Guthrie, and Squid took leave of the *Arrow* and went ashore.

The sun had begun to set and the weather had turned foul by the time our skiff made a landing. A good time to look for a tavern and some temporary lodgings. As the rain pelted down, I wished to be back in Dinesh's cozy cabin aboard the *Arrow*. I felt suitably protected in my present company, even though the chaos on the docks and the narrow dirt streets of the port town took me by surprise. I didn't know what I'd expected—I'd been in my share of dodgy areas, but Tortuga was different.

There were all sorts of people, dressed in all sorts of peculiar ways, but none to the fashion standards of the day. Not that I was an expert in any way, but the bright colours and strange clothing of so many people was blinding in its variability. The men, too, were of all different countenances, so many of indefinable race who worked or lounged or drank or gambled together. And women, with whom I wasn't used to dealing at all, didn't look to fall into either of the more obvious categories of honorable wives or daughters, and filthy harlots, by the cut of their clothing or their manner. They also flaunted the expectations of fashion and many acted more like men in their bearing. Absent the visual cues of the social structures I'd grown up with, while enlightening to observe people simply being themselves, my surroundings proved unsettling in their unfamiliarity.

Captain Martin checked in on me often with a glance of concern as we made our way along the busy streets. I acted like I was taking the chaos in stride, but he could probably see how skittish I was. At one point, he slowed and, when I caught up to him, bent to my ear.

"Quite the place, isn't it? Wait until you see the wonders on offer here." He grinned, with the devil in his eye, and winked.

"What on earth do you mean?" I asked, wrinkling my nose. "Whores?"

He must know by now that I wouldn't be interested in any woman who would spread her legs for coin. Or any woman at all.

"You'll see, my sweet Simon. I've got quite an evening planned for us."

He pulled away and clapped his hands together, gaining the attention of the others.

"Let's find us a likely tavern, shall we? I need a hearty meal and some drink after so long at sea!"

He lifted the leather pouch at his waist and shook the contents, and I was reminded of our first meeting at the Penny Whistle in Port Royal. The coin inside jingled and I followed him like a trusting lamb, whilst Squid cast his gaze about, as if we might be set upon at any moment.

"What are you looking so spooked for?" Hillier asked, but Squid only glanced his way before casting his gaze around us as we walked.

Captain Martin didn't appear concerned, Hillier neither, both talking to Guthrie as we made our way through the hustle and bustle of Cayonne.

"The island was settled by huntsmen and farmers of differing nationalities," Captain Martin said. "Then, when certain, ah, shall we say 'adventurers' began to stop by…"

"You mean, pirates," I stated.

He smiled. "Well. They have many names, you see, and little allegiance. Even the ones who had writs from the king didn't actually have any loyalty, beyond having the license to kill and plunder in the name of Britain. Or France. Or whomever had employed them."

"Mercenaries. Thieves and murderers," Hillier muttered.

"And what are we?" I asked, genuinely curious. If Dinesh didn't even think much of the men who'd called themselves privateers with some legitimacy, what did he think he was?

He shrugged. "We are in business for ourselves, it's true. I don't have a writ from anyone to give me leave. However, I like the word, 'privateer'. We work for ourselves, but we're not mercenaries. There are things I won't do for money."

"Well, I'm glad to hear it," I said. "But that doesn't surprise me."

He grinned wider. "Why? Do you consider me honourable?"

I regarded him with a hint of the lustful looks I often gave him. "Most of the time."

He laughed. "Aye, well, that's better than I'd hoped for." He walked beside me in silence for a moment, his steps measured. Then he spoke again. "I like to think I've created a unique sort of community on the *Arrow*. A kind of a utopia for the likes of us, and others, who refuse to live by the rules of an unjust society."

I nodded, thinking that he had done so, in my opinion.

We hadn't gone much farther before Captain Martin gave a happy shout.

"The Turnkey, Hillier! The place is still here. Let's hope the tavern offers the same entertainment we've found here in the past."

"Aye, Captain. Let's hope so."

"The Turnkey? What's that?" I asked, casting my gaze about the street that teemed with people of all sizes, shapes, and hues.

"Oh, Rooster. The Turnkey is an experience. That's all I can say at the moment, but I'm excited to show you."

Squid put a hand on my arm as the captain and Hillier hastened their steps.

"Fancy whores and molly boys," he said.

"Oh," I said, trying not to sound shocked. I was a man of the world, after all.

But what was Dinesh planning? Was he going to discard me for a bevy of handsome prostitutes that he could have for a few coins from that fat purse of his? Probably have me fed and filled with whiskey until I collapsed, then go dip his quill in some fresh ink. Well, perhaps not *fresh*. But new and different.

I frowned and looked up to see Captain Martin beckoning to me under a large sign that read TURNKEY in bold red letters, with an engraving of what looked like a fluffy fox tail coiled beneath the word.

Well, I would eat, but I'd resist his efforts to get me dizzy with drink. And when he tried to leave me for a room upstairs, I'd tell him that I didn't approve of his plan at all.

But would he listen? Would he care at all about my feelings?

Perhaps, now that he'd promoted me, he didn't see me the same way. He saw me as his equal instead of his 'boy' and bed-warmer. And Goddamn it if that didn't make me sad, so how fucked in the head was I? Maybe getting pissed with the drink was a good idea, after all.

Dinesh could do whatever, and whomever, he wanted, and who was I to have any say about his actions? He wasn't my husband and he never could be. I could never have a husband, and wasn't that simply the most depressing thought? The excitement I'd felt, combined with my uneasiness, evaporated in a haze of jealousy and melancholy. Why had I even left the *Arrow*?

Inside the Turnkey, we crowded the bar until spaces opened up at a rough-hewn table. There were so many people, the stink was incredible. Without the crisp sea air to disperse the grime, the tangy scent of a score of unbathed men was quite pungent. I tried not to wrinkle my nose.

"Captain Martin!"

The dulcet tones came from behind me, and I turned to come face-to-face with my worst nightmare.

"Domingo! *Como estas*?" Captain Martin said with a jubilant lilt.

I'd had no idea he spoke a different language to the King's English, so I gaped at him in surprise.

"Eh, you know. Getting by. Barely."

The young man in women's frilly undergarments, chemise gaping over pert red nipples, and a tight black corset emphasizing a trim waist, glanced at me with curiosity. His dark brown hair tumbled in silky, shiny curls to his shoulders, and his clean-shaven face was accentuated with touches of paint here and there to draw out his amber eyes and plump lips.

"Fuck," I said out loud.

He smiled—a knowing, alluring grin. "That'll be ten gold pieces."

"Ten!" I exclaimed.

Domingo's smile got wider, and he looked me over with an approving gaze.

"It'll be worth the coin, my pretty."

I sputtered with indignation, but Captain Martin wrapped stern fingers around my wrist and gave me a look. I forced myself to remain calm, although inwardly I bristled at the offer.

Captain Martin matched Domingo's grin. "How much for both of us?"

Squid, who had already gotten himself a tankard of ale, made a noise of disgust.

I gaped at Captain Martin, then studied Domingo with a fresh appreciation.

Both of us? I wasn't sure if that made the situation better or worse. Perhaps I should be glad he wasn't planning to exclude me from his exploits. My gaze strayed to Domingo's waist in the black corset, then over his shapely legs in short bloomers, black stockings, and soft leather shoes.

He frowned now, his pretty rouged lips turning down, and

gazed back and forth between us.

"Well, I don't know. That's a lot to take on."

"It is," Captain Martin agreed. "But I know you can handle the job, Domingo. Mr Simon White is my right-hand man, you see, and I don't go anywhere without him."

The tip of Domingo's pink tongue slid over the top of his lower lip as he assessed us, contemplating.

"Hmm. Since I know you very well already, Dinesh, I suppose I can do the both of you for fifteen. But three hours tops. You can't ruin me for tomorrow." He threw back his head and smirked with mischief, his beautiful and luxurious locks feathering back from his face in a charming way.

Captain Martin nodded. "Quite fair. Thank you so much. We'll need a meal first. Where shall we find you?"

"I'm still in room 18. I'm sure you remember."

"Oh yes," Captain Martin said, giving me a cheeky wink as I forced my mouth to close.

"That will give me time to prepare myself," Domingo said, giving a curt little nod. "I'll see you and Mr White very soon, then." He started away, then turned back. "That'll be fifteen pieces up front, you realize."

"Of course. I'll have the payment for you upstairs."

"Excellent." Domingo fluttered his hand and wove through the crowd, shoving men to the side so he could get through, swinging his saucy hips as he went.

"Fifteen gold pieces!" I exclaimed as a scantily clad person of the female persuasion approached with a pitcher and two tankards.

"Ale?" she asked, blowing a curl of black hair off her forehead.

"Yes, please," Captain Martin said. "And whatever you've got in the way of meat. Boar, perhaps?"

"There's a rich stew, or you can have a roasted hock with potatoes and carrots."

For a moment I forgot about Domingo and our future plans.

"Roasted hock?" I gasped. I could almost taste the delicate meat that would be falling off the bone. I might have drooled a little.

Captain Martin looked about for Squid and Hillier, but neither of us could locate them.

"Where on earth did the rest of them get to? Ah well, only us, then. Two of the hocks, if you please."

"Right. The girls and boys are around if you're looking for an evening's entertainment."

"Yes, well, we've made arrangements already," Captain Martin said. "Thank you."

"Fine. I'll bring the hocks."

I levered my mind away from the food and once again questioned the captain's judgement.

"You're going to spend fifteen gold pieces on a whore?" I asked, still finding the very idea to be outrageous.

Captain Martin frowned. "His name is Domingo."

"But he's a—"

Captain Martin silenced me with a finger over my lips.

"—very sweet young man with incredible talents and a malleable disposition. Don't judge me until after. That is, if you *do* want to join me. I won't force you."

I tried to think of some fitting words. Domingo was a very pretty man, for certain, but I couldn't decide if it would be worse, or better, to let Captain Martin enjoy him without me. I'd never been confronted with an opportunity like this before.

He leaned toward me. "Do you trust me?"

"I—I—I suppose so."

Captain Martin smiled. He was so handsome when he smiled, and I was helpless against his charm.

"Then let me help you to experience the beauty of Tortuga, Rooster, in the arms of Domingo and myself this evening. I promise you'll enjoy yourself."

"But to waste that much coin!" I couldn't get over the cost. Fifteen gold pieces would get you a team of good horses back where I'd come from.

"Oh, the expense won't be a waste. Domingo's skills are considerable."

"But..." I was distracted for a moment, wondering what some of those skills might be.

"The others have probably gambled all their gold away by now, or most certainly will have by morning. At least I'm betting on a sure thing," Captain Martin said, giving me a dreamy, anticipatory look that I'd not seen before.

"I thought... I thought..."

"Oh, I know. You thought I was going to let you sit in a crowded tavern by yourself, or with only Squid for company, and go off with Domingo on my own for a night of illicit passion."

"Well, yes."

"Oh no, Rooster. What I am most looking forward to this evening is watching you and Domingo perform various acrobatic maneuvers for my visual enjoyment."

"Oh..."

"Before I ravage you both, one after the other."

He lifted his tankard and gulped down a large swallow of ale.

I couldn't tear my gaze away from the bobbing of his Adam's apple. Suddenly parched, I grabbed my own tankard and downed gulps of the brown ale, as Dinesh laughed with unfettered glee.

And when our meal arrived, I forgot about everything except the hunk of rich meat in my bowl.

"Easy. We need to be ready for anything when we go up. Domingo is quite dedicated. Part of his popularity."

I nodded, trying to slow down and chew my food, taking sips of ale between bites. The portions were small, but hearty.

"When he said he needed to get ready…"

The captain gave me a knowing smile. "I imagine he's cleaning himself out somehow. They have lovely contraptions for that, you know."

"Wot? You mean… What do you mean?"

"A bladder filled with warm water and a tube will do the trick. Not complicated but very effective to get rid of any…inconvenience."

So the whore was cleaning himself of shit and any evidence of his last client. Well, that was kind of him, I supposed. Still, what a life. One I'd briefly contemplated out of desperation before making my bid to board the *Arrow*. I enjoyed bed exercises, certainly, perhaps more than most, but only when I could select my bedfellows. I wasn't sure I could give myself over for a price.

Domingo was either extremely good at his job, or he did actually find Dinesh and I appealing, which I supposed was a good day when it came to whoring. At least the gold pieces Captain Martin was to pay—fifteen gold pieces—would go a long way to keeping Domingo in some level of comfort, which eased my mind a bit. The world was a rough place, and if this was what Domingo had landed on as his best opportunity to live well, who was I to judge him?

Captain Martin took another swig of his ale and relaxed into his seat.

"So lovely to be off the *Arrow* for a bit. I do love the life I've been gifted, but it's a relief not to be in charge for a spell."

I smiled. "Aye, or worrying about marauders on the open sea. Are we truly safe here?"

"Aye. We're among the Brethren of the Coast now, and there are unwritten rules about bringing violence and crime into the port of Cayonne. Further inland you could run into trouble, but here things are managed pretty well. Nobody wants to deal with trouble, as most folks are after a good time. If you become known as someone who brings trouble, you can be barred from the island, and nobody wants that, trust me."

"So...you're not a gambling man, then, Dinesh?"

"Not like the rest of them, no. I bet on things that matter. Like bringing aboard my precious ship a bright young fellow with an attitude, who needed occupation and a good ravishing."

I couldn't help but smile, now that my belly was filling and the captain was being so charming.

"And who, underneath all the grime and desperation, proved..." He shrugged. "Well, a worthwhile associate."

"A worthwhile associate? Is that what you think of me?"

But Dinesh grinned, and his eyes sparkled. I realized he was baiting me.

"Oh, my cocky little rooster. I think many other things about you. All of them gracious, but some of them very, very perverse."

I cleared my throat, licking gravy off my lower lip, and wanting to climb into his lap for a passionate kiss. But, though we were amongst other social outcasts, I didn't dare. Not all of them would be supportive of two men being intimate in public, and I didn't want to take any chances.

"In fact," Dinesh continued, "if you'll finish your meal and drink your ale, we should go up and make some use of the lovely Domingo."

"Aye, Captain," I said, wanting nothing more than to fulfill his every fantasy.

When we were done, Captain Martin paid the innkeeper for the meal and arranged for a room upstairs, where we could stay the night once Domingo had entertained us. I'd never been treated to such luxury, nor had anyone spent this amount of coin on making me happy.

The room itself was adequate and quite clean for such a place. We left our fine jackets and hats, then went to find Domingo. On the lower two floors, we passed a good many closed doors, behind which came the sounds of carnal enjoyment. Captain Martin grinned and wagged his eyebrows at me, no doubt imagining what was to unfold behind Domingo's door this evening.

That feeling of unease I'd had on first coming to Cayonne had faded over a hot meal and a tankard of ale. But I was anxious once more, now that we were standing outside of room 18.

The captain raised his hand to knock.

"Wait," I said.

His relaxed fist hung in the air as he gave me a questioning look. "But why? What are you scared of?"

Are you truly asking me this?

"Captain... Dinesh..." I whispered.

His lips parted at the unusual use of his given name. I'd only ever used it once or twice.

"What if this changes things between us?"

His expression softened. "Oh, Rooster. How could it?"

I levelled my gaze at Dinesh. "Have you seen him?"

"Rooster. He's lovely and beautiful and sweet, but not any more than you."

I frowned.

"Not even *as much* as you. You are much prettier than Domingo."

I felt a bit better.

"Really?"

He didn't answer right away, as if he had to think on his assertion. The corners of my lips drew down.

"Yes. At least, to me, you are."

Wait a second. That was some backhanded compliment nonsense.

I sighed, giving up my protests, because I really did want to tup Domingo and put on a show for Captain Martin. He had no idea what he was in for, and I only hoped that Domingo was as acrobatic and creative as the captain had implied.

"Fine."

"If you really don't want to..." he said, his voice low.

"I do want to. I just needed to know I was prettier," I said with a saucy toss of my chin-length hair.

Captain Martin grinned and clapped his hands together. "Excellent."

He rapped on the door with his knuckles.

"It's Dinesh and Simon," he said, and I understood that we were suddenly on a first-name basis with Domingo. I suppose that made sense as we were about to be very intimate with him.

"*Pasa*", came a voice from inside the room.

Dinesh twisted the handle and pushed the door open. He moved into the dimly lit space and I followed.

We were greeted with a terrible high-pitched whistle that made us step back.

"Never mind. That's just Esmaralda."

"Pardon?" Captain Martin asked.

"My name is Esmaralda. Who the fuck are you?"

My breath caught, as I imagined we'd been found out. Not that we were doing anything illegal here. At least, I didn't think we were.

"Esmaralda. Stop it. That's enough."

"Who the fuck are you? Who the fuck are you?" Another whistle, some clicking noises, and then: "My name is Esmaralda. Esmaraaaalda. Esmaraaaalda."

"Never mind her; she's a rude-assed cunt."

"She's a rude-assed cunt. She's a rude-assed cunt." The words were spoken in a precise replication of Domingo's tones and cadence.

"Yes, you are, my darling, but I do love you so."

I finally determined where the strange words were coming from. Not another person, as I'd supposed, but—quite unbelievably—from a diminutive black bird, with white marks and a small pointy black beak, perched on the corner of a desk, bobbing its tiny head in agitation.

"What the fuck is that?" Captain Martin asked.

"I beg your pardon?" Domingo asked, putting a hand to his chest in shock.

"I'm so sorry. I mean, is that bird saying those things?"

"Yes, I'm afraid so. She's a rude-assed cunt, my Esmaralda."

"Rude-assed cunt," the bird said again, this time in a woman's voice with a slight French accent.

A man Carago had known had kept a parrot, and the brightly coloured bird had been able to repeat words and phrases, but not with the vocal perfection that Esmaralda possessed.

"Remarkable," Captain Martin said, staring at the bird as if she were the second coming of Christ. "How does she do that?"

"She's a mynah bird. They are excellent mimics."

"My name is Esmeraalda. My name is Esmeraaaaaalda!" said

in the woman's voice.

"All right, Essie. We all know your name now."

"Rude-assed cunt!" The bird echoed Domingo again.

Domingo laughed, a lovely sound. But I was off center about the bird who spoke in tones so reminiscent of a person. Esmaralda's talent was eerie and strange and almost unbelievable, but I was there to witness her skill.

"She was a gift from a friend who had to leave us," Domingo said, looking somber. "And I don't know that I quite realized what I was taking on. But at least I still get to hear Claire's voice every day."

Captain Martin smiled. "I take it Claire was also a…person in your line of work?"

"Of course. So the bird doesn't have fancy manners." Domingo shrugged. "Well, neither do I, so we get along well."

The room was not that big, but it had a large window with velvet curtains pulled to keep out the night, and was lit by a few pretty oil lamps in sconces. Incense burned on a side table, a wisp of smoke trailing upward and filling the room with the scent of orange and spices.

Domingo lay on a large bed that was positioned against one wall and covered with silks and pillows. He lounged on his back with one knee bent, his feet bare, and a chartreuse silk robe—the only thing he wore—sliding off one shoulder and belted loosely at his waist. The bright colour popped against his olive skin and gave him the air of a French courtesan.

He was as expensive as one, to be sure.

In one corner, I noticed a large wooden cage with perches placed at varying heights. The hinged gate was open as the bird had free run at the moment.

"Hello, Simon," Domingo purred.

I turned to face him.

"Is your belly quite full now?" he asked in his sultry baritone.

"Hello, Domingo. It's full of hock and potato. But there's room for more."

Domingo's eyes went wide at that, and he flashed a look at the captain.

"Oh, I like him already. And he's so very beautiful and small. Where did you find him, Dinesh?"

"Oh, he found me, actually. Begged to come aboard the *Arrow* and said he'd take any job I offered him."

"I see," Domingo said with a laugh. "And has he fulfilled that promise?"

Esmaralda chirped and then mimicked Domingo's melodic laugh with incredible accuracy.

Chapter Fourteen

Respite

Dinesh ignored Esmaralda and turned to me.

"In spades. Rooster has been absolutely invaluable to me and to the *Arrow*, both."

"Rooster?" Domingo asked. "Is your nickname Rooster because of your big—"

"Put it in! Put it in!" the bird shouted.

"Dear God," Captain Martin muttered. "Won't that bird shut up?"

Domingo regarded Captain Martin with much fondness and amusement.

"Only if I put her in her cage."

"Won't you?"

"That'll be an extra five gold pieces."

"For fuck's sake."

"Yes, exactly that."

"Take him out back! Pummel the blackguard!" Esmaralda squawked.

"I'll pay it! I'll pay the fee," Captain Martin said, eyeing the small black bird with distaste and fishing for more coin from his purse.

Meanwhile, my heart had warmed at the praise he'd given me.

"I appreciate what you said, Captain," I said, as he placed five more coins in Domingo's outstretched hand. "The feeling is...mutual."

Well, I loved him, in fact. But I didn't dare speak of my true feelings. I was supposed to be a heartless privateer officer and a witch, as well. If I spoke of love, what did that make me? Bad enough in the eyes of society that I was a sodomite, a pirate, and a witch. I could at least pretend that I didn't have feelings that could be hurt, or a heart that could be broken. Maybe if I didn't name it, the universe would let me keep it.

"Esmaralda. In your cage, darling," Domingo said.

Immediately, the bird hopped across the desk and through the open door of her cage.

"Time for bed. Time for bed," she sang.

"Yes, quite," Domingo muttered, reaching behind him for a string that, once pulled, lowered an opaque black cloth over the bird's cage. And all was quiet.

"Is that all it takes? To quiet her?"

"Generally. There's food in there, and she won't disturb us." He smiled. "She's quite used to hearing all sorts of sounds from this bed."

Domingo licked his bottom lip as his fingers moved to the

sash of his robe, playing with the knot until the belt came undone, and the edges of his robe fell away, revealing his completely naked body.

I gasped as the captain chuckled.

Domingo's skin contained nary a trace of dark hair, a fact which surprised me greatly. From his name and the fact that the hair on his head grew so thick, I had expected a similar level of coverage on his chest and in his private area. There was nothing but a sheen of oil covering him.

"Mmm. I see you're looking after yourself as well as always, Dom," the captain murmured, his gaze roaming over the beautiful man and flaring in a way with which I was familiar.

Domingo inclined his chin with a graceful and silent acknowledgement of Captain Martin's praise. He traced those long fingers along his throat and over his chest and then across his midriff, to where his cock lay half-hard and dark against his thigh, as he lifted his gaze to that of Dinesh.

"Take off your clothes, Rooster," Captain Martin said, holding Domingo's gaze, as he drew off his jacket and tossed it onto a chair.

The tension was thick in the room as I pulled off my jacket and started to unbutton my waistcoat. Domingo's words brought a halt to my actions.

"Oh, please, Dinesh, may I do it? I want to undress your pretty Rooster."

I glanced up to find both of them regarding me like they were ready to pounce. My cock had already swollen but got even bigger now, especially at the excited look in Captain Martin's eyes.

"Of course," Captain Martin said. "Slowly, whilst I watch."

Domingo smiled and stood with a feminine grace. He slunk towards me, chartreuse robe dragging on the wood floor, sleeves falling to his elbows, as the garment did nothing to conceal his nakedness.

I swallowed, my fingers frozen on the buttons as Domingo approached. I risked a quick glance at Dinesh, and almost moaned at the expression on his face as he worked at the fastenings on his waistcoat and then his shirt.

The scent of cinnamon and evergreen came from Domingo. The nostalgic fragrance calmed me at the same time that it ignited my blood. He stood before me like some kind of vision of beauty created from my own imagination. He placed a delicate hand on my frozen fingers, nudging them aside as he smiled seductively.

"Put yourself at ease, Rooster," he whispered. He raised his brows. "Do you mind if I call you that?"

I shook my head from side to side as quick breaths puffed from my mouth. I really didn't mind. I liked the captain's nickname for me.

"Just enjoy the fact that I am here to serve you in whatever way you desire."

"Or that I desire," Captain Martin added.

"Of course, Captain," Domingo said.

"Yes. Right. I know." I sounded like a dimwit. I didn't know why I was so unsure of myself. Normally I was full of confidence when it came to this sort of thing, although I'd never received the attentions of an expensive—*or inexpensive*—whore before.

Domingo smiled as he unbuttoned my fine waistcoat and pushed the garment over my shoulders. His fingers went to the buttons of my shirt as my arms hung helplessly at my sides.

"What can I do to ease you, Rooster darling? What can I possibly do to make you feel more comfortable?" Domingo asked in a teasing voice as he finished with the buttons and pushed my shirt off.

"Oh…I…well…" I stuttered, my gaze fixed on Domingo's lips.

"Swallow his cock, perhaps?" Dinesh offered.

My gaze flashed to the captain as he settled himself—bare from the waist, a distinct bulge in his breeches—into a lush armchair with a view of the proceedings.

"Yes, I was going to suggest it," Domingo murmured as flames shot up my spine.

My breaths came even quicker, and when Domingo's fingers worked the buttons on my fall-front breeches, I moaned as his knuckles brushed against the iron brand within.

Domingo gasped in exaggerated surprise.

"Oh! Goodness me, he's hard as fucking rock already."

"Yes, that's my randy Rooster. He can rise in an instant. He's awfully young, you know."

"How young?" Domingo asked. "Younger than me?"

"I'm twenty-two," I said, my voice catching with a gasp.

Domingo smiled. "I've only just turned twenty-one. But I've lived a hundred lifetimes already." He made the statement with a laugh and a toss of his hair, but I saw a flicker of pain in those eyes.

I watched with parted lips as Domingo let the flap of my breeches fall, revealing my prick in all its turgid glory. To be honest, my prick looked like a wee noodle most of the time, but I was rather proud of the thing in this state. Not a truncheon like the captain's, but my cock had its own sort of charm.

Domingo hissed and glanced up at me.

"Oooh, what a fine example of a man you are, Rooster," he purred, before wrapping his elegant fingers around me and bending to tongue the tip.

As wet warmth surrounded me, I met the captain's intense gaze and moaned.

Domingo whimpered as he pulled off me, looking over his shoulder at the captain.

"Well, aren't you the lucky man? He's really lovely, isn't he?"

"Mmm," Dinesh murmured. "Wait until you see his sweet little—"

I coughed and cleared my throat, embarrassed to be spoken about in such a way.

"Oh, I can't wait. But first I want to sample this lovely sabre he's waving at me. Are you quite comfortable over there, Captain?"

"Aye. Never mind me. Give the lad a suck to remember. And one that's worth the price I paid for the pleasure."

Domingo rolled his eyes. Then he turned back to me and let go long enough to shrug out of his robe completely. He dug in one pocket and pulled out a length of ribbon, with which he spent a moment tying back his lovely hair. I waited in some kind of erotic thrall, caught between the two of them—a helpless plaything to be spoken of and entertained. A role I'd been born to play.

"Now then," Domingo said, placing his delicate hands—as dainty as any woman's—on his bare thighs as he regarded the salute before him. "Do tell me when you're about to overflow, will you?"

I didn't have a chance to respond before he'd gripped my cock at the base and swallowed me down. I fought against finishing so soon and barely managed to hold back. Breaths stuttered out of my mouth, along with broken cries and long moans as I closed my eyes and enjoyed his attentions.

Domingo's skills were considerable. There was an air about him too—a vulnerability and sincerity—even though he worked in a brothel. I lost myself in the feel of Domingo's warm, soft mouth. When I opened my eyes, I saw Captain Martin watching us with his lips parted and his hand down his breeches. A surge of pleasure hit me so hard, I let my hand drop to Domingo's head and gave him the warning.

"I'm going to—" I gasped just before my cock overflowed.

Domingo slid off me, quite elegantly for someone with an unexpected load of spend in his mouth—although I supposed he'd been somewhat ready. He let the milky fluid spill down his chin, as if he'd drunk a jug of milk too quickly, then wrapped his fingers around me to stroke me through my culmination, his eyes like firebrands.

Then Captain Martin was there, bending down and guiding Domingo's mouth to his, kissing him hard, licking my seed from Domingo's lips and chin whilst I watched in a dazed and depleted state.

I drifted in a comfortable haze, watching Dinesh and Domingo as they embraced with passion before me. Domingo melted like a cherished bride against Captain Martin, succumbing to him, either in sincere thrall, or very well-acted forbearance. The captain devoured him with his kisses, glancing at me as if wanting to enjoy us both in any way he could.

My desire returned quickly, watching the two of them together.

I stepped out of my boots and breeches and leaned against the mantel of the small fireplace, in which a low fire burned. I wrapped my arms around my chest and watched while Captain Martin sucked two fingers into his mouth, then slid them down the crack of Domingo's shapely arse as he held him still in his embrace.

Domingo gasped as Dinesh breached him, going up on his toes against the taller man and letting his face slide to the side as he gazed at me with intensity and hunger.

"Won't your right-hand man deign to fuck me?" Domingo

asked in a voice roughened by passion.

"He will if I tell him to," Captain Martin said.

"And will you?"

"Of course."

"Oh, wonderful. Let's have some fun, Dinesh. I haven't been properly ravished in ages."

"I find that hard to believe," Captain Martin murmured.

"I said *properly*. I've been disappointed quite enough, thank you."

I was focused on not acting like a star-struck innocent, which I most assuredly was not. However, the sense of professionalism and experience that Domingo exuded was intimidating. He appeared an expert in his field.

"Rooster, has the cat got your goddamned tongue?" Captain Martin asked, pumping his fingers in and out of Domingo with undisguised delight and enthusiasm. "Normally I can't get you to shut up unless I gag you."

Well, that did it.

"I beg your pardon, Captain," I said, straightening up and scowling at his audacity. "I'm in the process of recovering from a masterly suck, I'll have you know. And there isn't much to say now, is there? Unless you want a blow-by-blow account of my experience as a side piece to you and this beautiful molly who hordes a bevy of secrets in his lovely brown eyes."

But the captain grinned and nodded.

"There he is. That's the cocky rooster I've grown to love."

I blinked, cut off by the captain's unexpected use of the endearment.

"Love, is it?" Domingo gasped, riding Dinesh's fingers as if that were his lifelong occupation. "I could have guessed."

"Truly?" I whispered, looking at Domingo and the captain

both for confirmation that I'd heard Dinesh correctly.

Domingo looked smug, and Captain Martin benignly satisfied.

"Of course. I knew your feelings for him immediately. They are written on your annoyingly handsome face." Domingo waved his fingers in the air and then surged against Dinesh on another jab of those long fingers. "Oh God, Dinesh, you're such a fucking tease. Give over to your right-hand man. I want you to watch him ravish me and imagine him doing the same to you."

Captain Martin grinned. "Well, he'd have to beg me for a very long time. I don't give over my arse to just anyone, you know."

Dinesh and I stared at one another, the import of his recent words echoing in the room.

Did I want to fuck Dinesh? It had been such a long time since I'd fucked anyone. Truly, I was better on the receiving end, and I enjoyed taking a man's cock so much. But, on the cusp of fucking Domingo, the possibility of eventually having such a chance with Dinesh intrigued me. I'd had no idea he'd even consider the option.

Now, looking at Domingo, a flushed and oiled and alluring rag doll in Captain Martin's embrace, I wanted to prove to the captain that I could do the deed, and do it well.

My desire had returned in spades and I nodded.

"Fine," I said. "I might as well drill the pretty whore. We've paid enough."

Domingo's eyes went wide, and then he threw back his head and cackled as Captain Martin withdrew his attentions and pushed Domingo onto the bed, gazing at me with pride.

"On your hands and knees then, beautiful boy," he said as Domingo hastened to obey.

"And *you*," he said, pushing his trousers off as he gave me a look of lust and emotion and dominance. "Do me proud. Show him what my right-hand man is made of."

I found myself grinning, then laughing. My unease had vanished, and I had begun to appreciate the unique dynamic contained in these four walls.

"Oh, I'll show you," I said, grabbing my cock and waving it at Domingo, who lay in a seductive position on the bed, gazing at me with a smirk and heavy eyelids, idly touching himself.

The captain winked, and I let go of myself, becoming serious and moving towards the sultry boy on the bedsheets.

"Oooh, Officer White," Domingo moaned. "Please show me how a privateer officer deals with a paid whore, if you please?"

Well, I really had no idea how a privateer officer would act in any situation. I desired to be fierce and passionate, but I also wanted to take care that I didn't overstep Domingo's graciousness. Yes, we had paid a pretty penny for him, but he wasn't an object to be bartered with. He was a person, the same as me or the captain. He'd been dealt a rotten hand in life, as had I. Our bad fortune didn't make us any less deserving of good treatment.

Dinesh had thrown a blanket over the armchair and settled his naked self in the comfy spot. He gave me a nod to go ahead.

"If I remember correctly, Domingo likes a good slap to the arse."

Domingo went to all fours, pulling his hair over one shoulder so its bulk didn't obscure the length of his slim torso and petite waist. He gazed at me over the other one.

"Do it, Mr White. I've been ever so naughty."

"I'm certain that's true," I said. "How's this?"

I hauled my arm back and brought my hand down on his right arse cheek. The sound of flesh-on-flesh reverberated off the walls as Domingo's buttock bounced and quivered.

"Oooh, yes. Again!"

I slapped him again, to the sounds of Captain Martin's laughter.

"Take it from behind!"

We froze at Esmaralda's sudden statement from under the black cloth, then all burst out laughing.

"Take it from behind! Put it in! Put it in!" the bird continued as Captain Martin and I tried to curb our hilarity.

"Shut the fuck up, you bloody cunt!" Domingo yelled, throwing a pillow at the cage. The yellow cushion bounced off and luckily didn't dislodge the cover.

"You are a cunt. Nasty cunt!" the bird replied.

"Fuck," Domingo muttered, hanging his head in frustration. "Never mind. Keep going, but harder. I'm not made of china."

"Pummel the blackguard!" Esmaralda yelled, but we ignored her.

"You heard him, Rooster. Go harder. He's had a better spanking at the hands of a maiden, I reckon."

I scowled at Dinesh, not enjoying my manhood being made sport of, then doubled down on the pretty tart's arse.

"Oh yes. Yes! Fuck, yes. Thats... Oh! God!"

Esmaralda gave a whistle, then yelled, "What a trollop!"

"Enough," Captain Martin said to me, finally. "Now I want to watch you fuck him."

Domingo was panting hard, his chest and cheek pressed to the mattress, his rosy arse in the air. He spread his knees and sighed. "Oooh, yes."

Esmaralda was quiet. Perhaps she was intent on listening.

Domingo moaned and made eager sounds as he gazed back at me, his puckered hole visible and glistening with oil. "See? I'm ready for you, Rooster."

Captain Martin took a seat on the bed beside us, facing me. He used his hands to spread Domingo's cheeks further so his hole stretched and he made a vulnerable sound.

"Pass me that oil. I'll make sure he's slick enough for you."

My fingers trembled as I passed him the bottle. Now that we were getting down to the act, I was plagued with unease. The idea of being watched by Dinesh was, on the one hand, exhilarating and perverse, but on the other, intimidating. What if I made a mess of this? It had been such a long time since I'd used my prick this way. Yes, fucking was fucking, and I was, at heart, an animal with base instincts—that couldn't be argued.

I shook my head, trying to get the unwelcome thoughts to leave me be. I focused on the rising lust and the image of oil dripping down Domingo's crack as Dinesh tipped the bottle.

"Put it in! Put it in!" Esmaralda ordered from her cage, which added insult to injury.

Domingo groaned as the oil made a path along his skin, then gasped as the captain spread the slick over his hole and taint and pushed two fingers inside.

"Oh, fuck me, Captain Martin. You do know how to touch a man."

"Yes, well, I've had years of practice."

"Slattern," Domingo muttered.

"Beautiful, dirty, whore," Captain Martin said in the sweetest of tones as if he were conferring upon Domingo the highest of praises.

"Nasty cunt!" Esmaralda screamed.

But we were getting used to her rude interruptions and didn't pay her any mind, although the fact that she sounded so human remained unsettling to a degree.

The captain used his other hand to spread Domingo again so

the oil pooled and moistened every bit of him.

"There you go, Rooster. Have at it."

"Fuck," I said. Now that I was staring at the beautiful arse of the sweetest whore I'd ever laid eyes on, I wanted nothing more than to fuck him. The intimacy of what the three of us were about to do was intoxicating.

I got on my knees behind Domingo, and met Dinesh's gaze as I nudged the head of my cock where it yearned to go.

"You'd better watch what you're doing, Rooster," Captain Martin suggested. "Don't look at me. Look at the man beneath you."

I mean, he had a point.

I swallowed and dug my fingers into Domingo's hip to keep him steady as I pushed my cock inside him.

Captain Martin cursed. Domingo moaned. Esmaralda whistled and clucked.

As my prick sank into Domingo's velvety warmth, my eyes rolled back in my head from the pleasure. Had topping another man ever been this good? My instincts and my lust took over as I pushed in all the way.

"Oh my God..." I gasped, as I gave Domingo soft thrusts that elicited gorgeous sounds and a comment from Captain Martin.

"Jesus Christ and all the angels," Dinesh murmured in awe as I opened my eyes to meet his gaze. A surge of excitement hit me, solely from our connection. I moved into a quicker rhythm, encouraged by Domingo's vocal reaction. The sounds he made could have been an act, but I chose to believe he was enjoying himself.

Chapter Fifteen

Escape

"Wait," Dinesh said, and I froze, because I was used to obeying him. "Don't move."

He let go of Domingo and surged onto his knees beside me. His mouth found mine, and he breathed into me, plunging his tongue inside as he slid his slick fingers down my back and into the crack of my arse. Before I could comprehend what was happening, he'd breached me with two fingers and sank them deep.

I let out a surprised whimper that became a low groan of intense pleasure.

I cursed, my hips moving of their own accord to get the needed friction from Domingo's passage, as the captain pushed his long fingers in and out of me.

"Oh fuck, fuck, fuck...Captain!" I yelled as I spent, jerking and clutching Domingo's hips to keep him close as I thrust impossibly deep.

"Aaaah!" Domingo cried. "Oh, yes. Yes!"

Esmaralda whistled and muttered, "What a trollop," in annoyed tones.

Dinesh gave me two final jabs and withdrew his fingers.

"Out. Now."

His voice was strangled and urgent, and I knew what he wanted.

I pulled out of Domingo and collapsed onto the bed beside him, watching as Dinesh spread Domingo wide and pushed in, his way eased by the copious amounts of oil and spunk that lingered.

That sight would stay with me—Dinesh bollocks deep in the gorgeous olive-skinned whore, Domingo given up to genuine pleasure, moving together as one excited beast.

Strangely, I wasn't jealous. Instead, I was filled with an appreciation for the beauty and rawness of the tableau—two men joining in shameless intimacy and passion, rising above this dreary plane of existence into an ecstatic realm, where physical pleasure and human connection were the only things that mattered.

Domingo's luxurious dark hair stuck against his face, his head turned to the side on the sheets, eyes closed and mouth open, as Captain Martin caged him with his powerful arms and thrust quick and hard, his forehead resting between Domingo's shoulders. As I watched, he brought one hand to Domingo's swollen prick, and stroked fast, helping the younger man to reach his pinnacle in moments. Domingo gave an inhuman cry as his cock erupted with streams of white onto the sheets. Captain Martin spent soon after, groaning and gasping as the intensity took his breath away.

Domingo recovered quickly, opening his eyes and giving me a lazy, satisfied smile.

"I can see how you claimed the position of right-hand man on the *Arrow*, Officer White."

"Aye," I said, smiling and blushing. "'Tis one I'm made for."

Captain Martin gave another little groan and pulled out of Domingo, wiping himself with a corner of the sheet.

"Stay as you are, Domingo. Rooster, come and see."

He crooked a finger, beckoning me to where he sat on his heels behind Domingo's splayed knees. Once I had a good viewing angle, he spread the globes of Domingo's arse and used his thumbs to stretch the glistening hole. A glob of thick fluid pushed out and slid down Domingo's taint as Dinesh sighed and gathered the substance with his finger.

"Fuck," I murmured, as he used the digit to shove his spunk back in.

Domingo whimpered as the captain played with his hole, causing more fluid to ooze out. Such a filthy sight that I couldn't stop watching. The desire rose within me again.

I grabbed the captain's chin, turning his face to me. I kissed him hard, surging up against him.

His arms wrapped around me, and he held me close as he plundered my mouth. We lost ourselves to each other, and after a short time, our renewed excitement made itself known.

"Mmm, my sweet little witch. How about we show Domingo how we fuck *each other*?"

"Yes, please. Please, please, please."

"Put it in! Put it in!" Esmaralda sang.

Dinesh rolled his eyes. "I intend to, you bloody bird. Now shut the fuck up."

He spoke so sternly that, even though we waited for a

response from the bird, nothing came. Only the sounds of rustling as she—hopefully—settled herself down to sleep.

Domingo sat demurely against the carved headboard of his large bed, wrapped in the chartreuse robe, knees bent and lying to one side. He combed his tumble of hair lazily with his fingers.

"Oh yes." He nodded. "I would like that very much."

"I don't suppose you have any soft rope or leather cords?" Captain Martin asked, his eyebrows raised as he clutched me to him.

"Oh, fuck," I muttered.

"As a matter fact, you will find just the thing in the second drawer of that cabinet," Domingo said, gesturing to a chest of drawers with elaborate wood scrollwork that stood against the wall on the other side of the room.

After several moments, the captain had me trussed up like a roasting hen, much to Domingo's amusement.

The beguiling man crawled over to examine my predicament more closely and leaned down to kiss the corner of my mouth where the cloth gag, which the captain had fashioned from a silk scarf, stretched my lips.

"Oh, he has quite a skill with knots, our captain, doesn't he?"

Dinesh laughed. "I should think so. Rope work is an important skill for any mariner."

I whimpered as Domingo trailed his fingers down to tickle my balls and cock before returning to his former spot and making himself comfortable again.

"This is what we like, isn't it, little witch?" Captain Martin said, his expression smug and his eyes filled with heat.

I nodded, filled with both a sense of safety in my rope confines, and an anticipation of imminent danger. Well, danger in the form of whatever indignity the captain had in mind for me this evening. With another man in the room, I still had no issue giving myself to Dinesh in this way. Domingo's presence made everything more exciting now.

"Excuse me for being daft, Dinesh," Domingo said, "but why do you call him your little witch? Has your little rooster put a hex on you?"

My eyes went wide. I entreated Dinesh with no words, only the trepidation in my eyes, not to reveal my secret.

"Well," he murmured, leaning down to brush the hair out of my eyes. "My rooster has bewitched me for certain, and I shall never recover."

My chest flooded with heat as my body ached with the need to spend my passion. I made a pitiful, submissive sound.

"You best get on with your tupping, then. I don't think he's going to last very long. We've had a stimulating evening."

"Haven't we, just?" Dinesh replied. "And, yes, I think you're right. Are you ready, Simon? I'm going to ravish you in front of Domingo, so you'd best close your eyes and pretend we're in our rooms on the *Arrow*."

I made a desperate sound and did as he'd bid, closing my eyes and giving myself over, thinking of Domingo watching. What followed was a thorough and lazy fucking that made the most of my captured position and allowed the captain full access to any part of me.

I thought I might die, as the screwing went on and on, and Domingo's prediction was proved wrong in the extreme. The captain tortured me for ages, not in an urgent state himself after having already achieved satisfaction earlier. I, however, went into a state of pure submission and floated on a haze of desperation, need, and waning and rising excitement.

Finally, *finally*, after he satisfied himself with a restrained and cursory grunt, he pulled out and descended on me with three fingers up my hole and his mouth around my cock until I convulsed and screamed, emptying down his throat.

I must have lost consciousness for a brief time. I heard the sound of Domingo's laughter and slow clapping as I came to and blinked my eyes open to the captain's concerned face.

"There he is. Welcome back, my darling," Captain Martin said as he untied the gag and pulled the soaked cloth from my mouth.

"You fucking bastard," I whispered, completely spent and utterly exhausted.

"Yes, that I am," he agreed as he gazed upon me fondly and with much satisfaction.

"That was quite the sight, I'll admit," Domingo said. "I rarely get the chance to sit back and enjoy the torment of another. Thank you both very much."

"Entirely *our* pleasure, to be sure," Captain Martin said, untying the knots that had held me still for him. "We've been on the ship a long spell. Jolly to fuck on solid land for a change."

I had to agree with that. We hadn't had to worry about the rocking of the ship, or any of the crew needing us. Once I was loose, and the captain had rubbed the blood back into my limbs, I accepted his offer of a glass of water that Domingo had brought.

"Your rude bird has gone quiet, at last," Dinesh said, eyeing the covered cage in the corner.

"Yes. She's rude, I'll admit, but I love her dearly." He shrugged. "No accounting for taste, I suppose."

"We should go up to our room and sleep," the captain said to me. "You look like you're barely awake as it is."

I gave him an incredulous look. "I beg your pardon. You try being taken to the edge of heaven and pulled back multiple times, after having fucked the most lovely whore on earth, and then experiencing the closest thing to God and the angels in a moment of release, and tell me how *you* feel."

"'The most lovely whore on earth'?" Domingo said, gazing at where I lay near him. "Well, I thank you very much for that compliment, Rooster," he said, brushing the hair off my forehead. "I have had a wonderful time, which isn't always the case when you run a business out of your arse. I shall remember you fondly, as I remember Dinesh. You've been absolutely wonderful clients."

And, in the end, that was all that we were to Domingo. Yet I went away from our encounter with an appreciation and a fondness for the beautiful man in the chartreuse robe who had entertained us and watched us enjoy each other.

Captain Martin took me upstairs and tucked me in with a kiss and a murmur of profound affection.

"Aren't you coming to bed?" I said, barely able to speak. I was so tired.

"Soon, my love. I want to take a walk on the streets of Cayonne and check in on the crew. We need to be back on the *Arrow* in a few days, and they may need reminding not to completely demolish themselves with the drink."

"All right. But don't be long."

*

I jolted up in bed and stared at the wall, where flashes of light splashed the cracking plaster and explosions rang in my ears. I barely had time to parse it when the door burst open and Captain Martin charged in.

"Get dressed. Now."

"What's the matter?" I asked, springing into panicked action, as the captain helped me find my clothes and get into them.

"The Spanish, damn their hides. They want the island back."

"Is it theirs?" I asked, still barely awake and unsure of what was happening.

"Used to be. They ceded to the French, but they're sore about losing the territory. Bad luck that we happen to be here during a raid."

"Dinesh!"

We looked up to see Domingo, his hair wild and the knotted chartreuse robe the only thing covering his nakedness, except that now he wore a pair of leather boots and carried a square object in one hand.

"Put it in! Put it in!"

Captain Martin frowned at the covered cage from which the voice of Esmaralda, Domingo's mouthy mynah, was issuing.

"Not the bird, Domingo."

"I'm not leaving her."

"For fuck's sake."

"I'll take my chances in the streets without you, if you make me give her up."

I stared at the captain, honestly wondering as to his response.

"Fuck it. Fine. Bring her, then." He turned to me. "Hurry."

"Domingo's coming?" I asked.

"Aye. He'll be killed if he stays here," Dinesh muttered.

I didn't want Domingo killed. I wasn't sure I wanted him on the *Arrow*, either, but at this point we'd be lucky to get out of Cayonne. My gut roiled with fear.

"I'm sorry, *chica*," Domingo said. "I won't be a burden, I promise," he said.

He looked pale and frightened, and that, more than anything else, made me hurry even more as a panicked sweat broke on my neck. I pulled my jacket over my unbuttoned shirt and grabbed the captain's outstretched hand.

"Let's go."

We raced down the stairs, colliding with other scantily clad whores who had decided their best bet was outside.

"Domingo!" A dark-skinned woman yelled. "Where are you going? Don't leave us, you scoundrel!"

Domingo turned briefly and blew the woman a kiss. "I'm sorry, Beulah, but I've a new assignment! Thanks for the memories, darling!"

And we were gone.

Coming out of the Turnkey into the dim city streets, where people ran to and fro, and bursts of fire lit up the night was terrifying, and I clutched Dinesh's hand like a frightened child as he pulled me along, Domingo keeping close to both of us, the covered cage clutched under his arm.

"This is not how my night was supposed to go," he panted, tucking a length of hair behind his ear and rushing along next to us.

"Nor mine," Dinesh muttered, guiding me past multiple desperate people who ran in all directions.

"Will we make the docks?" I voiced my main fear.

"They're our best bet. We must."

"But the crew..."

"They're all making a run for the skiffs. I was with some of them when the attack began, but I ran back to get you and Domingo."

"Thank the Gods!" A strike of fear shot up my spine imagining him not coming back for me and what that would have been like.

"I wasn't leaving without you, Rooster. If that meant my

death, then I was prepared for the end."

"Don't speak of such things, Dinesh. We'll be all right," Domingo said, and I'd never appreciated him more.

"Yes, we will," Captain Martin agreed.

When we got to the docks, someone yelled the captain's name.

"There's Guthrie! Thank God," he said and tugged me forward.

My hand slipped from his grip and I yelled out, but no sooner had I noticed, than I was immediately grabbed by Domingo and practically lifted off my feet.

"I've got you!" he said as he pulled me up.

Captain Martin had stopped when he'd lost hold, but seeing that Domingo had me, he gave a smile and a nod, and we all continued on at a fast pace.

I grasped Domingo's hand, so thankful he was with us, as we spied the waiting skiff filled with half the crew.

"The others are already at the ship. Let's make haste and leave this blasted place," Guthrie muttered.

"Quite!" The captain agreed, helping Domingo to get me into the boat as another voice shouted above the din.

"Wait! Wait!"

I looked in the direction of the cry to see none other than Squid racing towards us. He was dodging between frantic people and almost fell off the dock in a moment of carelessness.

"Come on, man!" the captain yelled. "Watch yourself!"

"We have to cast off, sir," Hillier said. "We daren't wait for anyone else!"

"He's almost here," I cried. "Just one more moment!"

I gazed at Dinesh with desperation in my eyes. We couldn't leave Squid. Not like this.

Captain Martin stood and leaned over the side of the skiff, reaching for Squid, who grabbed his hand like a lifeline and was tugged forward, falling into the boat as the captain yelled out, "Now! Go!"

The men on the oars managed to pull us away from the dock, far enough that we thought we'd make our getaway. We gazed onto the port city of Cayonne, where multiple structures burned and smoke obscured the stars.

Then came a drawn-out whistle of impending doom and hell was upon us.

Everyone shouted at once before a huge explosion shattered my eardrums and knocked me into the water. The world turned to fire and cold and darkness. I held my breath out of instinct, but I didn't know which way was up. As I lost my bearings and began to panic, a flame lit inside me, a white-hot rage taking me over before I had any chance to stop the rising power.

Again.

I burned like a fireball and the water lit up around me. I looked at my hands under the water, even as my lungs screamed for air. They were nothing but two balls of blue flame as the water around me became a maelstrom and propelled me in one direction with incredible force. I caught a glimpse of Dinesh through the waves, leaning over the side of the skiff, ready to dive for me. But then I surfaced and gasped a lungful of air, and he saw me.

"Rooster! Simon!" he yelled, reaching an arm out, but I was already there, and I couldn't grab onto him because my hands were on fire.

Instead, I grasped the edge of the skiff as the men looked on with palpable horror, and Domingo made the sign of the cross, his eyes wide.

My blue-fire fingers gripped the wood like strange claws, as

I recited the ancient words:

"Bring me the fire and the flame,
O'er the ocean, in my name.
Give me the lightning and the storm,
From the heavens, let it be borne.
Smite those who threaten what's mine.
They'll not have anyone this time.
Let the sea and the flame rejoice.
Let the ocean and sky make the choice."

I chanted them over and over as a storm of my making caused the wind to whip and the waves to toss. Rain pelted my face and sizzled against the heat of my hands. Flashes of lightning lit the sky as the storm surrounded us. I was bringing the wrath of hell upon us all. I didn't know what was happening, but I held the image of Captain Martin in my mind and repeated the words over and over again until, after a long time, everything became calm again.

I recognized the chant as some ancient incantation, long forgotten. Perhaps my mother had taught it me, or an unseen force had placed it deep within my memory. I kept saying the words, even as I was pulled aboard the small boat and cradled in someone's warm lap, a cold cloth placed over my hands that still burned with a hot fire.

"It's all right, my love. Rooster, you're safe now. We're safe." The captain's voice sounded in my ear, his arms around me.

I sobbed and turned my face into his clothes, inhaling his familiar scent like that alone would save me.

Where? Where are we? In hell, or in heaven, or someplace else?

Time became fluid. The skiff rocked and hands pulled at me, and the world turned upside down. I went up, up, and up. Then found darkness and peace, at last.

Chapter Sixteen

Aftermath

I woke with pounding pain between my ears and confusion.

Where am I? The water... Did I drown? Am I dead?

"He's awake, Dinesh. Look."

Domingo's voice.

Then I heard the captain's frantic tones as I struggled to open my eyes.

"Rooster! Dear God, Simon. Talk to me. Wake up! Please..."

A hand pressed to my forehead and then warm palms against my cheeks, and the softest touch of lips to mine.

My eyelids fluttered open. Dinesh's face came into focus as his frown turned into a jubilant smile. If I'd doubted his love before this moment, the truth was plain in the look he gave me now.

"Oh, thank heavens."

"My dear, you gave us quite the fright," Domingo murmured, and even he was gazing upon me with much affection and relief.

"Where am I?" I croaked.

"In my rooms, where you should be. Always. I've a mind to keep you here under lock and key." They were harsh words uttered lovingly.

Domingo laughed. "Now, now. Don't be ridiculous."

"What happened?" I asked, trying to make sense of what I remembered.

An explosion. Then I was drowning, then I was… Oh no…

Captain Martin put a steadying hand on my arm.

"We're safe on the *Arrow*, Simon. We're away."

"I unleashed my power again, didn't I? The storm…"

Domingo and Dinesh glanced at each other.

"Is everyone all right?" I whispered.

Captain Martin nodded, but he looked grave. "Most of them. There are a couple of men who—" He glanced at Domingo again, and Domingo frowned and gave his head a little shake. "—we don't know what happened to…"

I felt sick. "Because of me?"

"No, Rooster. You saved us. Again," Captain Martin said. "But two men are missing. They didn't get to the skiff in time."

I took in this information. But I needed to know. "Who?"

"Mr Silk, the carpenter's mate. And Duncan, the coxswain."

Mr Silk could tell a yarn like no other, and Duncan played his hornpipe for anyone who asked. They'd be missed.

"Are they still on the isle?"

No one answered me. Then Captain Martin smiled in a reassuring way.

"The ordeal is over now. Rest. How are you feeling?"

He was distracting me from my worry, and I decided to go

along with his plan, at least for now.

"My head feels like my brains got blown to pieces," I said. "My ears are ringing."

"Yes, there was an explosion. Most of us are dealing with that. Faraday says the sound will go away."

I lifted a hand from the bedcover to put my fingers to my head, but I froze when I saw the linen bandage wrapped around my palm. I looked at Dinesh.

"The storm. It helped us get away?"

"It did."

Domingo snorted with disdain. "Fuck, White, you brought down a vicious blast from the heavens. I wouldn't call that a storm."

"What would you call it, Domingo?" I asked.

"A judgement," he said, quite definitively.

He and Dinesh looked at each other again, and the gravity of their expressions worried me.

"What are you not telling me?"

Captain Martin's expression melded into one of exaggerated unconcern.

"Oh, no, don't worry. You saved us, once again. That's all."

"But the last time this happened, I obliterated an entire ship and its crew. Was there no damage done?" I stared at Captain Martin, who continued to smile, although the sentiment didn't reach his eyes.

"Are you a witch, Rooster?" Domingo asked in hushed tones.

"I have no idea," I said, tired of the question. Tired of wondering myself.

"Never mind," Captain Martin said. "Simon needs to eat. I'll go see Guthrie."

"There was some damage," Domingo said then, and Dinesh

levelled a sober stare his way. "To the dock. Enough that they couldn't come after us."

Captain Martin sighed.

"Yes. Well done," he said, but there was no enthusiasm to his words.

My stomach rumbled, and I wondered if some food might help my head. I couldn't worry about the secrets they were keeping, not right now.

"Could you please ask Guthrie if he's had time to make any of his raisin scones? How long have I been out of it?"

"You've been sleeping for nigh on two days, I'm afraid. I'm sure he's made all your favorite foods. Everyone's worried about you," he said.

"Truly?"

"Yes, Rooster. You've made many friends here."

Domingo stood. He'd changed from his robe into a pair of linen trousers and one of the captain's white shirts. The garment, much too big for him, made him look sweet and small. His dark hair was tied back with a ribbon, and the look suited him.

He lifted his chin and spread his arms, showing off. "I'm a buccaneer now, Mr White, ain't I? Perhaps I'll try living a different life."

"I think you'll have to," Captain Martin said. "You must have some skills beyond..." His face turned red, and he coughed.

Domingo grinned. "Beyond sodomy and prick eating, you mean?"

"Well..."

"Perhaps I do, but I don't know what they are."

That made me smile. I was pleased that Domingo was on board the *Arrow* and safe from harm, either from the Spanish invaders or from the men who bought his services. Perhaps he could find some skill that would serve him well in the future. For now, I supposed, he was crew.

As if reading my mind, Captain Martin turned to Domingo.

"I'll make an announcement to the crew that you're not to be trifled with. They respect and admire me, and I'll have your back, don't worry."

"Thank you, Dinesh."

"Guthrie has a spacious room near the kitchens. Perhaps you can bunk with him. The man is committed to celibacy, believe me. I've challenged that position for years but he won't budge. You'll be safe with him."

My eyes went wide. "What do you mean? Have you tried to bed *Mr Guthrie?*"

"Oh my goodness, no. For heaven's sake." He waved his hand in the air. "Merely philosophical discussions, around the idea and practice of celibacy. Don't be ridiculous."

I frowned. "He ain't a bad looking man, Mr Guthrie. I'd tup him."

The fib was worth seeing the look on the captain's shocked face and hearing Domingo's laughter.

Dinesh soon realized I was having him on.

"Shit disturber," he said.

"Philanderer."

"I'm not a—" Captain Martin started, then saw the grin on my face. "Dear God, nothing can keep you down for long, Rooster. I'm glad to see."

"I am honoured to be under your protection, Captain Martin," Domingo said with grace and inclined his head as the captain left for the kitchens.

Domingo glanced at my wrapped hands with some concern. "How are they?" he asked.

I shrugged. "The last time they were burned well and truly," I muttered. "Blistered and broken."

"Are they sore?"

"A bit. Raw, you know? Like when you stay in the sun for far too long."

Domingo nodded and opened his mouth but then closed it.

"You want to know what I am."

His gaze met mine. "I'm...curious. And a little...frightened, to be frank. And there's not a lot that frightens me anymore."

"There's nothing to be frightened of though. Everyone I care for turns out all right after. At least, they have so far."

Domingo's face betrayed astonishment. "Do you... Do you *care* for me, Simon White?"

"Of course, I do."

Domingo gave an astonished little laugh. "You'd be surprised how few ever have."

"That's horrible."

He shrugged. "Goes with the life I lead, I'm afraid." He frowned. "Led, I suppose. Perhaps that's all over now." His tone held a somber note.

"Will you miss that life?"

He pondered my question, tracing a finger along the seam of his trousers. "It's only that I've been living that way for so long. I feel...unmoored. I'll miss the silks and the finery, for certain. That part of the lifestyle I quite enjoyed."

I gazed on him with concern. "I'm certain we can find some fancy clothes for you, Domingo. Somehow."

"I'm not sure how practical that would be here on the ship."

I snorted. "Fuck practicality. Do what you want."

Domingo grinned, his eyes sparking. "Oh, I do like you, Rooster."

I smiled, too, my head beginning to feel much better and the ringing in my ears lessened.

*

The first time I ventured on deck after our escape, the men were predictably avoidant.

The *Arrow* had departed from parts near Tortuga and now sailed freely to the east, towards the Turks Islands. The morning had turned from overcast to bright, and the winds were steady. The creaking of her hull and the splashes of spray against her solid sides as the *Arrow* surged forward through the waves were a reassuring accompaniment.

Most of the men paid me as little attention as possible, pretending to be busy with important tasks. I'm sure they were busy, but the avoidance was intentional. They made sure they knew where I was.

Others were kinder.

Squid came right up to me and put his hand on my arm. "I thank you very much, Mr White. I thought I was a goner."

"We couldn't have left you, Squid. You're one of us now."

Then Lahiri and Martinez brought me some flowers.

I blinked in surprise at the kind gesture. "But where did you get them?"

"They're herbs, really. Mr Guthrie threatened to serve us up for supper when he saw us in his kitchen. But we grabbed these and ran."

I looked at the pretty sprigs that had been tied with a length of blue ribbon and thought about Guthrie in his galley watching them running away.

"You braved Guthrie's wrath for me? I'm honored. I hope he doesn't shit in your soup."

Their mouths gaped, and they glanced at each other in horror.

"Oh, I'm sure he won't. Probably," I added.

"We was wondering about that long-haired fellow youse brought aboard," Martinez said, glancing at Lahiri. "Is he what...we think he is?"

"What do you think he is?" I asked, blinking benignly.

Lahiri looked down and shook his head, but Martinez continued.

"A whore?" he said in hushed tones.

I stared at Martinez and frowned.

"Well, he doesn't do that any longer," I asserted.

Lahiri glanced up from his ropework nearby. "Aye. He's crew now. Whatever he did before don't matter."

I nodded and Martinez gave me a long look, then nodded in return.

"S'pose that makes sense. Most of us have pasts with some shame tied to 'em, I reckon."

"I reckon," I agreed. "His name is Domingo, and he's very sweet. Also tough. So I wouldn't say anything untoward to the man. He'll have you hung on the mainsail. He's tight with Captain Martin."

Martinez chuckled, then frowned. "Wait. How tight?"

"Never mind. We're friends, the three of us. That's all."

Martinez looked skeptical, and Lahiri rolled his eyes.

The captain's voice came from behind me.

"Ah, Rooster, there you are."

I turned around and was delighted to see him in his fancy captain's garb again. I couldn't help but admire the fine figure he cut.

"Do you need me, Captain?" I asked with exaggerated

innocence, my gaze dragging down his body like a fishnet dropping over a swimming shark.

"Most urgently, Roost—" He cleared his throat, smiling. "—Mr White." He corrected himself, a slight pink hue to his cheeks. He put his hands on his hips, trying to look sober and businesslike. "Ah, there's a...situation that I need you to...uh...address."

Snickers from Martinez and Lahiri as they took their leave.

"A situation?" I asked, my face a mask of concern. "My God, what kind of situation?"

Captain Martin checked his surroundings as he approached me. When he got close—too close for a regular gentleman's chat—he leaned in to my ear.

"The usual one."

I couldn't help the laugh that escaped me, and the smug look on Captain Martin's face was my reward.

"Oh, I see." I folded my arms across my chest and leaned against the rail. "And I'm supposed to simply jump, whenever you come to me asking for help with this?"

The captain said nothing, simply gazed at me with lust and longing. He shrugged.

I rolled my eyes. "Fine. Come along. I'll have you sorted in a moment."

"A moment!" he exclaimed, true shock on his handsome face. "I should hope it'll take longer than that."

I smirked. "If you're lucky."

Back in the captain's cabin, I took charge. Captain Martin observed me with amusement as I prepared the bed and bade him stand still whilst I took my time removing his lovely vestments.

"You know, my sweet red rooster, watching you fuck Domingo was a treat. I think on that evening often."

I grinned at him. "Do you?"

"I do. And you?"

I sighed. "Aye. But, to be honest, I only enjoyed our romp because *you* were there. I don't know if I'd have liked such an encounter as much otherwise."

"That's just as well," Captain Martin said.

"Is it?"

"Aye. Because I don't want you in another man's arms unless I'm involved somehow. Does that make me a terrible person?"

"Not at all. As I feel the same about you."

"Well, then."

"Well, then."

I folded his jacket neatly and put the garment on the chair. Then I stood before him and took my time unbuttoning his shirt.

"How are your hands?" Dinesh asked, gazing down at them.

When I'd removed the linen bandages, my palms had looked completely normal, which I had anticipated, as the same thing had happened previously. I showed him.

He took my wrist in his fingers and brought my palm towards him to examine the surface. Then he pressed his lips to the skin briefly and released me. He did the same to the other one.

I'd not known a kiss in that particular place could go straight to my cock, but it shot through me like lightning. I gasped and smiled. I went back to my unbuttoning. When I pulled the tails of his shirt out of his breeches, his hands wandered around my waist and went to cup my behind.

"No, no. Hands off. Let me do this. It's like Christmas morning."

He laughed. "Fine."

"Once you're naked you can take over. All right?"

"All right. Meanwhile, I shall contemplate all the horrible things I'm going to do to you."

"I'm sure they will be shocking and terrible."

"Most surely. You will be wracked with agony."

"As always." I grinned at him.

"As always." He matched my smile.

Although an agonizing trial to float in a haze of intense arousal, whilst not being allowed to finish, the experience also proved euphoric and blissful in a strange way, so I couldn't complain. Suffering at the hands of this man was everything.

I think letting me take my time with his disrobing was giving the captain a taste of his own medicine. He tried to go for me again, and I twisted away.

"No. Stop. Not yet."

He rolled his eyes and made a frustrated sound.

"Huh. Not much fun being on the other side of such torment?"

"Ah, but you see, it's against my dominant nature."

"Hmm. You think I'm naturally submissive?"

"Aren't you?"

"I suppose so," I admitted, not in the mood to argue. And he was probably right. "Yes, I'll give you that."

I unfastened his breeches and tugged them down, noticing that he had forgone the cotton undergarments he usually wore underneath.

"My goodness, Captain. How daring. What if we were suddenly set upon by vagabonds?"

"I'd wave my prick at them."

"They'd want to stay."

"No doubt."

The prick in question was full and standing, I was pleased to see. I went to my knees, hearing his sudden intake of breath.

"Rooster..."

"Yes, Captain?" I asked, gazing up and blinking innocently.

His expression was sober. "I want to thank you...for saving us all once again."

I stared at him in silence for a moment, unwilling to think on what had occurred—not right at this moment.

"Don't. I can't think about that."

"But you must. We need to figure out a way to control your powers."

I couldn't believe he was talking about this now.

"*We?* You mean, *I* need to."

"Well, I'll help you."

"I don't want to talk about this now."

"We will need to at some point," he insisted, and I wondered why he was insisting on a future conversation about something that confused and horrified me.

I lifted my hand. "Fine. But not now. Right now, I want to make your knees weak as you spend down my throat."

He gasped and nodded quite vigorously.

"Quite right. We can talk later."

However, I hoped that by the time we were done here, he would be too exhausted and satisfied to remember.

*

Domingo made friends easily.

He had taken to wearing the linen pants and too-large shirt with panache, by tying a red sash that he'd gotten somewhere around his slim waist and wearing bedroom slippers on deck. He must have brought the slippers with him somehow, because I recalled him wearing them in the room of our passionate encounter. I wasn't sure where they'd been tucked away on his person when he'd escaped with us, but I didn't want to contemplate it.

He'd also asked Lahiri to pierce one of his ears and now had a hammered metal fish hook hanging from his dainty lobe. He liked to tilt his head this way and that to have the charm glimmer in the sunshine. A vainer person I'd never met, yet he charmed the fuck out of us all. Perhaps that was why he'd been so good at his previous employment.

Esmaralda often hopped about on Domingo's shoulder as he walked around the ship and offered rude comments on the regular to the absolute delight of the crew. They'd even been teaching her new ones, which could scare the shit out of a person if you didn't know the bird was near, as she sounded just like the person who taught her.

"Got a fag? Got a fag?" she would say in Martinéz's voice, or, "Give over, Your Highness," in a perfect replication of Lahiri's sardonic tones. I was extremely proud of the "Your prick's the size of a gnat!" that I'd taught her. I knew for a fact that one fellow had been ready to pummel me for the insult as he'd not been aware of Esmaralda's presence and thought the speaker was me. The captain had had to demand that we stop teaching her these things because he anticipated the situation would end in bedlam and bruised egos.

But it proved impossible to *unteach* her what she'd learned, so we had to put up with the damage that had been done. I was secretly pleased that the endeavour had already earned me one spanking, and I had big plans to go against Dinesh's wishes and teach her to say, "The captain's dick is a truncheon!" because that would amuse me and certainly wouldn't lead to any misconstrued slights.

Mr Guthrie had been resistant to the idea of having help in the galley, but since Domingo didn't have any hands-on skills other than, as he himself described his proficiencies, 'sodomy and prick eating', Mr Guthrie agreed to the posting on a trial basis. He had also been reluctant to share his quarters with Domingo, knowing of his background, but they had soon eased into a benign association that might even be called a friendship.

Perhaps Domingo was relieved to be staying with a man who had sworn off sexual adventures of any kind and Mr Guthrie had realized that Domingo had had more than enough intimate encounters in his past to look for them now.

Our way was fairly easy. We avoided other vessels as much as possible, and if we did see any, we made sure to fly our decoy Dutch flag so we didn't become a target and were able to continue on without issue. The captain and Hillier had made the decision to sail eastward toward China.

Captain Martin had grand ideas about exploring the Asian lands. He said attitudes toward men tupping other men were different there, and he wanted to see if that was true and what that might mean for the two of us. Whether the crew realized that their beloved captain was thinking about abandoning his ship in favor of a land adventure, I wasn't sure.

I didn't say a thing about the captain's plans to anybody, but I was excited at the possibility of making a new life somewhere that wasn't on the ocean. I was grateful to be aboard the *Arrow*; don't get me wrong. The captain and his ship had saved me when I was most desperate and lost, and I treasured my place here. But I wasn't sure I wanted to live the rest of my life on this ship, and I had come to understand that neither was Captain Martin.

Chapter Seventeen

The Storm

On a subsequent afternoon, following an intensive rendezvous with the captain in his quarters, in between meetings that he had arranged with Hillier and Guthrie to discuss strategies and plans, I wandered up on deck to catch a breath of air.

The weather had been agreeable over the past few weeks, but as I came out of the sheltered hold, I spied skies like old porridge. The winds had picked up, and the *Arrow* was coursing like a thoroughbred over the waves. My hair had grown longer, and the wind whipped the feathery strands as I made my way over to Hanes, who stood at the rail with a worried look on his face.

"That don't look good," I said, starting to share his concern.

"No, it don't. Not at all. We're in for a pounding, I reckon."

I frowned, not wanting to consider a storm at all. "The

Arrow's got through bad weather before…"

She was a sturdy ship, her crew experienced and competent.

"Aye, but this looks worse than anything I've seen in months. Just before you came aboard, we had a terrible time. We'd docked at Port Royal to take our bearings and conduct repairs. I don't like the look of that out there."

Neither did I.

He cocked his head. "This ain't one of yours, is it?"

"Pardon?"

He gestured at me vaguely. "This ain't one of your vengeance spells? Like the one you summoned at Cayonne?"

I blinked. "No, of course not. It's a…a natural storm, I suppose."

"You got any power over that kind of weather? Because that might be handy."

"I don't think so. Those others… They're not really storms. I don't think. The truth is, Hanes, I don't know."

He nodded. "Well, why don't you go find Captain Martin, then, and let him know we'll need to batten down the hatches in—" He looked into the distance again, and shrugged. "—a few hours. I reckon the gale will hit just before dusk. Which ain't ideal to begin with. But nothing about that looks ideal."

He made the sign of the cross over his chest.

"I will. I'll go now," I said and hastened down the stairs to find the captain.

He wasn't in his chambers, or the meeting rooms that were attached. I tried the galley and found Domingo chopping limes.

"Oy," he said, tossing me half of one. "Suck on that, why don't ya. Stop the scurvy, right?"

I caught the piece of fruit and thanked him. "We'll need more than limes though."

"What do you mean?"

"Storm's coming. Big one."

His face went white. "Ah, fuck."

"Not a fan of storms?" I asked, feeling the same, honestly.

"Not at sea. I'm just getting used to the whole floating all day and night thing. Not sure I want to try sinking."

"We won't sink," I said, with more conviction than I felt. "But the situation could get dangerous."

"You are a cunt!" Esmaralda shouted from the rooms behind.

"Shut your fucking twat, you sorry pile of feathers!" Mr Guthrie yelled back from nearby.

Esmaralda laughed, sounding like Domingo when someone told a good joke.

"Wonderful." Domingo pointed the tip of his knife at me. "See, that was one good thing about being a whore, White. If the weather was bad, there weren't any clients, so we had a chance to rest. But I can tell you, I'm not looking forward to weathering a storm on this floating pile of timber."

I snorted. "Don't let Dinesh hear you talking about his ship like that."

Domingo laughed. "Oh, I say all kinds of things to Captain Martin. I don't exactly watch my words with him, if you get me. But he knows I don't mean half of what I say."

"Do you know where I'll find him?" I asked.

Domingo nodded toward the stern. "He went with Hillier to check the stores."

"Thank you."

"White?"

"Yeah?"

"Where's the safest part of the ship during a storm?"

"I...don't really know. Anywhere but on deck, I suppose?"

"Right." He went back to his work, but his forehead furrowed, and he muttered under his breath.

I took my leave and found the captain and Hillier where Domingo had said they'd be. Hillier was standing before a wall of shelves, holding a clipboard and a pencil. Dinesh was reclined on a pile of burlap bags that had the word 'FLOUR' printed on them, one knee bent and the other leg stretched out.

"Ah, there he is, Hillier. Tell me, does he look taller to you?" Captain Martin asked with genuine curiosity.

"What?" I said, coming to a halt.

Captain Martin smiled benignly with amusement in his eyes.

Hillier examined me and nodded. "He's carrying himself a bit straighter, now he's an officer."

"Captain, I was just on deck, and Hanes wanted me to tell you that he's very worried about the weather."

"The weather?"

"Aye. There's a big storm coming. Well, the sky looks very nasty; that's for certain."

He frowned. "Hmm. We haven't had a big one in a while. Apart from—" He gestured to me vaguely as he stood.

"Yes. He asked me if the coming storm was one of mine."

Hillier and Captain Martin gazed at me with questions in their eyes.

"What?" I asked.

"Did you, uh... Has anyone made you cross, Rooster?" Dinesh asked, while Hillier listened attentively, his pencil poised over his paper.

I narrowed my eyes at Captain Martin.

"'Has anyone made me cross'? Of all the—" I folded my arms over my chest. "*You're* making me cross right now, but I ain't gonna call a storm."

He gave a forced laugh.

"Right," Hillier said.

I stomped my foot in frustration. "For fuck's sake, my bloody powers ain't like that. They ain't a conscious thing I do. They just...happen."

"When someone you love is threatened," Dinesh agreed. "I know. But I wonder..."

I frowned. "You wonder what?"

But Captain Martin shook his head. "Never mind."

He turned to Hillier. "Well, Hillier, I suppose we'd best batten down the hatches and warn the crew. If this is as bad as that beast several months ago, we're going to need all of our luck and more."

*

The storm hit as the sun went down, just as Hanes had predicted. We'd prepared as much as we were able, rolling up most of the sails and only using the storm jibs to keep us pointed in the right direction.

The ship lurched and jerked in the midst of the horrible gale. Hillier, Guthrie, and the captain were on deck, shouting orders as men hastened to follow them. Hillier had the wheel, fighting the wind to keep the ship steady, and Captain Martin stood nearby, holding onto the mizzen mast to keep his feet, both of them soaked to the skin. Strangely though, they seemed to know what to do and had an air of authority, as if they would get us through in one piece, which I chose to believe.

As an officer myself, I should have stayed with them, but since my sailing skills were abysmal, the captain had sent me downstairs, ostensibly to keep his rooms in order, although how I was supposed to stop things from tumbling off his desk and out of his cabinets, when the *Arrow* rocked and lunged, I didn't half know. The larger pieces of furniture were bolted down and didn't present a problem, but the straight chair kept sliding back and forth, and eventually tipped over. I held onto one of the oak bedposts and prayed to a God, whom I didn't believe in, to be merciful. I was sick with worry for the men up top, but I knew I wouldn't be any good to anyone up there, and Dinesh would have been distracted with worry for me.

I was quite damp, still, and not very comfortable but glad to be below deck. The cabin was dim and dark with dancing shadows. Lightning lit the space in frequent bursts as thunder boomed with terrifying intensity. I daren't light any of the lamps in case they fell from their hooks and caused a fire. Perhaps that was unlikely— what did I know, really?—but I wasn't taking any chances.

I mumbled some barely remembered prayers and tried to remain calm. I didn't want my desperation and fear to cause me to summon a supernatural tempest because that might be a bad idea in this situation. So I closed my eyes and tried to imagine blue skies and good times.

Then the cabin door slammed open, and I almost shit myself.

Domingo stood there, with his chartreuse robe belted over top of his shirt and trousers, and the small cage containing a frantic Esmaralda tucked under his arm.

"Oh, thank God, you're here, Rooster!"

He shut the door and ran to the bed, wrapping his free arm around the footpost.

"Is the ship going to sink?" he asked, eyes wide with panic. "I don't want to die!"

From somewhere, I summoned the pretence of calm.

"We're not going to die. Everything's going to be fine," I said, hoping those words would soothe me as well.

"Pummel the blackguard! Take him out back!" Esmaralda shouted as if she could intimidate the weather into easing.

"Shh, my pretty girl," Domingo cooed. He gazed at me in apology. "I didn't have time to cover her cage."

"Perhaps she can distract us," I suggested.

Domingo gave me a mean look. "You're fucking delusional. We're all going to die. We're going to end up on the bottom of the sea and the fishes will feast on our bones!"

I sighed and then shouted a little too loudly, even with the crashing of the storm and shouting above us.

"Get a hold of yourself, man!"

He looked at me as if I'd grown another head. I was a little surprised myself.

Esmaralda said, "You are a cunt!" but I knew she didn't mean the insult. She was frightened as well and flapped about restlessly in the confines of the carrying cage.

I continued in a volume somewhat more controlled.

"For one thing, you almost caused a literal shitstorm when you barged in here. I'm barely controlling my bowels right now. And I know the captain has this under control. *And* Hillier. The crew will keep us afloat."

I tried hard to believe my words.

"Do you think so? But—"

"They *will*. They have to," I said, tightening my grasp on the bedpost as the sextant tumbled off the captain's desk.

"Oooh, that's his favourite thing to play with—other than me," I commented, watching the instrument slide to the other side of the room.

Domingo barked a laugh that was half amusement and half cry of terror. Mostly tension relief.

The ship lurched in the other direction, and the sextant went sliding across the floor, along with a selection of other items.

"You're remarkably calm for someone holding onto this bed for dear life," Domingo commented.

"It's called self-control, Domingo. You should try it."

"What a trollop!" Esmaralda said, then gave a whistle of appreciation.

"I'm calmer already just being near you. Even though I think you're deluded if you think we're going to be fine."

"What's the point of expecting the worst? Besides, you don't want me to panic."

"Why not? The bowels?"

I gave a half-hearted laugh. "Not only. If I panic and feel like our lives are in danger, I could call up another storm on top of this one."

Domingo's face went even paler. "Fuck. I hadn't thought of that."

"It's *all* I've been thinking of."

There was a tremendous crash of thunder and a flash of light that illuminated the very struts of the groaning ship. Esmaralda was struck to silence, and Domingo and I found ourselves in a frantic embrace, holding each other like these were the end times. It certainly felt that way.

When the world didn't end and the shouting and lurching of the ship continued, we released each other and uttered embarrassed apologies.

"All right. Go back to your own bedpost," I muttered, ashamed to have lost my composure.

"No, I want to stay near you," Domingo said, clutching the same sturdy post as I and sounding determined.

"As you like." Perhaps we *had* better stay close to each other.

"Do you smell smoke?" Domingo asked, sniffing the air.

I sniffed and caught a whiff of woodsmoke. "Fuck. Is the ship on fire?"

Then I heard the sound of running men and a voice—Hanes, possibly—yelled to clear the way. I met Domingo's gaze, and we turned toward the door as it swung open.

Two men carried the captain inside.

"Put him on the bed!" Hanes instructed Lahiri, who was helping him.

"What happened?" I cried, letting go of the bedpost and rushing forward.

Dinesh!

"Lightning strike," Hanes said.

"Lightning strike!" Domingo gasped. "The ship's been struck? We're all going down!"

"Nah, it glanced off the side. We snuffed the fire," Lahiri said with a calm and confidence I envied.

"Shard of the rail came off and went through his leg," Hanes explained. "He's bleeding pretty bad."

I grabbed one of the oil lamps, struck a match, and lit the wick, then adjusted the flame and hung the lantern back on the hook. I stared at the blood soaking the cloth wrapped around Dinesh's thigh.

"I'm all right, White. I'm fine," Dinesh said, with a brave attempt at a smile.

He was alert but looked pale as a ghost as he gazed up at me before turning to Hanes. "Go back on deck and help Hillier. We've got to be at the back of this weather soon."

"Aye, Captain," Hanes said. "Here, White. Look after him. Keep pressure on that wound. Faraday's on his way."

My blood ran cold, but I wasn't giving in to despair.

"All right," I said, steeling my nerves and calling all the last vestiges of my bravery. "Go on, then."

They left and I kept my hand firmly on the cloth that covered the captain's wound.

"Figures the two of you'd be canoodling," Dinesh said. "Found some time whilst I was otherwise occupied, I see?"

I frowned at his ill-timed humour. "We were terrified and trying to convince each other we'd live to see tomorrow."

He nodded and looked chastened. But I didn't like his sudden lack of confidence.

"Are you truly going to be all right?" I asked him.

"Of course. Merely a flesh wound. But if this storm doesn't let up…"

"It'll stop," I stated, not willing to consider other options.

"Here," Dinesh said. "I can hold this."

I lifted my hand from the bandage on his thigh, and Dinesh replaced it with his own, holding the fabric firmly.

"I'm not sure the *Arrow* will withstand this," Captain Martin said. "Why don't you try to call on your powers?"

"My…powers?"

I knew what he meant but pretended I didn't to buy myself some time.

"Well, we might all very well die today, Rooster. And it might not make an ounce of difference if this wound isn't fatal, because sinking to the bottom surely will be."

"Mother Mary and Jesus!" Domingo whispered. "Not drowning. I'm too pretty to drown."

As if on cue, Esmaralda said, "You are a cunt!"

I waved my hand at Domingo and his annoying bird.

"Shush." I glared at the captain. "What do you mean 'why don't I try to call one of mine'?"

"Rooster, the past two times we've been in a life or death

situation, you've called on your powers, and we've gotten out of a very sticky spot."

"But I don't—" I said. "It's not—"

"Well, that's a fucking shame because we could really use that magic right now."

"For fuck's sake, Dinesh, I've been trying *not* to call a storm! There already *is* a storm! You want to suffer under the weight of two storms?"

"We never *suffer* under yours. Whatever powers you call upon, when you do summon them, we are never harmed. And I'm not sure we're going to survive this. Whatever magic you possess, what arises is *not* a natural phenomenon. And *this* natural phenomenon is trying its bloody best to kill us."

We stared at each other. I didn't want to admit that he was right, but he was. There was still one problem.

"I don't know how, Dinesh," I said, holding onto the bedpost as he did the same. Even though he lay in the bed, the ship was pitching and rocking so much he could easily roll off. I held my free arm out, palm up. "I can't just *call upon* my powers as I like."

"How do you know?" he asked, his eyes entreating me. "Have you tried?"

"Well, no, but…" I covered one ear and bent the other to my shoulder to shut out the shouting from above. Another flash lit the room. The gas lamp swung on its hook and gave the cabin an eerie feel in the darkness as shadows shifted and moved.

The captain lifted his free hand and reached for me, then flinched in pain.

"Please try. I think it's the only way to survive this."

Domingo wailed and clutched the bedpost like a lover.

"No, no, no, no, no. I'm not going down to the depths of the ocean. I'm *not* going to die like this!"

"Take it from behind!" Esmaralda ordered, then clucked and chirped, the flutter of her wings against the wood cage a frantic accompaniment.

Fear swirled in my belly as an ember of heat warmed deep inside me. A sensation that had become familiar, but didn't help me to summon my powers with intention.

"I don't know how!"

"Think about me dying in some horrible way," Captain Martin suggested. "And Domingo too."

"Noooo!" Domingo cried. "I'm too young to die! Don't let me die!"

Dinesh's words did what they needed to, as harsh as they had been. The glow of heat and the sharp knife of fear grew and grew.

"And Lahiri and Squid. Hillier and Guthrie. All of us plunging to our deaths."

The fear and the heat increased, a storm inside of me. I turned my free hand palm up. There was a faint blue glow there, under the skin. I looked at my hand on the bedpost. Blue light shone against the wood.

Dinesh continued, his tone eager. "The *goats*, Simon. The *chickens*! All sunk to the bottom of the sea. Elizabeth and Henrietta!"

I stared, horrified, at Dinesh. Then I planted my feet apart for purchase and brought my free hand to the bedpost to grip the polished wood, wrapping both together in seeming prayer as the words of the ancient spell came to my lips:

> *"Bring me the fire and the flame,*
> *O'er the ocean, in my name.*
> *Give me the lightning and the storm,*
> *From the heavens, let it be borne.*

Smite those who threaten what's mine.
They'll not have anyone this time.
Let the sea and the flame rejoice.
Let the ocean and sky make the choice."

Maybe this *was* a mistake, but I was too far gone to stop, and the sense of power flowing through me was heady and new.

I opened my eyes and lifted my head from where I'd had my forehead pressed against the bedpost. Through a blue haze, I saw Dinesh gazing at me with abject terror or possibly awe that looked like terror. Anyway, whatever emotion was displayed across his features didn't matter because I couldn't stop now.

I closed my eyes, put my forehead against the wood again, and repeated the chant, whilst the sounds of chaos echoed around us, and somewhere at the edge of my hearing, Esmaralda shouted, "Pummel the blackguard! Pass him around!"

A whirlwind surrounded me. I couldn't hear Domingo's bird anymore, nor anything but the shrieking of the wind and the creaking of the ship as I waited for the saltwater to suck us down to the depths because, surely, that was going to happen. I'd only hastened our imminent end with my ridiculous attempt at a rescue.

If only the captain hadn't pushed me to call upon my magic. I'd blame him because that was easier than blaming myself.

A strange buzzing filled my ears. I lifted my head and gazed at my hands where they clutched the bedpost.

Translucent blue fire engulfed my hands and the bedpost. My first thought was to let go, but I couldn't, and the flame didn't hurt me. The blaze coursed through me, around the post and up through the ceiling, melding with the ship and with time itself. None of this experience felt real, and the spell went on forever.

There was a terrible ringing in my ears, worse than after the explosion at Cayonne. I opened my mouth to scream, but I couldn't tell if anything came out of me but blue fire.

Time meant nothing, but at some point, the ringing in my ears lessened, and a sense of peace descended as if a cool cloth had been placed over me. My breathing, which had been heavy and laboured, calmed and fell into a gentler rhythm. The world around me quieted, and I wondered if I was on the bottom of the ocean. Or in heaven.

I gasped out a laugh. As if I'd end up in *that* place, after all I'd done.

Then Domingo's voice whispered in my ear, and soft arms wrapped around me.

"You did it, Rooster. You did it. *Dios mio*, we're saved!"

"What a cunt!" Esmaralda exclaimed.

I opened my eyes.

Captain Martin gazed at me from the pillow, his loose hair a halo, his face a picture of reverence and awe—a strange and somewhat awful expression, but much better than fear.

The peaceful feeling expanded, and I realized that the room was filled with moonlight. I heard cheering from above and the cawing of gulls.

"Well done, Rooster," the captain said. "You were magnificent."

Chapter Eighteen

Taking Good Care

Somehow, I had saved us all.

On purpose this time. I didn't know quite how or why I had these powers. But I'd been able to channel them in a way that had eluded me up to this point.

I was a hero. I didn't know how to deal with the unfamiliar role.

Faraday had ushered me out of the captain's rooms so he could deal with Dinesh's injury, and then go and attend to some other minor wounds that had been suffered by the crew. The captain's had been the most serious. By some miracle, no one had gone overboard or been struck down.

Domingo had kissed me on the cheek and gone to the galley to return Esmaralda to her bigger cage, then help Guthrie put everything to rights. Everywhere below decks was a shambles and would take some time to clean up.

I tried to find out what had actually happened from the men who'd been on deck.

"I don't rightly know," Hillier admitted, shaking his head. "One moment the sky came all dark and exploding with lightning and thunder, worse than anything we'd seen yet, and the next moment it all snuffed out like a candlewick. So quickly, we stood there in a bit of shock for a time. I've never seen a storm go down like that."

"Two of them, you mean," I said.

"Never saw more than one. Whatever you called down on us took the storm away, White. Don't quite understand, but I ain't gonna worry about it."

Everyone wanted to shake my hand. Nobody was afraid of me. But now I felt an enormous sense of responsibility and wondered if this would be my new job and whether I could actually call up my magic again.

I ended up in my old hammock down in the hold, where I fell asleep for the remainder of the night and woke up feeling worse. I found Domingo in the galley, helping Mr Guthrie tidy up.

The mess table was bolted to the floor, and the counters were built into the ship. But the chairs had been in piles, and the pantry was a mess of spilled food and flour. I helped Domingo restore order, whilst Guthrie tossed random things into a giant pot of boiling water and made a stew. There was no lack of fresh rainwater, collected in strategically placed items on deck and also from unintended sources. There had been such a downpour that rain had gathered where no rain had gathered before, and members of the crew had collected the fresh water in syphons and bottles, then poured it into barrels. We'd replenished our regular water stores whilst on Tortuga, so there was no worry on that end.

Domingo had been quiet, likely due to embarrassment at losing his habitual confidence and take-it-as-it-comes demeanor. So I tried to chit-chat as we mopped and cleaned the galley while the doctor tended to Dinesh.

"You know, I was terrified. I really did almost shit myself when you came into the captain's rooms."

He might as well know I was embarrassed about the whole thing too.

Domingo didn't respond, simply renewed the force of his scrubbing. Which was unusual for a man who didn't normally enjoy manual labour, or shutting his mouth.

I kept talking.

"I hope the captain's all right. The wound wasn't deep, and I know he lost some blood, but his colour was good when I left him."

Domingo and I scrubbed harder. He still didn't say anything. So I chose a different tactic.

"I hope he's not laid up for too long. He was talking about inviting you to his bedchamber to have another go…"

This was a total lie, but I thought my words might get a reaction.

When they didn't, I threw the mopstick down and stood before him, with my hands on my hips and the angriest expression I could summon.

"Domingo! Why won't you talk to me?"

I hadn't expected him to look at me the way he did then. He made the sign of the cross over his chest.

"Oh, what the fuck now? You're not scared of me. You're not scared of anything!"

He sat back on his heels and gazed at me. Licked his lips. Frowned.

"I don't want to be! But your powers are—"

I folded my arms across my chest. "My powers are a gigantic pain in my arse, Domingo. I figured you should know that."

His frown wavered. "How do you mean?"

"Well, for one thing, every time I use them I feel like I've died or travelled to another plane of existence. Nothing looks right, and everything goes very strange. It's not a fun feeling."

He considered this.

I crouched down so we were eye level.

"And the crew thinks I need to be handled with kid gloves, or avoided. Or they need to make me happy all the time. It's... strange."

A thought occurred to me.

"Oh God, Domingo, what if the captain starts coddling me? I don't know if I can handle that." I sat on my arse and put my head in my hands. "He knows just how to deal with me, and I like things rough and wild." I jerked up and raised a finger, as if I were teaching a lesson. "There shall be no coddling in the captain's quarters, not when we're together in our sins."

Domingo fought a smile but still appeared guarded.

"Are you a witch, in truth, Rooster? Are you a godless thing?" Domingo asked carefully in hushed tones.

I shrugged. "I don't think so. Not sure I believe in God or the devil, to be honest."

He didn't tumble in shock, so at least he'd probably realized that.

"I'm surprised *you* do," I admitted.

"What? Believe in God?"

"Well, yes."

"Because I'm a whore?" Domingo said, enunciating the word with a certain relish.

"Were a whore. You ain't one now."

Domingo shrugged, but he didn't look particularly happy.

"Then what am I, Rooster? If I'm not a dirty whore, I don't know what I am."

My heart ached for the look in his sad eyes, and I hastened to reassure him. I needed all the friends I could get.

"Oh, Domingo. You're a part of the *Arrow's* crew. You're a friend of mine, *and* of Captain Martin's. And Guthrie's assistant. You've made a name for yourself aboard this ship, and your reputation doesn't have anything to do with that life."

Domingo nodded, blinking back emotion. "I miss some things. For one thing, there were significantly fewer possibilities of winding up at the bottom of the sea."

I shook a finger at him. "*Fewer*. Not none."

He smiled this time. "No, Rooster, my dear. Not none."

"The way I see things, you're better off aboard this ship, with your friends."

"*Are* you my friend? *Truly*?"

"Domingo, of course I am," I said, taking a step toward him. He didn't flinch, but he still looked wary. "If you can handle being friends with a witch or whatever the fuck I am."

"Well, I suppose I'll have to be. I'm sort of stuck here, at least for the moment."

"Aye, that's true," I said.

"You've been nothing but kind to me, Rooster. And you fuck like an angel. I'm not used to being treated so gently as part of a monetary transaction. I've wanted to tell you that for a long time."

I was truly touched, both at his compliment, but also at the thought of what the reality of his life had been.

"Thank you, Domingo. You're very easy to like, you know.

And I shall always remember that night as being very special."

"Thank you."

"Friends again?" I said, holding out my hand.

"Friends again," Domingo agreed, standing and enfolding my fingers with his own. "What you said about Captain Martin wanting to…" He waggled his eyebrows and gestured in the direction of the captain's chambers.

"I was trying to get a rise out of you. But I won't say another go with the both of us isn't a thought he's had."

Domingo grinned. "Hmm."

"Or that *I* have had…"

Now he laughed. "Well, well, well. Never been tupped by a witch before."

I met his gaze with a smug look. "Well, in actuality…"

"Oh, fuck. Yes, I have. Although you struck me more like an angel at the time."

"Not so bad, then?"

"Not at all."

"Now look, we'd better get on with this cleaning, or Guthrie'll have my arse," I said. "And he's not the one I want dealing with that part of my anatomy, to be frank."

Once we'd made a dent in the cleaning, I asked for permission, from Mr Guthrie, to fill two bowls with stew. I grabbed two spoons and carried them to the captain's cabin.

Boone was in his regular post outside the captain's quarters with his arm in a sling.

"Oh dear, what happened?" I asked.

"One of the men fell on me. The break is a clean one, Faraday said. Didn't you hear me scream when he set the bones?"

"No. Did it hurt that much?"

"Aye, and more. Still aches like a bastard. But I've got a

ration of rum here that's helping. And Faraday says my arm'll heal well."

Since my hands were occupied, Boone used his good hand to rap on the captain's door.

"Yer witch is here, Captain, with your supper," Boone barked.

"Thank you, Boone. Let him in, please."

Boone ushered me in, then shut the door behind me.

The space had been put to rights, I was pleased to see. The errant sextant was in its place on the captain's desk. Dinesh himself was laid out in bed, propped up on some pillows that, the last time I'd seen them, had been halfway across the floor. A miracle everything had stayed dry. He was wearing one of his everyday linen shirts, with the ties undone at his neck.

I placed the bowls of stew and the spoons on the dresser.

"Come here, Simon," Captain Martin said, beckoning me over.

"How are you feeling, Dinesh?" I asked. "How is your leg?"

"I've had enough rum to keep me from despair and to dull most of the pain. Faraday stitched the wound and says if I can keep the puncture clean the injury should heal completely in a few weeks."

"Can you walk, do you think?"

"Aye. I might have a limp, though, if the pain is great."

I made a face. "Oooh. I don't know if I can love a man with only *one* good leg," I said, with much gravity and a pretence of distaste.

He looked taken aback until I gave him a broad smile and confessed to the joke. He rolled his eyes.

"You are a cheeky little devil."

"Correction: a cheeky little *witch*."

"*My* little witch."

"Will you eat some stew? Mr Guthrie said you might."

"I'd love some. Thank you."

I brought his bowl over, the scent of the rich broth seeping into my nostrils. My stomach growled.

"Here, I've got that," he said, taking his bowl and spoon. "You get yours. Sit beside me, please?"

"Of course."

I got my bowl of stew and settled myself on the bed. We didn't have to wait for the liquid to cool as the trip from the kitchens had done that already. My first bite proved the perfect temperature: hot enough to warm us, but cool enough to eat with haste.

"Fuck, this is good," I muttered, chewing and swallowing.

"What's this made from? Chicken? The flavour's wonderful," Captain Martin muttered, slurping the broth from his spoon.

I froze.

"I...didn't ask. Oh God, it *is* chicken..."

The captain met my horrified gaze.

"Oh, Rooster..."

"It's fine," I said, lowering my spoon into the bowl.

"Squid popped in to see how I was and said two of the chickens had perished in the hubbub of the storm. I wasn't going to tell you. I suppose Mr Guthrie decided to make use of them."

I nodded. I wanted to eat the rest of my stew, but now I was filled with sadness and regret. Of all the things that could have brought me to tears over the past twelve hours, a meal wasn't what I'd expected to affect me.

I turned away from him. I'd tried to be so brave all this time.

"Are you crying, my darling?" Captain Martin asked.

"Not because of the chickens."

Well, not solely because of that.

An arm circled me and pulled me against the captain's warm chest. He nuzzled me and kissed my face. "It's been a hell of a day," he whispered in my ear.

And I released what I'd been holding so close, all the tension from thinking I would perish in the storm, the stress of trying to call up my powers, when I had never done so before, and seeing the captain injured. The effect of all these things had piled up and now spilled over.

"Oh, fuck, I'm sorry. You need to eat your stew and get well," I blubbered.

"It'll keep. I want to make sure you're all right."

"I just... I don't know *who,* or *what* I am. Or what I can *do.* Or if I *should* do it." I tried to explain. "I'd assumed the magic to be out of my control. Now, I've been proven to have some, but that brings with it all kinds of other considerations."

"Yes, I suppose that's true. You've a lot to bear, Rooster. I do see that."

"Thank you."

"And I will be with you and stand by you to help you learn more about these powers. They've done nothing but good for me. I wouldn't be here right now if you didn't have them."

I started sobbing again, thinking about that very valid fact.

After a bit, I recovered my emotions, wiped my face with Dinesh's handkerchief, and we ate the rest of our meal.

"How is Domingo faring? That storm frightened him," Dinesh said.

"He's all right now. Except that I had to explain to him that I wasn't the devil's child, only as confused about my fucking powers as everyone else."

"I don't know how he could think you had anything to do with the devil."

I shrugged. "He believes in God, and heaven and hell, and all that malarkey. I can't fault him for his beliefs, but they do make him quick to jump to conclusions."

"Do you not believe in God, Rooster?"

I looked at him funny. "I...do not. I didn't think you did, either, to be honest. I hope my words haven't offended you."

"Not at all. I'm still open to the...well, to the idea of God, I suppose. Perhaps not an old man looking down on us from above, but a greater force in the universe. Some entity that might have blessed a beautiful young man with great powers because he loves so much and so ferociously."

"Do I?" I asked, sitting on the bed beside him and leaning in. "Love ferociously?"

"Most ferociously," he said. "I'm afraid you wear your heart on your sleeve, Rooster. You try not to, with your rough talk and rude words, but your sweet, soft heart is plain to see by everyone around you."

I frowned. "That's a load of bull."

He laughed. "Ask anyone. I dare you."

"All right. I will."

He gazed at me in benign surprise when I stood and went to the door.

I opened it.

"Boone."

"What?"

I glanced over my shoulder at Captain Martin, who had an amused look on his face, then turned back to Boone.

"Do you think I'm fucking sweet, or a foul-mouthed and belligerent rascal?" I asked, folding my arms over my chest and planting my feet apart.

Boone thought about that for longer than I'd expected him to.

"Well, though I think the captain should wash your mouth out with soap, then put you over the rail for a good hiding, your nasty words ain't but a cover for the loveliest heart I've encountered on these open seas."

Well, that made me mad. How dare he prove the captain right about me?

"Boone! For fuck's sake!"

He smiled and made a kissy face at me. I slammed the door and turned to the captain.

"That proves nothing."

The captain threw back his head, laughing with delight. Then he gazed upon me with so much love I thought I might explode, even after hearing the cruel words he'd said about my heart.

"I can assure you that if I *were* to bend you over the rail, it would be for a very different purpose," he promised.

"Oh my God. In front of everyone?"

He sighed with regret. "I suppose that *would* be a little much."

"Although, they probably wouldn't be as intimidated by my powers after seeing me in such a position."

He nodded. "Truly. We must consider the idea."

I went up to the bed and lifted the blankets, peering underneath. As I'd suspected, Dinesh was completely naked below the waist, but for a wide bandage wrapped around his injured thigh. The dressing made him look vulnerable and helpless, especially with his poor cock standing at the ready after that conversation.

"Would you like me to help you with that, Captain?" I asked.

"Only if you want to, my dear Rooster."

"My God, man, how can I resist?"

"You can't possibly. I've manifested it just for you."

"Mmm," I said, folding the blankets down at his knees, exposing him. The most adorable bubble of fluid sat at the very tip of his pink prick.

For one moment, I felt guilty about taking the time to have fun with the captain, when the rest of the crew repaired the damage the storm had caused. But then I decided that making sure our beloved captain would be comfortable and at ease so his leg might heal well didn't feel such a wayward occupation. I convinced myself I was doing a valued duty for the entire crew.

"Wait," he said, as I zeroed in on his rampant appendage.

"Why?" I whined, gazing at him in frustration.

"Well, because I had a rather filthy thought."

I feigned surprise. "You? Never."

"Mmm. Would you do something for me?"

"I was *about* to."

"Something *else*."

I put a hand on my hip and narrowed my eyes at him. "You can't move around, you know. You have a lightning injury."

"A splinter, nothing more. But, yes, you're right. This wouldn't involve me moving at all."

"Oh. Then what do you want, you confusing, confounding man?" I asked, with put-upon frustration.

He seemed suddenly bashful. "Well, if you wouldn't mind..."

I raised my eyebrows.

"I'd rather like to see you...bare from the waist..."

Not too shocking.

"And kneeling at the foot of the bed..."

Still, nothing we hadn't done before.

"Playing with yourself, I'd really like to watch that."

Oh, I see. That was different. But would such an activity fulfil the requirements?

"With my cock, you mean?"

"If you'd like..."

"What would *you* like?"

"I'd like to see you—" He took a deep breath, closed his eyes, and sighed, as if contemplating a religious ritual. "—playing with that sweet hole of yours. *That* is what I would like."

"Is that all?"

He opened his eyes and smiled beatifically. "Yes. That is all."

"A simple request."

"I thought so."

"But specific."

"Mmm."

"And then you want your prick sucked?"

"Yes, that would be lovely," he said, as if I'd just offered to serve him afternoon tea.

Chapter Nineteen

Reckoning

I took off my clothes, laying them neatly on the chair.

"Get the oil, will you?" Captain Martin suggested.

"Yes, Captain," I said, falling back into our habitual dynamic during these sorts of games. It felt good and right to be here with him, following his orders. His amorous attention made me feel safe and cherished, and I could forget for the moment about everything else.

"Oh, and tell Boone not to let anyone in," he added.

I looked down. "But I'm naked! You could have asked me before."

"I didn't think of it. Just talk to him through the door." He shrugged.

I walked to the door and crossed my arms.

"Boone," I said.

No answer.

"Boone!" I repeated with more volume.

"He's probably fallen asleep," Captain Martin said.

"Some bodyguard," I muttered. I cupped my hands over my mouth, braced my elbows against the wood of the door, and yelled at the top of my voice.

"Boone!"

There was some muttering and then Boone's voice. Thank goodness.

"Aye!"

"Please make sure the captain is not disturbed until morning, will you?" I asked.

"Oh, aye. Not disturbed. Of course."

"And don't fall asleep!"

"What? All night?"

"Well, at least for the next—" I glanced at the captain who raised his eyebrows. "—couple of hours."

The captain's eyes went wide. He must be more tired than I'd thought.

I turned back to the door. "One hour. Maybe even half an hour."

I heard the captain's laughter and rested my forehead against the door in defeat.

"What the bloody fuck?" Boone muttered under his breath. Then said, loudly, "Aye, fine! Got it."

"Thank you."

"You're welcome. Enjoy yourself."

I glared at the door, wanting to shoot a bullet into Boone for being so vexing when the captain was truly at fault. He should have thought of this earlier.

He was still laughing as I marched over to the bed, got up onto the mattress with my back to him, squirted oil into my hand, and got to work. The laughter behind me died, and a curse replaced it as I stuck two fingers inside myself up to the knuckles.

I craned my neck to see him.

He gaped at my fingers as they worked my hole, his eyes wide, his mouth open, and a look of entrancement on his handsome face. As he should.

I faced forward and redoubled my efforts at revenge for what he had put me through. A strange way to get back at him, I grant you, but effective in wiping all traces of smug amusement from his face.

"Oh my God," Dinesh whispered.

The next time I looked, he had a fist working his cock and was gazing at my arse like he wanted to bronze the thing.

The only hitch to my plan to drive Captain Martin mad with desire this way was that I'd turned myself into a writhing mess of need. I had been play-acting when we started, but I wasn't pretending now. My moans and groans were real, and I wished the captain didn't have a fresh wound that needed healing so he could take me against the cabin wall whilst Boone tried not to fall asleep. In fact, I was frigging myself so skillfully that I almost forgot about the captain until he reminded me he was there and expecting attention.

"Rooster...are you going to...? I need you to... Jesus, get over here...please. How are you so bloody profane and delightful?"

I had a sudden flash of my tombstone: *Here lies Simon White. He was profane and delightful, and he died by not getting fucked in the year of 1781. May he rest in peace.*

I needed to get a hold of myself. By not getting a hold of myself. And by getting a hold of someone else.

I pulled my fingers out of my arse, though saddened to do so, wiped them on the bedcover, and turned to the captain. He had his prick in hand and looked ready to go over the edge. At least this would be quick.

"Well, if you want me to swallow that thing, you'd best let go," I said, crawling forward.

"Fuck, fuck, fuck," Captain Martin muttered, letting go and putting his hands behind his head. His prick bobbed against his belly, a spidery strand of fluid connecting them.

I sighed. "I wish we *could* fuck. I want to climb on top of you."

"You could do that..." he said with hope in his eyes.

"Perhaps, if the wound wasn't so high up on your thigh. But I'd only hurt you and delay its healing. Never mind. I'll just do this..."

I bent and lifted his cock up off his belly, then took his turgid flesh in my mouth with a voraciousness that caught Captain Martin by surprise.

He cried out as I took him to the root.

I circled him with my fingers and hummed a song as I jerked and sucked, jerked and sucked. He uttered a long groan as he dumped a gallon of seed into my gullet.

"Oh...my...god..." he muttered, gazing at the ceiling whilst I cleaned a bit of seed that had leaked from my lips. "You are the damnedest creature, Rooster. And so very fucking talented."

Now I was the one who looked smug.

"Yes, I know."

I swallowed and licked my lips, then gazed at the window, where the sun was not visibly lower than when we'd started. "I doubt that was half an hour."

"No," the captain said. "But that's just as well. I do need to rest."

"Yes."

"And now that you've taken care of that, I think I shall. Thank you very much, Rooster."

"You're very welcome, Dinesh."

I was feeling rather exhausted myself. It had been a trying day.

"Do you mind if I rest here, with you? I'm quite tired and a bit fragile, if I'm being honest."

He levelled a stern gaze at me. "You should always be honest with me, Rooster."

"I shall try," I said, and snugged myself under the covers with him. "Oh, I forgot to snuff the lamp," I said, preparing to get up again.

"Never mind. It's a proper hurricane lantern, hanging on a hook. The thing'll burn out before morning."

I was more than happy to stay under the covers with my captain, savouring the peaceful rocking of the ship, and the hum of activity and conversation from the deck. I fell asleep snuggled into the captain's side, listening to his light snoring.

*

Shouts woke me at the crack of dawn. Someone was pounding on the captain's door.

I shot out of bed and cowered with fear against the wall, abandoning poor Dinesh in a selfish panic. The captain very calmly slid a hand beneath his pillow and pulled out a pistol as my eyes widened. Had the weapon been there all along?

He cocked the hammer.

More pounding and then...laughter.

"What the fuck is going on out there?" the captain yelled. "Simon's about to throw himself overboard, he's so frightened."

"Oh, sorry, Captain Martin," Lahiri's voice came loudly. "We didn't mean to scare anyone."

"Why? Did we interrupt the two of you?" Domingo said.

Voices and cheering could be heard. The captain eased the hammer back and lowered his gun as we exchanged puzzled looks. I hopped back into bed and covered my nakedness, trying to slow the rapid pounding of my heart.

Lahiri's laughter sounded outside the door. "It's Mr Silk and Duncan! They're alive!"

The captain moved to get up and then remembered his wound. He settled back.

"Jesus! Rooster, can you get the door?"

"Yes, of course," I said, grabbing the captain's shirt off the floor and pulling the garment over my nakedness.

I went and tugged open the door.

Half the crew were there, and they all yelled, "Heya!"

Lahiri gazed at me with happiness, and Domingo's eyes took in my lack of clothing with barely hidden amusement.

I smiled and lifted my hand, feeling rather exposed, even though my very private bits were somewhat concealed.

Squid pushed through the mass of men, many with bottles in their hands, and now drifting away to go back to where the real party was.

"Is this true?" I asked, looking at him and Lahiri and Domingo. "Mr Silk and Duncan?"

Squid nodded ferociously, then frowned. "Well, they found us, more like. Poor blokes have been rowing for days."

His words didn't make sense.

"But...Squid...the storm. If the gale almost sent the *Arrow* down, how did they survive the weather?"

"They must have been a day behind us. The captain ordered us to stay put as best we can so the *Arrow* could be repaired. There ain't much wind, and we don't have the sails unfurled."

"Well, I'm glad they're alive."

"So am I," the captain said, his voice at my ear.

I turned and gaped at him. "Get back to bed! You're wounded!"

"I'm fine, Rooster. Good as gold after a night's rest and...well, you know."

"I'm sure I know," Domingo said.

I frowned. "I don't think you should be up," I said to the captain.

Squid laughed. "Well, you'll both miss the celebrations if you don't join us. You must come and welcome them back aboard. You must!"

"Of course, we will. Save us some rum, will you?" Captain Martin said.

"Yes, Captain," Squid said, turning to follow the rest of the men to the deck. Lahiri went as well, but Domingo remained.

"That's the happiest I've ever seen that fellow," Captain Martin commented.

"I don't actually think Squid's a 'fellow'," I said, giving voice to an idea that had been niggling at my brain since we'd brought him aboard.

Domingo said nothing, just gave me a soft smile that felt like agreement.

I glanced at Captain Martin. He looked flummoxed.

"What on earth do you mean?"

"Well, I don't know. Doesn't matter..."

"You think Squid is a maid?" Captain Martin asked, doubtful, because Squid was quite unladylike.

"Ain't my business, really, and I don't give a flying fuck, to be honest."

Domingo laughed.

"Well, then, neither do I. Let's have a look at our two re-turned crew members. I couldn't be happier about this unexpected development."

"You'd better put some clothes on," Domingo muttered, scanning us in our undressed state. "There's quite a crowd up there. Oh, and here."

He brought his hand from behind him and held out a polished walking stick to Captain Martin. "One of the crew told me to give this to you. He found it in the hold."

"Oh, thank you, but I don't think I'm quite that—"

I took the stick from Domingo and thanked him.

We hastened to dress. I had to help Dinesh as his leg was stiff and sore.

When we were ready, I passed him the walking stick. He took the aid from me with an expression of peeved indulgence, and we made our way up to the deck.

He managed well with the wood staff, and I was reassured about the mild nature of his injury. When we reached the others, there were more cheers, and the men brought Mr Silk and Duncan to greet us.

They had rather awful sunburns, and their lips were cracked and parched, but they hadn't fared too badly other than that.

When they saw Captain Martin, they stumbled forward. But then Duncan stopped Mr Silk and whispered a curse as they noticed me.

"My God, we're glad to have you back!" Captain Martin said.

I looked down at myself to see if I had a big glob of dirt on my coat. But I looked fine. When I lifted my gaze, they were taking turns shaking the captain's hand and keeping a wary eye on me. Perhaps they were still spooked from the summoning at Cayonne.

Well, they'd get over the shock. The rest of the crew had.

"Thank you, Captain. We're immensely relieved, of course," Mr Silk said. "We were lucky to get away." He glanced at me. "The port was—"

"Oh yes," Captain Martin spoke overtop of Mr Silk, whilst Duncan regarded me with visible horror. "Terrible business. But 'twas necessary, or we would all have perished."

He glanced at me with a look on his face I'd never seen there before—sheepish and deceptive.

What the fuck was going on?

I glanced at Domingo, who stood near to Squid by the mizzenmast. Neither of them looked at me, and I wondered what was suddenly so fascinating about the wooden planks at their feet.

"Necessary?" Duncan spoke up now, his voice rough from dehydration, no doubt. "Truly? Necessary to demolish the entire town of Cayonne?"

Hushed silence followed. The captain coughed, his cheeks red with embarrassment.

Hillier spoke up, "No, no. Not as bad as that," he said, looking at the captain and then at me.

Captain Martin got a hold of himself and smiled, the way he did when he was trying to appease an enemy. "Please tell me there's a bottle of rum for your captain? And his right-hand man, of course—" He flourished a hand at me. "—who saved us all from certain death, so many times! To Simon White! Hip, hip, hooray!"

Hanes passed him a bottle, and he lifted it high, repeating the chant that no one took up on my behalf.

"Hip, hip, hooray!" he said, gazing about him with a silent entreaty.

Then the crew took up the chant with feigned enthusiasm, and everyone acted as if nothing had happened.

"What is going on?" I asked in a voice barely above a whisper.

Nobody heard me, of course. I watched the crew dance and jig and tipple. Dinesh spoke with put-upon joviality with a still wary and confused Silk and Duncan, and so I shouted at the top of my lungs.

"What the fuck is going on!"

Everyone heard me. Domingo and Squid looked at me now, their eyes wide.

And the rest, as a group, stopped celebrating and stared at the deck as if they wanted the boards to swallow them up. I caught a few looks of abject terror at my outburst. But most didn't even see me. A few glanced at the captain with questions in their eyes, then looked down again.

And Captain Martin watched me with the saddest look in his eyes—as if I'd just learned I had a horrible disease and was on my deathbed.

"What the fuck is wrong with everyone?" I asked Captain Martin, not in a loud or demanding way, but in genuine bafflement.

"Just tell him," Hillier said, sounding weary and forlorn.

"Aye. You've got to," Mr Guthrie agreed, whilst Squid came through and stood at my side.

Domingo joined him and reached for my hand. I let him wrap my fingers with his because I'd wager whatever truth was about to be revealed was going to be hard to hear.

"Tell me what?" I asked, quaking to hear the secret.

What had I done at Cayonne? What had they not told me?

"Let's go to my rooms," Captain Martin said in a gentle voice.

"No. Tell me here. Now."

Captain Martin looked at Hillier, who spoke next, as Dinesh couldn't get the words out.

"That storm you called up to save all of us, when you fell into the sea and came up and clutched onto the skiff…"

I nodded. I remembered that part. I repeated what they'd told me: "I burned the docks. That's what the captain said. I burned the docks."

Maybe if I kept saying the words, they would be the truth, not what they were about to tell me.

Domingo squeezed my hand as Hillier kept talking. Dinesh looked at the boards of the *Arrow's* deck in silent regret.

"That storm… It ravaged the entire port," Hillier said in low tones.

"Aye," Mr Guthrie agreed. "The town itself. Cayonne."

Horror filled me at his words.

I looked at the captain. "Is that true?"

He nodded. "Yes."

I pulled my hand from Domingo's grip and stepped toward Dinesh. "Then…you lied to me."

He hesitated but then said, "Yes."

"We thought it for the best," Mr Guthrie explained.

The three of them looked at each other, as if wondering if that had been the best idea, after all.

I stared at Dinesh for a long moment, my heart lurching in my chest, both at this shocking information and at the sense of betrayal I felt. I blinked and shook my head as if I could deny the truth.

Then I marched to the rail, staring in the direction from which we'd come, feeling my bowels coil and my stomach reject the stew I'd eaten earlier. I saw the scorched handprints in the wood and placed my hands over them. So much death and destruction. Innocent lives lost. What had I done?

A hand came to rest on the small of my back as bile rose inside me. I leaned over the rail and retched.

The captain supported me, but when I was able, I wrenched myself away and ran for the only place I truly felt safe and at peace and alone. And where I could empty my protesting bowels without anyone watching.

I sat on the toilet in the privy, once my bowels had voided themselves in angry and violent protest, and thought about all the lives I'd ended. What was I that I could so easily kill so many, only to save those I loved? Could I keep saving our skins if my triumph meant that so many others would perish? Should I even try?

What a heavy burden to carry. And they'd known I'd have a hard time doing so. I couldn't blame them for keeping the facts from me, but at the same time, I wished I'd known.

After some time, a knock came at the door.

"Go away," I muttered.

There was a pause and then another two knocks.

"Christ, can't a man take a shit in peace? Go. Away."

There was a sigh and then Guthrie's voice.

"I need to use the privy, Simon. Are you going to be done soon?"

For fuck's sake. After what I'd been through, I wished I could have gotten some grace. There were other places where a man could take a shit. But I supposed that Guthrie, the ship's cook, couldn't be expected to use the hole tucked in the corner of the bow.

I put myself to rights, at least in terms of my appearance, got up, and opened the door.

"Thank you," Mr Guthrie said, giving me a look of gratitude so sincere that I promptly burst into tears. I went to step aside, but he grabbed me and pulled me into his arms, circling them around me and holding me tight.

This proved to be exactly what I needed. My sobs came then,

huge wracking cries that I worried might topple us both to the deck.

"I'm sorry. I'm so sorry," I blubbered. "You need to use the privy..."

"Nah, I don't. That was a lie so you'd open the door."

That made me cry harder. "Why is everyone *lying* to me?"

"Because we love you, Simon. Not just the captain. But he's so far gone he couldn't bear to tell you the truth himself. He had to let Hillier confess."

Fine. All right. That did make me feel somewhat better. He did love me. I knew he did. But the rest of them? Why should *they*?

"*Everyone?*"

"Simon, you've saved our lives three times now."

The black cloud over me threatened to return.

"Yes, by killing loads of other people," I muttered, feeling sick to my stomach again at the thought of all of those deaths.

"We're *pirates*, Simon," Mr Guthrie said. "We kill people all the time. The captain might like to use a fancier word for us, but that's what we are. We're all thieves and murderers."

I made a sound like a laugh that turned into another sob.

"Not like me."

He sighed. "No, not like you. But, you know, that there's a cruel world, Simon White. An awfully cruel world. I don't know where your magic comes from, or how you came into these abilities, or what they make you, but I thank God for them every day. I really do."

"Truly? You don't worry about...everything else?"

There was movement in the corner of my vision, and I spied Dinesh walking towards us with the aid of the walking stick. The walking stick he needed because of the wound he'd suffered. My heart filled, and I forgave him in that moment.

"No, I don't," Guthrie continued. "Because whatever powers you have, they ain't a gift you have much control of, are they?"

"No," I admitted.

Even when I'd deliberately called the storm on top of the storm, I hadn't any idea of the breadth or the power of the result.

"Then it's not your fault."

I nodded and relaxed my grip on Guthrie's jacket. "I suppose...perhaps..."

"I've got him, Mr Guthrie. You can go back on deck. The party's resumed," Captain Martin said.

Mr Guthrie stepped back and tipped his head to the captain. As he walked past, Captain Martin stopped him with a hand to his arm. "Thank you."

"Aye. Well, he's like a son to me now," Guthrie muttered, and I almost started crying again.

Mr Guthrie took his leave, and Dinesh stood there, gazing at me with so much love and affection I could hardly bear it.

"I'm sorry I lied to you, Simon," he said. "I was trying to protect you."

I nodded, afraid to speak. If I opened my mouth I might lose the precarious control I had over myself.

I pointed at the walking stick.

He looked at the staff with a sigh. "The blasted thing's turned out to be quite handy, in fact." He focused on me with a look of concern. "Are you all right?"

The tears coursed down my cheeks, and I shook my head, and the captain came forward and caught me in his arms as my knees gave way. He held me close and whispered kind things into my ear and stroked the hair back from my forehead and kissed me all over my face. And I'd never felt so loved and cherished, ever in my whole life, except for when my mam had been alive.

Chapter Twenty

In Good Hands

I was helping Squid with the animals. He was good with them, I had to admit. We were down to three chickens, of course, but Mr Guthrie was getting an average of four eggs a day, which he used for the captain's and my breakfast. I was a little embarrassed to be hogging the eggs, but then again, they were still thriving thanks to me.

The goats, however, remained a challenge.

I was telling Squid what the captain had said to me that morning—that he was tired of picking my clothes up off the floor and was thinking of making me his cabin boy, slash, housekeeper again.

The cheek!

Squid agreed that the captain's words were way out of line

and said I should complain about the captain's prick being so needy and say I was thinking about taking a break from his appetites. I laughed so hard at that because, whilst it might honestly be a very effective bargaining tool, I wasn't sure that decision wouldn't punish me more than the captain.

During this stimulating intellectual discussion, Lillith got free of her tether and charged past us, heading down the hall toward the stairs.

"Oh, for fuck's sake," I muttered as Squid cursed and made chase. I followed behind, watching Lillith scramble up the steps and Squid follow in quick pursuit.

"Excuse me, pardon me," I said as I followed them up onto the deck, colliding with a crew member who cursed me, then made the sign of the cross, muttering apologies.

"Oh stop! I'm not going to smite you down for being in the way," I said, irritated with the way some of the crew steered clear of me. In a way, it was nice to have a little more respect. But on the other hand, I didn't want the crew worried that at any moment I might call up a sudden storm to solve a minor dispute.

The young man scurried off, and I rolled my eyes, then continued the chase.

"Take it from behind!" a familiar bird voice yelled out.

"Oh fuck off, Esmaralda!" I yelled, spying Domingo and his pet watching us with much amusement.

"Oy!"

The captain's terse shout pulled me right up, and I skidded to a stop near to where he stood by the rail speaking with Hillier. Hillier was holding an unrolled map between his hands so they could both regard it.

"Mr White," Captain Martin said, with a stern look at me as his gaze tracked down my body in a way that made my cock stand up and say please. Until his attention landed on my bare feet.

"No shoes, I see," he said with obvious disapproval. "And scrambling after a runaway goat. Some things never change."

"You are a cunt!" Esmaralda shouted.

I straightened up and crossed my arms over my chest. I had on my pants and a shirt and even my jacket, so I wasn't sure why he was grouching at me about my lack of shoes.

"I'm helping Squid. Lillith got away again."

"I'm sure Squid can handle the animal," he said. He was using his stern, no-nonsense voice, and my entire body turned into a panting tongue.

Captain Martin turned back to the quartermaster.

"That's enough, Hillier. Let's continue on to the Turks Islands. We must go somewhere, and I'm not going to dither about where. We're fully manned and we have—" He glanced at me with a little smirk, then turned back to Hillier. "—our secret weapon. We'll be able to deal with whatever comes our way, I trust."

"Aye, Cap'n."

"And you," Captain Martin said, turning to where I was pinned to the spot, waiting for him to take charge of me. "In my cabin. This instant."

"Yes, Captain," I said, bashful all of a sudden, knowing full well what was coming.

Esmaralda chose that moment to yell out "The Captain's cock is a truncheon!" in an excellent appropriation of my voice.

I closed my eyes, knowing that now I was in even more trouble.

Muffled laughter came from the crew who were nearby, and Domingo said, "Shut your trap, you bloody bird."

I opened my eyes in time to see Domingo hastening away, the rude mynah scrambling for purchase on his shoulder.

The captain's cheeks flushed but he pretended he hadn't heard the remark. His gaze was fixed on me, at any rate.

"I need to teach you about the value of wearing shoes on deck, since you insist on behaving like a vagabond."

I put a hand to my chest, my eyes going wide. "A vagabond! I'm dressed better than—"

"Enough. Go to my cabin and sit in the chair. I'll be there momentarily."

I knew enough not to push my luck so I obeyed the captain's orders.

Boone was sitting on his chair outside the captain's cabin.

"Hello, Simon," he said.

"Boone," I replied and went into the captain's rooms, slamming the door behind me, so hard that the thing bounced open.

"I'm very fine, thanks. You?" Boone said sarcastically.

"Piss off."

"I'm going to tell the captain you were rude to me," Boone said

"Do as you like."

I tore off my jacket, mad now that the captain had used his stern voice to captivate me into doing as he said. I'd been having fun with Squid. The banter had reminded me of a more carefree time when I hadn't known my powers were about to make a reappearance and turn me into more than the *Arrow's* animal handler.

I sat in the chair because I knew better than to disobey Dinesh in his own chambers. But I crossed my arms over my chest and scowled. My feet were still bare, and he could go to hell about it.

I sat there fuming but also feeling desperately aroused, which made me even angrier. How dare he be so tempting and handsome and make me do things I didn't want to do? Well, I actually did want to do most of the things he insisted upon, but sitting in this chair and waiting was not one of them.

Finally, I heard him speaking to Boone outside the closed door.

"Good luck with him. He's in a mood," Boone muttered.

"There's nothing I like better."

"You're a strange one, Captain Martin."

"You're not the first person to say so."

Boone laughed and the door pushed open.

"I am not in a mood," I growled.

Captain Martin closed the door and stood there, staring at me whilst I glared at him.

"Simon White."

I didn't answer right away. He narrowed his eyes.

"What?" I said, not daring to defy him by remaining silent.

"Come here."

"Why?"

"Because I want to kiss you."

I narrowed my eyes. "Is this a trick?"

He moved toward me, slowly, like he was stalking a helpless animal. Which I wasn't, but at the moment, I certainly felt like one.

"Do you think running about on the deck with no shoes on is a safe thing to do, Rooster?"

He was staring at my feet now with a hunger he generally reserved for my arse.

"Well, I don't—"

"Yes, or no?"

"No," I squeaked as he came closer. What was he going to do? My breath hitched, and I held onto the chair edge even harder.

He sank to his knees, my gaze following him in shock. What on earth?

He picked up one of my bare feet and rubbed his stubbled cheek against the bottom, which felt...well, *incredible*, to be honest. I might have whimpered.

"What are you doing?" I asked, suddenly breathless.

"I'm showing you what I want you to protect by wearing shoes on deck and most other places."

"But I—" I started to protest, but he sucked my big toe into his mouth, staring at me with big, dark eyes, laving the sensitive pad with his silky tongue.

"But...my feet are filthy," I sighed.

He grinned and sucked harder. "Mmm."

I made a strange noise as each rub of his tongue and suck of his cheeks worked their magic on a more intimate part of me.

"Oh my fucking God..." I said as my eyes rolled back in my head, and my body went limp.

And then he sucked all of my toes into his mouth, and I groaned in erotic agony, my prick filling with blood, and my bollocks coiling in readiness. I was going to spend from this if I didn't speak up.

"Captain," I whispered, barely able to make words. "Captain..."

He groaned around my toes as I made a desperate noise and barely held on.

"Please...please..." I begged.

I didn't know what I was begging for. Did I want him to stop, or did I want him to continue? How humiliating to ejaculate from having my toes sucked. Then again, humiliation was kind of my thing.

I made a soft sound and took my fingers off the chair, reaching for the tent in my breeches.

The captain let my toes slide out of his warm mouth. But he

held my foot still.

"No, no. Hands off, my boy. That there's mine, just like these five pretty babies," he said, sliding a finger along my toes. "Unbutton yourself and pull your prick out. But then let go. I just want to see how much you want my attention."

"Oh God," I moaned, doing as he bade me. How could I resist touching myself now?

"Keep those hands on the arms of that chair."

"But Captain, I—"

"I don't care a whit. I'm going to take my time and enjoy you, and I don't give a good goddamn what you do. If you need to finish, finish. If you'd rather try to hold off, I'll do my best to make it good for you. Either way, I'm going to take my own pleasure, so you might as well hang on for the ride."

He gave me a look of such wickedness it took my breath away.

"You want me to stop?" he asked in a quiet voice that demanded a genuine answer.

I shook my head from side to side. "No, Captain."

"Good. Because I have a whole afternoon to waste whilst Hillier charts our course."

I didn't know exactly where we were going, or what we might do when we got there, but for the next several hours I didn't care about anything except the feel of the captain's lips and tongue touching me everywhere. I floated in a quiet, blissful place whilst eventually attaining a well-earned release, then drifted off to sleep in the arms of my beloved captain.

Acknowledgements

My family, for helping me to be the person I am, and for encouraging me to write my stories.

About the Author

AE Lister is a Canadian non-binary author with a vivid imagination and a head full of unique and interesting characters. They write explicit, adult LGBTQ+ romance. They also write much less graphic Young Adult LGBTQ+ romance under Alison Lister.

Email
alison@aelisterauthor.com

Facebook
www.facebook.com/aelisterauthor

Instagram
www.instagram.com/aelisterauthor

Website
www.aelisterauthor.com

Blog
substack.com/@aelisterauthor

Linktr.ee
linktr.ee/aelisterauthor

Bookbub
www.bookbub.com/authors/ae-lister

Goodreads
www.goodreads.com/author/show/20851633.A_E_Lister

Newsletter Sign-up
stats.sender.net/forms/dPOr6b/view

Other NineStar books by this author

The Braided Crop Ranch

Stable Hand
Ponyboy
Dark Horse
Hotblood

Connect with NineStar Press

Website: NineStarPress.com

Facebook: NineStarPress

X: @ninestarpress

Instagram: NineStarPress

BlueSky: NineStarPress

Threads: @ninestarpress

www.ingramcontent.com/pod-product-compliance
Lightning Source LLC
Chambersburg PA
CBHW060231100726
47907CB00003B/593